THE MYSTERY OF THE LOST HUSBANDS

GINA CHEYNE

First Published in 2021 by Fly Fizzi Ltd,
Pyers Croft
Compton, Chichester,
West Sussex PO18 9EX
www.flyfizzi.co.uk

Cover design by Kari Brownlie

ISBN 978-1-915138-00-2 (eBook)
ISBN 978-1-915138-01-9 (Paperback)
ISBN 978-1-915138-02-6 (Hardback)

For my husbands

"Things are not always what they seem."

— Plato

CONTENTS

CHAPTER 1

MARBELLA MARCH 1987

Anastasia balanced her camera daringly on the horse's withers, but even when he increased his pace from dawdle to stroll, it was not in jeopardy: this cob was built for comfort and had been swapped for a broken racing bike.

'*Coño estúpido!* Move, move!'

She kicked her heels into his side, ineffectively. The horse shook his head lazily and the flies that clung to his eyes flew off and outpaced him up the hill.

The horse and his girl meandered up the hill to the village, completely unaware they were being viewed through a pair of binoculars, from a villa roof less than a mile away. Had Anastasia known, she would have shaken her head too, but only with indifference: no flies on her.

The girl reached the village and disappeared from his view behind the sun-bleached adobe houses. Her brother put down the binoculars.

'Well?' said his mother. 'She's just going to get eggs from the village. You worry too much.'

'Do I? She's seventeen, she does nothing but party and

ride over to visit her friends. If you won't send her to school, you should be finding her a husband, not leaving her to misbehave like a vagrant. It won't do, Mother.'

Mrs Rodriguez sighed. Bogdan knew very well that they couldn't afford the school fees for Ana because all their money went on schooling him and his four brothers. Was it her fault she had had a daughter so late in life? Why didn't he bother his father the way he cursed her? As for a husband! *Who*? They couldn't afford a dowry and Ana didn't like any of the boys who would take her without. She said the Russians were ugly, that Spaniards were all obsessed by Franco (one way or the other) and she hated the tourists – as she called anyone not born in Marbella. Did other mothers have such difficult children?

'She takes lovely photographs.'

'Photographs!' Bogdan scoffed. 'You give her a camera, so she can wander around the beaches and villages unattended and now she is David Bailey. Photography, my dear Mama, is not a career for a woman.'

'But ...'

'OK,' said Bogdan, 'if you are not going to do anything about Ana, I will.'

'Where are you going?'

His mother looked fearfully at her son as he jumped off the roof and headed away, past the pool to the gate. He used to be the easiest of children, but then his wife absconded with a Portuguese sailor from Lisbon and he had become a one-man martinet of moral values.

He stopped. Looked back at his mother. 'I'm going to talk to the priest. If you don't understand, he will. He has seen the beaches since Franco died. The pornography, the licentiousness ...'

'Bogdan darling ...'

'Don't try and stop me, Mother. I will not have my sister turn into a whore like my wife.'

Who would Bodgan's confessor suggest? She smiled at the thought of the novitiates told to leave their vocation and marry a headstrong young girl: for the love of God. Or was there some elderly layman at the church who, now widowed, would like a younger wife? How did Bogdan think she would entice Ana to accept that? Or was he suggesting a forced marriage?

CHAPTER 2

OWLY VALE AUGUST 2018

'How does a woman kill four husbands, take their money and get away with it?' asked a bloke with dreadlocks, finishing his beer and putting it down precisely on the edge of the mat.

'To lose one husband,' said his heavily tattooed friend, known in Owly Vale building circles as a bit of a literary critic, 'is a misfortune, to lose four looks dead dodgy.'

The Owly Vale pub was typical of its generation: the 1980s. The cigarette-stained flock wallpaper and the imbedded scents gave evidence to four decades of happy drinkers enjoying cheap, if sometimes skunky, beer.

Miranda, in her usual position on a stool at the centre of the bar, was on her phone but with the other ear switched to listening mode. She put down the phone. She recognised the raconteur as one of the Drayton builders, and swaying slightly on her stool, tried to make eye contact. She seldom forgot a face, but what was his name? Mike? Martin? Something with an 'M'?

He nodded in recognition.

'Hello, dog lady, isn't it?' he barked at her, and she remembered: Mark the Bark.

'That's me,' she said, visualising herself as a skinny woman, twice her age with legs poking out under a Barbour.

Mark's empty glass fell off the mat and rolled onto the floor. Miranda picked it up.

'Ready for another?'

'Don't mind if I do, love,' he said. He smiled while the pint was pulled, adding, 'I'll have some scratchings too, Dave. And crisps. Couple of scotch eggs.' He winked.

Miranda added a white wine to the list and raised her eyes at the man with tattoos.

'Anything for you?'

'Well,' he said, uncrossing his arms so the tattoos smiled. 'Rude not to, wouldn't it?'

'Where's your Cat, tonight?' barked Mark. 'Stood you up, has she? Toy boy come home?'

She considered barking herself: that the toy boy was fifty at least but remembered in time that she wanted information, and instead laughed sweetly.

'So, what was this story about the rich widow who murdered four husbands?'

Mark turned to his friend, raising an eyebrow.

'Miranda here has a detective gig; they look for lost dogs. I fancy she's thinking of getting a new client.'

His friend laughed loudly wagging his bottom. 'Ooh, a Dog Gig ... is the widow a bit of a *bitch*? Those hubbies certainly got *lost*! Was she *leading* them on?'

Mark turned to Miranda, tipping his head. 'Scuse him. Phil's a plumber, they have shitferbrains.'

'Ha, ha,' said Phil, 'that's colourful coming from a painter!'

'We have a Dog-Finding Agency called SeeMs,' said

Miranda, her smile showing her teeth. 'Lost dogs are very important family members.'

The plumber was still looking sceptical, so she turned her back on him.

'How did you find out about the killing widow, Mark?'

Privately, she thought this would be a fascinating job for the agency and give them a bit of kudos. The plumber wasn't alone. People did mock a dog-finding detective agency.

'Her last victim was our boss,' said Mark, 'Tom Drayton. Bitch got half the business when he died.'

'I remember,' said the plumber pushing back into their conversation. 'I know who you are, you go around with the Cougar Cat. She's a MILF.'

Now both Mark and Miranda turned their backs on Phil. Mark raised his eyebrows. 'See what I mean,' he mouthed. 'Plumber!'

'How did she get the business?' Miranda persisted, 'you said she took half Drayton's business. Why half?'

'Pete owned the rest. You know him, don't you?'

Miranda nodded, feeling a flash of sadness: Pete had been a friend of her father's. 'Yes. Go on.'

'Yeah, well Tom Drayton was her fourth husband. He was seventy-three. She was nice! No need for Viagra there.' He whistled.

'But,' said Miranda, 'what about the previous husbands, wasn't he worried about that? I mean ... if he knew they had been murdered?'

'He didn't. It's hardly a pick-up line, is it love?' Mark put on a poodle voice. 'Hello darling, just killed my last old man, fancy a job?'

Miranda laughed encouragingly. 'OK, so how do you know she killed Tom?'

'Stands to reason, don't it? He was thirty years older and rich, last husbands all dead. How does she make her money? Killing 'em. Obvious.'

Miranda drained her glass and wondered what Cat was doing. She had said she'd be in the pub by nine latest. They were supposed to be discussing the recent bout of dog thefts and who was doing them.

She turned back to the gossip source. 'So did he leave his share of the business to her? Was that it?'

'No,' Mark began but the plumber broke in: 'That's right, I remember now. Miranda's Cat! That's her. Over at the Round House. Older Husband. Nasty death. And then the old ladies tried to get her to join the book club and she freaked. Started dressing like a ...'

'Yes, yes, yes,' said Miranda, 'that's the one. Now, Mark, how did the widow? Any idea of her name, Mark?'

'Anastasia. Can't be right with a name like that, can it. Russian. Since Salisbury we all know about them and their games. Probably a spy too.'

Miranda sighed internally. It was much easier getting information on lost dogs. She took a gulp from her empty glass, and tried again. 'Did you get a surname, Mark?'

'Something foreign. I forget, but it would be Drayton now anyway. Good English name.'

'So, how did Anastasia kill Tom?'

'Pillow over the head,' said Mark imaginatively, 'died in bed, held it until he had a heart attack.'

'Oh, then why isn't she in prison?' She tried to keep her voice softly inquiring but her eyes kept threatening to roll.

'Yeah, you know what they're like. Got away with it, didn't she? Pretty girls get away with everything these days.'

'I see. When did they get married?'

'2017. I don't usually talk about my boss, but for you I'll tell the story!'

He finished his beer and looked at Miranda invitingly. She ordered another round.

'We was at the wedding. The reception was at The Tithe Barn, you know big place up near Petersfield. Grade 2 listed, we worked on it couple of years back. Tricky paint job that one with architraves everywhere ...'

Miranda had to keep her eyes very still. What was it Cat had told her? Keep quiet, let others do the talking, most people don't feel comfortable in silence and their excess of words may well give something away.

'Anyway, love, Tom insisted that the whole workforce came to the reception. Even let me bring my mate Marvin. He was a good man Tom, got in extra beer ...'

Miranda pouted.

'OK, posh totty, not everyone likes champagne ... some of us have more refined tastes.'

Miranda laughed. 'Go on.'

Mark drank some beer. 'The actual ceremony, like, was elsewhere ... she's Catholic wanted a proper service ... I don't think Tom cared one way or other. He's normal like us. You should've seen the size of the tents, must've had a thousand or more people in them. They was crammed ... and the catering ... sixty to seventy vans, at least ... and the guests ... films stars, hundreds of politicians ... lords, ladies, royalty ... you name 'em they was there ... ha! Them and their morals!'

He looked at Miranda suddenly thoughtful.

'You be careful love. She's well connected that one. That Anastasia! Poisonous spiders are much more deadly than dogs.'

CHAPTER 3
MARBELLA 1987

Bogdan's priest had found a lovely Scottish laird called Johnny Holmes who was looking for a wife. A tall handsome man with straight teeth, he owned a small island north of Scotland called Fetlar. He was busy showing Bogdan and his mother pictures of his nineteenth-century Gothic castle, when Anastasia arrived back on her horse.

He rose immediately.

'*Privetstviye*' he said, with an elegant flourish that captured not only a seventeen-year-old girl's heart, but her mother.

Her father and brother had already been captured by his Mercedes, his castle and the tales of vanquishing clans on the islands, back in family history. Nobody in the Rodriguez family could find anything wrong with the rich handsome Johnny Holmes from Brough Lodge, and the way he generously spent his money on anything they required endeared them even further.

For Anastasia, whose experience of men was limited to those who prayed with her parents, Johnny was a revelation straight from the pop and film magazines of her village friends: magazines not allowed at home.

'He looks like Thomas Anders,' Anastasia told her girl-friends.

When Johnny heard that, he went out and hired a Cadillac. Drove Anastasia around Marbella and the local villages with 'Geronimo's Cadillac' playing on the cassette player. Anastasia, at first awed, was soon waving at the tourists and locals like a film star, basking in the jealous looks, and the admiring ones.

Three weeks later, the debonair Johnny Holmes and his beautiful fiancée Anastasia Rodriguez were married in El Encarnación. One of the best churches in Marbella, it was built in the sixteenth century and was formerly a mosque.

The Rodriguez family had been delightedly surprised to find a Catholic Scottish laird, and Johnny admitted he was unusual, especially in his devotion. This, he said sadly, although he did not like to traduce his peers, was very rare in the Highlands and Islands, which could be cruel, lawless places.

'Ah,' said his future mother-in-law, 'it sounds like Russia.'

Johnny had found some bagpipers to play at the wedding, and the reception was so lavish that it captured the hearts of the Rodriguez friends, as well as the family. No one was left out. This wedding would still be talked about in years to come. Even Bogdan knew he was doing the right thing by his sister.

They spent their honeymoon in Marbella. Johnny insisted on entertaining his in-laws, Bodgan and his priest to every dinner. Three weeks of constant celebration.

The newly married couple stayed in the family house and here Johnny distinguished himself by his sensitivity.

'Of course,' he said to his mother-in-law, 'Anastasia must remain in her bedroom and I will take the spare room. She is still young, will need time to get used to the change of circumstances and her changing role to wife, and hopefully, mother.'

Eventually though, much to the sadness of all concerned, the happy couple had to drive north, to go back to the laird's Castle in Shetland. How glad, Johnny said, his mother would be to welcome her new daughter-in-law. How pleased she would be that he had finally married. She had been worried for the succession. Now she would find contentment at last.

With flowing tears and laughing hearts the grandchildren ran after the Mercedes as it gathered speed away from the warm sunlight of the south, towards the cold but wealthy charms of the north.

CHAPTER 4

OWLY VALE 2018

All night Miranda mused on whether the Black Widow was a potential case, or simply a pub assumption: unfounded and unfair. This after all was the agency motto:

Looking beyond the assumption and what SeeMs to be true.

In the morning, she dashed over to see Cat and their other colleague Stevie, only to discover they had gone flying.

Miranda hurried through the field behind the house to the airstrip, cleverly created by Stevie with a borrowed tractor, hoping they hadn't left yet. Too late! Miranda hated flying and couldn't believe anyone would voluntarily go up in a shaky old biplane that didn't even have a roof. OK, Stevie was an airline pilot, but did that really mean she needed to practice loops and rolls? Ha ha! Miranda rolled her eyes: even that made her feel queasy.

When she looked up again, she saw, to her relief, they were circling down, leaving little trails against the blue sky, clearly preparing to land. Hurrah! They would be so thrilled by what she was about to tell them. She nearly tripped in her haste to get over to the plane.

The Moth had bumped its way to a stop by the time Miranda dodged through the fence and walked over. Cat leapt out of the front seat, balancing for a moment on the walkway on the wing and jumping down with such a lithe movement that Miranda bit her lip. How could anyone be so slim when they were pushing sixty years old? It was insulting to younger, normal(ish)-sized women.

Hastily Miranda reminded herself that the agency had a unique way of operating: in collaboration. One for all and all for one! They had even considered calling the agency The Three Dogateers, before adopting a less derivative name: SeeMs, a combination of their names and their belief.

Cat picked up the puppy who was tagging along behind Miranda and hugged it.

'Hello, darling, has Miri been nice to you while we were away?'

'No!' said Miranda. 'Little brute chewed up Peta's shoes and Felix's homework last night.'

Cat laughed.

Stevie cleaned the oil off the Tiger Moth's cowling, wiping her hands on her grey cotton flying suit and muttering to herself about overfilling and leaks.

'Are you girls ready yet?' asked Miranda impatiently. 'I've got something so, so thrilling to discuss. A potential new case.'

Cat looked sideways. 'One you found in the pub last night, by any chance.'

Miranda ignored her. There were a lot of annoying things about Cat, not just the fact she was so much thinner than she should be given her love of doughnuts. Still, you could only feel sorry for her: Cat had problems with her children, whereas Miranda's were little saints.

'You go ahead,' said Stevie, fetching a rag from her pocket and starting to wipe the Moth's nose. 'I'll join you in a few minutes.'

'OK,' said Cat, moving away.

Miranda paused, watching the younger girl.

'It is really fascinating news,' she said hopefully. 'Multiple murderess! You will hurry?'

'OK,' said Stevie, opening the cowling. 'Ten minutes. OK?'

Cat and Miranda walked towards Stevie's house. They could see Stevie's mother peering out the window, watching them approach. She was wearing a long velvet dress, her hair done up in an elegant costume-jewellery diamond tiara and waving a lorgnette.

'Going to a party?' Miranda asked Cat, her eyes widening.

'Who knows? Maybe today she's organising a do for her husband. Last week, she told me he was travelling in the Caribbean, and he's been dead over ten years.'

Cat opened the door and Blinkey came forward.

'Password?' she said.

Miranda jumped back, her hands in front of her.

'Hello Blinkey, darling,' said Cat.

'Password!' repeated Blinkey, waving her lorgnette aggressively at them. 'No entry without the password.'

'Blinkey darling, would you like a coffee? I've brought doughnuts.'

Cat leant forward and kissed the old woman.

'Darlings,' said Blinkey warmly. 'Lovely outfits, very New Look.'

'Phew,' said Miranda hurrying past to the kitchen, 'she

gave me a dog bowl of wine last time and I didn't know what to do with it.'

'Just put it in the sink, that's what I do. Or, if you're desperate drink it.'

'Ha ha.'

Miranda moved some of Stevie's tools from the table, frowning. She considered a doughnut, keeping her eyes away from the mirror visible through the door.

'Shall I tell you what I learnt in the pub, not wait for Stevie?'

Cat put the kettle on the hob and began searching for the coffee beans, finding them under the dog food, behind a Tesco's delivery crate.

'I would. You know she'll be hours once she starts looking for leaks.'

'OK, since you didn't come, I started talking to various of the chaps. And, apparently, thanks to the murder, they had to sell half the company.'

'Which company? What murder?'

Cat gave the puppy some water.

'Drayton's. You know the huge builder in Petersfield, been around for yonks, owned by three brothers? The great great or several more greats, grandchildren of the founder. The one who built the pub in—'

'OK, slow down ... who murdered whom and why?'

'Well, one of the three brothers died of a massive heart attack only three weeks after his wedding.'

'And ... you think it was murder? Or the pub does? How is the poor bride?'

Miranda sneered. 'Mark says she 100%! This is her fourth hubby, and each time she's walked off with the lolly. And she was Russian!'

Cat stared at Miranda, waving her doughnut absent-mindedly. 'So, is this massive news? That a Russian woman had four husbands all of whom died?'

'No! That she killed them all and moved to Spain.'

'Have I missed anything?' Stevie came in, taking off her helmet and gloves and dropping them on the table. 'What's the news?'

'Yes,' said Cat sarcastically, 'we are planning to fly to Spain to catch a Russian Black Widow in her web.'

Stevie raised her eyebrows. 'Oh, her. The woman who stuffed Pete.'

The other two stared at her. 'What?'

Stevie stared at that. 'Yes, when the guy brought over the tractor, so I could mow the strip, he mentioned the court case has just ended and Pete's brother's widow got half the business. Pete was incandescent. Apparently, he said that if he got his hands on her there'd be another stiff in the business.'

CHAPTER 5
ABERDEEN 1987

Dear Mother and Father,
England is very green. It has been raining since we arrived in Portsmouth and all the way to Aberdeen. There are lots of cows here.

I took some photographs on the ferry from Bilbao, some on the way and I have taken more here, which I will send you when we arrive in Lerwick.

Lerwick is the main town of Shetland.

We are about to go on another ferry to Shetland, which is not one place but loads of islands. Johnny said he only owns one island, but perhaps he is about to surprise me with a gift of an island for myself. How exciting.

The people here in Scotland don't speak English. Actually, they do, but it is not English like we speak in Spain. They use lots of strange words and their accent pulls the language at length so it sounds as though they are singing. Examples: they say Aye, instead of Yes, and Dinnae (pronounced dinner) instead of Do Not. They keep calling Johnny a Chancer, which, he says, means he is very lucky, particularly in his new wife. He is so sweet and looks more like Thomas Anders every day.

Johnny says everybody here is Peely Wally, which, he says, means they have not been to Spain and are very jealous. He also tells me very often that my Heid is Full o' Mince, which he says means I am very imaginative and unusual.

Ah well. I must Skedaddle Aff. (It is a way of saying goodbye in Scotland).

XX

CHAPTER 6

OWLY VALE 2018

Somewhat to Cat's surprise, Stevie also thought there might be a case to answer here. Something for the SeeMs Agency to work on.

Cat's remonstration: 'But we don't have a client!' fell on determinedly deaf ears.

'I'll do some research on the internet,' said Stevie. 'Costs nothing and who knows what I'll find?'

'And I'll return to the pub,' said Miranda, 'also free info!'

Cat sighed. 'Two against one. OK, I agree.'

This collaborative working could be so frustrating!

While Miranda planned her later trip to the pub and Cat went out to interview someone whose dog had been stolen, Stevie settled down on the computer in the corner of the kitchen.

She started by putting the name Anastasia in the computer. Immediately swamped by historical information and films, Stevie decided to change tack. Going on to Instagram she found details of the 2017 Drayton wedding. Although the family themselves put nothing on the site, plenty of their friends had been excited by the important event and there were many pictures, and even short videos, posted by guests.

A tall, beautiful woman in her mid-forties, wearing a light blue tailor-made wedding gown of lace over silk, glided around the room, with two equally tall younger people, in matching blue outfits. *Must be Anastasia. Did she have children? Or were these some other friends or relations?*

Stevie scanned through pictures and videos hoping to see anybody she recognised. All those tall, beautiful people, even the way they strode across the room marked them out as Top Dogs in their own kennels. Stevie might work for them, or invent things for them, but never be one or own one. In her pre-pilot days, otherwise known as her childhood, her parents enjoyed planning her wedding to this kind of person but Stevie was not interested. She wanted to make her own life, not live the life of her parent's ambition.

Luckily Miranda was different. Miranda *did* people, all people: big time. Miranda revelled in conversation, the way Stevie was invigorated by flying. 'And Cat,' thought Stevie, smiling, 'Cat was their Tiger Mother, defender of the young, flamboyant dresser.' Stevie shook her head, smiling, she loved Cat like a daughter, even with all her eccentricities.

One of the social-media comments drew Stevie's attention back to the screen. Someone called Mateo Perez Rodriguez had provided the wine for the wedding. *Why?* Looking at the pictures of the tall woman in blue with the matching youngsters, one was labelled Mateo. *Was it possible that Spanish children took both parents' names?* In which case Anastasia was either Perez or Rodriguez. That seemed rather more of a Spanish name than the Russian nationality suggested by Miranda's pub informant, Mark, but, perhaps because of her first name, he had just assumed she was Russian.

Assumptions. She hated it when people assumed all pilots were male, and yet, when she first met Miranda Zielinski, she had assumed she was Russian.

Miranda had replied: 'Imagine how irritating it is for a trans person to be asked "are you really male or female?" Then multiply that by the population of Poland: that is about half the amount you have pissed me off.'

Stevie decided not to ask Miranda if Anastasia was Russian.

Tapping in 'wine makers of Spain' Stevie discovered the Perez family had a vineyard just outside Jerez.

Intriguing and something for the multilingual Cat, if they took this further?

Mateo Perez Rodrigues, who owned the vineyard, had a business profile. Stevie discovered he was born in 1993, making him twenty-five. Young to be running what looked like a vast empire. However, looking at the history on Perez vineyard site, it was clear that his father, Carlos Perez, who was described as the innovator and genius of the vineyard, had died in 2012. There was also the information that Carlos married Anastasia Rodriguez in 1992. *Could this be our Anastasia and either her first or second husband?* A check showed that Anastasia was born in 1970, so she would have been twenty-two when she married Perez.

Could anyone be getting married for the third time at the age of twenty-two? *Seemed unlikely.*

More details on a Señor Perez, father of Mateo Perez Rodriguez and his sister Isabella, showed that Señor Perez appeared to be liable for some special tax that was a required payment for those who insisted on keeping a title in Spain.

She twirled her chair around, thinking. Spanish? Russ-

ian? Scottish? What other nationalities did Anastasia have?
What would her DNA test show?

Stevie gave up speculating and went out to the airstrip.
Pushed out the Tiger Moth and hand swung it from behind
the prop for safety. Claire had taught her that, just as she
taught her everything else.

Flying relaxed her, made her think more clearly. As she
looped gently over the local farmland, Stevie wondered
what age Anastasia was in marriage one. Cat first married at
just 19, so Anastasia might well have done the same or
younger. A runaway love marriage?

Stevie knew about absconding for love.

One day, biking back from school, Stevie saw an old
Tiger Moth running up in a field near the road. Curious, she
left her bike, ducked under the fence and walked over.

An old woman looked at her from the back seat. She
pulled the power when she saw Stevie walking over. She
reached into the cockpit under her seat.

'Wanna come?' she asked, handing the young girl a cloth
helmet.

Stevie put it on, clambered up the black-painted
walkway and into the front cockpit, qualmless.

As they took off Stevie felt the reality of dancing
between sun-split clouds; of slipping the surly bonds of
earth; of chasing the shouting wind. Stevie too trod the high
untrespassed sanctity of space ... and touched the face of
God. Beauty learnt from Pilot Officer Magee: a man killed
forty years before she was born and now forever embedded
in her heart.

After that, Stevie, playing truant from school, flew every
day from the local airfield. Claire taught her, laughed with

her, enjoyed their flights as much as her pupil. In no time, Stevie had soloed, learnt aerobatics and was on to navigation. Neither of them thought about licences or legality, only about the fun and beauty of flight.

Then, one Thursday, she arrived at the hangar to find it locked. No sign of Claire or her car. Stevie went to the café to wait. Perhaps Claire was late, it was unusual, but not impossible, things did happen at the last minute.

As she ordered a tea, a young boy from the aero club touched her on the shoulder.

'You Stevie?'

'Yes.'

'Thought I saw you around with Claire. They said to let you know she died.'

'Died!'

Stevie stared at him. Too numb to understand.

'Died? How? What happened?'

Had Clare had an accident?

'No idea. She was old. Maybe a heart attack ... er ... sorry ... like.'

This was the end: her parents had no money for flying. Anyway, they wanted her to marry well. Did well-born husbands crave a wife who wanted to fly? Fly. And then fly some more.

Two weeks later she received a phone call from Claire's lawyer. Claire had left Stevie the Tiger Moth in her will. Stevie, refusing to accept a little nagging question in her brain that it might not be legal, continued flying on her own.

When Stevie reached eighteen, she told her parents she wanted to be an airline pilot. Their reaction meant she walked out of the house that day taking nothing but her car and a few clothes.

Chapter 7

As Stevie looped and rolled in the Heavens, Cat was on her way home after an unproductive discussion with Miranda about finding a client for 'this Black Widow sideline of yours, when we really need to concentrate on the lost dogs'.

'Something will crop up,' said Miranda brushing the puppy, 'it always does. You know life has this marvellous way of providing answers when you start looking for them.'

'Huh! Says you,' said Cat, performing the incredible feat of rolling her eyes while hurrying next door.

Frank and his friend Angelo were drinking gin and tonic in the garden. Frank was wearing Cat's apron, and as she passed through the kitchen, she could smell spices and lamb in the oven.

'Hey, sweetheart, we're out here.'

As soon as they saw her, the sheep in the neighbouring field pushed their heads against the garden gate baaing loudly. Frank laughed.

'She feeds them apples,' he said to Angelo, 'so they've

become like dogs. Every time they see her, they start crazy woofing.'

One of the fat dogs opened an eye, only to immediately shut it and return to sleep.

Cat gave Angelo her hand. 'They don't have much grass and even the dogs have eaten enough apples. But I've met you before ... only you were the world's expert on snails then, and on some safety committee with Frank.'

Angelo gave a huge guffaw of laughter. 'Guilty as charged! And you were a beautiful woman then, and still are a beautiful woman, but also with a good memory.'

'So now art?'

'Yes, I started painting the snails and diversified.'

Frank laughed, getting up to go inside. 'I bet you are not even joking. If I tried that in a gig, I'd get booed off stage.'

Angelo laughed. 'Nothing new there! But I'm not joking, it was the best thing that ever happened to me. I shared an exhibition with a photographer, who turned out to be the love of my life.'

'How nice,' said Cat politely, as she and Angelo followed Frank into the house. 'I hope we will meet her soon.'

Although Angelo was still talking as they walked into the kitchen Cat focused on a bottle of champagne in a bucket on the island.

'Have you sold a book?' she asked her boyfriend.

'So many that champagne would be unnecessary.' He smiled at her. 'But seriously, Angelo brought it, he has news.'

Cat turned to Angelo raising her eyebrows. 'Must be good to bring us Veuve Clicquot.'

'It is indeed. The best news ever! And concerns a widow, if not the Widow Clicquot.'

Angelo grasped the champagne, fumbling briefly with

its top. It opened with a pop and the cork flew off into the air, hitting a kitchen cabinet and crashing to the ground.

Seemingly unaware of the stopper's shenanigans, Angelo gave them each a glass and still standing, lifted his glass to his friends:

'I'm getting married. The love of my life loves me, even more than a snail. What happiness!'

Frank laughed. 'Do we get her name?'

Angelo guffawed. 'Now this is really "a rose by any name would smell as sweet". My love has had five surnames in her career. Luckily she very early on decided to do all her photography under her maiden name or she'd never sell a picture but simply have a bemused fan club.'

Cat stiffened nervously, staring down at the grounded cork sitting in the dust.

'What is her name, Angelo?'

'Oh, so keen, Mama Cat, she goes under the glorious beautiful exotic name of Anastasia Rodriguez.'

CHAPTER 8

SHETLAND NOVEMBER 1987

The forty-knot wind forced the November downpour into harsh curtains that reversed into spray guns as they hit the tarmac. Inside the Scatsta Airport hut, a young boy looked intently out into the maelstrom. Weather like this was not unusual in Shetland, but why was the helicopter flying out to the oilrigs tonight? What could be so important that they needed to fly in a storm?

Yes, even the best pilots got caught out, but Clement was better than the best. He was infallible.

Peering out into the fading light, the boy rubbed the pane automatically, willing the visibility to improve. Clement *will* be back, he told himself, his leg tapping up and down in a curiously constant rhythm. Ignoring the goosebumps growing on his arms and legs, his eyes searched the sky, but there was no sign of the helicopter.

The airfield cat rubbed itself against his leg. The boy reached down and stroked it; his gaze still glued to the horizon.

'Don't worry Cashy,' he told the cat, 'he'll be here soon.

He's the best pilot in Shetland. And he knows the helicopter and the weather like ... like ... like you know which cat food is best.'

The cat gave a soft meow and the boy smiled.

'Sorry, Cashy, are you hungry? We'll just wait a bit more.'

Then, through the crashing cascades and howling wind, the boy recognised the whoop whoop beat of Bolkow blades. His whole body shuddered and relaxed.

'See, Cashy,' he said. 'I told you Clement would be OK. I told you he was the best pilot in the world.'

The cat rubbed itself on his leg, purring. The helicopter nosed out of the rain curtain, arcs of steam around its blades reflected in the hangar lights. The boy grabbed the cat and, his clothes immediately saturated by the downpour, ran like a gazelle, arriving at the heliport ready with the trolley, just as Clement landed.

Measuring the moment to drive the trolley under the helicopter's belly, the boy's heart gave a jolt of surprise. Clement was not alone in the helicopter. The boy recognised the people with him and knew it was against regulations.

Why? Clement never broke the rules. He would lose his licence if he was caught, and for Clement flying was life. What could Clement and his passengers have been doing that would be worth risking his licence for?

CHAPTER 9

OWLY VALE 2018

L anding the Tiger and pushing it into the hangar she'd constructed from leftover building material, Stevie was smiling inside and out. It was one of those soft pure evenings when the air was still and warm and flying the Tiger Moth felt like a small preview of Heaven.

Forcing herself to resist the temptation to check the Moth for leaks, Stevie headed towards the house. She needed to do more research on Anastasia, before she went back to work next week. Her shifts at British Airways were pretty good, but her ten days of leave were nearly over, and the 777, mini-jumbo, was calling. Now life had morphed into the Laptop Age, she could still do her detective research for SeeMs wherever she was in the world: but it was definitely her second job, flying would always be her first love.

As she walked towards the house her phone went off.

'Cat?' She was surprised because she knew Cat and Frank had a visitor this evening.

'Stevie. Disaster!'

'What?' Stevie wasn't that worried. Both Cat and Miranda tended to think losing a shoe was disastrous.

'Angelo is about to become the fifth dead husband.'

'What? What are you talking about?'

OK, not a lost shoe but a fantasy instead. 'Who is Angelo and why is he going to die?'

'He,' said Cat, her voice edging on hysteria, 'is Frank's best friend and he has just become engaged to Anastasia Rodriguez!'

'I see,' said Stevie calmly, 'well, we'd better find out if she is a killer of husbands or just unlucky. See what information about her you can glean from the loving fiancé.'

Stevie walked into the house, got herself a glass of water and settled down by the computer. She was pretty certain from the date line that Anastasia's Perez husband was the second of the four men. They already had the fourth husband, since that was where they came in. So, now Stevie needed to find the first and third husbands and see how they died, or, indeed, if they were still alive. Rumours have a way of imitating rubbish.

As Stevie began looking for an Anastasia Rodriguez marriage in the 1980s, Blinkey walked in carrying a feather duster. This was unusual, Blinkey normally thought herself too grand to search for spider's webs. Her words emphasised this confusion.

'Good morning, me lady. I don't think I've had me wages this month.'

Stevie shook her head. 'Mummy ...'

Blinkey shot round waving her duster. 'Mummy? Mummy? Why are you calling me Mummy, I'm not pregnant?'

Stevie wished Cat was here. She was so good with Blinkey, while Stevie herself alternated between wanting to cry or run away, back to the safety of the engineering shed. She tried again. Perhaps she should remind Blinkey that this was her house, so she was in charge and didn't need to look for spiders.

'No Mummy, the boot is on the other foot ...'

To Stevie's amazement Blinkey sat down and took off her shoes, swapping them left to right and right to left. She got up and tried to walk, but immediately sat down again.

'No, you are wrong! I was right. The boot was on the right foot.'

She swapped her shoes back while Stevie looked on silently: people were not her thing.

Chapter 10

When Cat (carrying a bag of doughnuts) and Miranda (plus puppy) came over the next morning, Stevie had still not found anything on the third husband. However, she had found a lot about the first one, including that he lived on a small island within Shetland called Fetlar: population sixty people.

'She went to some diverse places,' remarked Miranda, throwing off her shoes, which the puppy immediately stole and started to chew. 'How many Spanish people go up to The Shetlands? Come to that, I've never been there.'

'Ah, that was with the husband,' said Stevie. 'He worked on the Brent platform as an oilman or a diver, not sure which. Also, small point but they are called Shetland or The Shetland Islands, not a combination of both.'

Miranda threw the dog brush at her. 'How did you find out? About the husband.'

'Once I discovered which year she married the fourth husband, I could find her birthday and then look for previous marriages. There was one for an Anastasia Rodriguez in 1987, when she was seventeen.'

'Seventeen's very young to marry,' said Miranda, 'doesn't sound like she had much education. Was she like me? Leaving school at sixteen because ... because I had to?'

Stevie nodded. 'Seventeen: The age when you can, just, hold a driving or pilot's licence. Too young to buy cigarettes, alcoholic drinks in a bar, or get a tattoo. At seventeen, in England, you need the consent of a parent or guardian to marry. So, it cannot have been a runaway marriage: unless Scotland was majorly different.'

'Perhaps that was why Anastasia was in Shetland,' said Miranda. 'In Georgette Heyer novels heroines are always eloping to the borders, so clearly in Scotland you can or could marry without parental consent at sixteen years old.'

'On the other hand,' said Stevie, 'before 2015 a girl of fourteen could marry in Spain. And Anastasia was married in Marbella in Spain.'

'Oh,' said Cat, 'like me. Married before twenty but in her case a widow by ... when?'

'Same year she married,' said Stevie. 'He died in 1987. Married in March, widow by November.'

'Wow, that's quick! How did you find out?'

'By magic. Internet magic. *The New York Times* ran an article in 1988, about the dangers of working on oilrigs in the North Sea. It was written shortly after his death and his was listed. An accident. Vague on the details but looked like a fall off the rig.'

'Really?' said Cat. 'I went onto a rig once, doing a translation job, and they had nets all-round the place. You couldn't just fall off that platform.'

'Now, you may be right,' said Stevie. 'But back in the 1980s things were very different! Looking at the stats on the Brent platform, it happened more than once. Even, on one occasion, three people fell off in quick succession, and no one noticed.'

'Are you serious?' said Cat, wrinkling her brow. 'Their work must have been important!'

'On no,' broke in Miranda, fighting the puppy for her shoe, 'that's typical 1980s.'

'What is?' asked Cat, 'people falling off rigs?'

'Ha, ha! No, lack of regulation. In the pub last night, a journalist was pointed out who didn't go into the office throughout the 1980s, but was still on a full salary. The company were that rich they never noticed.'

Cat waved her hand dismissively.

'OK,' said Stevie, 'There were all sorts of other deaths too, on rigs and platforms over the world. Helicopters accounted for a few deaths and injuries. Injury from instruments, falls, even a couple blown off platforms by the wind while going up ladders. Cop that! Brent can't have been the easiest place to work with some three-and-a-half thousand people working there.'

'Three-and-a-half thousand people,' said Miranda, now hopping around in one shoe while the puppy evaded her, 'quite a party. All at once or shifts?'

'Shifts. And that was at the zenith. By the 1980s they were down to two thousand eight hundred.'

'So do we think it was an accident?' asked Miranda. 'Or could one of the two thousand eight hundred people have pushed him off? Even his wife?'

'Maybe so, but at the time Anastasia was not there, so not her.'

'How do you know?'

'Rigs and platforms didn't allow women.'

Miranda narrowed her eyes. 'Bet there were some, for all that – smuggled in for a party!'

Cat ignored her. 'When did they let women on to the rigs?'

'Looks like sometime in the 1990s.'

'So late.'

'Not so odd,' said Stevie, 'the UK didn't allow women RAF pilots until the 90s either.'

'And yet, they still had parties ...' Miranda threw her remaining shoe at the puppy.

Chapter 11

C at stared at the globe in her office. At the top of the UK were The Shetland Islands, so far north they could have been part of Scandinavia, while at the bottom of Spain was Jerez, so far south you could wave at Africa. Google Maps told her it would take twenty-two hours to drive to Lerwick (which wasn't even as far north as she needed to go) and that included a ferry and tolls. The map showed that The Shetlands were made up of hundreds of small and medium-sized islands, and not just one great big island like Lewis and Harris over on the west coast.

However, when she researched how to get to The Shetlands, her heart sank. It was easier and cheaper to fly to the south of Spain than get to the little islands north of Aberdeen and parallel with Bergen in Norway. It was hard to believe that it was still part of the UK.

But they had to do it. They had to find out if Angelo was safe to marry Anastasia or not.

For a wild moment she considered hiring a Cessna and getting Stevie to fly her up to Shetland. Then she remembered the cost of flying a small plane in a previous case. In that case the client had refused to pay the bill.

Perhaps she should just take her car.

'I might drive,' she told Miranda, 'take the ferry, it would be cheaper.'

'And you'd be too done-in to interview. Forget it Cat! Remember how exhausted you were after the lost French bulldog incident, when you insisted on driving back from Cannes. Let the plane take the strain. Make a bit of a holiday while you are there. Are you ever likely to visit Shetland again?'

'Attractive idea, but we still need a paying client. Someone who wants to ensure Angelo survives his first marriage.'

Sometimes in life, amazing coincidences happen: you think of calling a friend, only to discover she has just picked up the phone to call you; you long for a client and one arrives as if by magic. However, this was not one of those times.

What did happen, however, was that Blinkey decided to give her daughter some money.

'I've been listening to Money Box Live on the radio,' she told Stevie, confounding her daughter: clearly this was one of her lucid days. 'Paul Lewis says old people have too much money and should give it away.'

'Did he?'

Stevie's heart sank, where did Blinkey try and send money? And how much?

On a previous occasion, Blinkey had become obsessed by the women of Afghanistan and insisted on wearing a burqa (actually a blanket with a hole cut in it, as she didn't have a burqa) twenty-four hours a day in support.

'Yes, and he says then you must live seven years. So, if I give you money, I'll live another seven years.'

'Mum! That was not what he meant.'

'How do you know? You weren't listening, were you? Anyway, it's my money, I'll do what I like with it.'

'No, Mum, you need it to pay the carers.'

'I'd much rather have you, darling. Why don't you give up that funny little job and come and look after me?'

Stevie sighed; luckily, she had power of attorney. But her mother's demented wisdom had put an idea into her mind.

'Has Angelo,' she asked Cat, 'got any relations?'

'No idea.'

'You could ask Frank.'

The girls found their client: Angelo had a younger sister.

Chapter 12

Angelo's sister, Gia, was a scientist. She was currently working on a project at King's College Hospital in London. While Angelo was a tubby enthusiast on life, who loved talking, joking and spending time with people, Gia preferred facts. However, she did tolerate people enough to agree to meet Frank and his detective friend. They took a train out to Denmark Hill in London.

'King's has a helipad,' said Frank, swinging into his train seat like a performing monkey. 'If you were a proper detective, like James Bond, we could steal a helicopter, land on the helipad, abseil down the side of the building and arrive in her office through the window in triumph. She would immediately sign us for a million-dollar deal.'

'Or stare at us in disbelief before sending us packing. From the way you described her, she's not likely to be impressed by that kind of bravado.'

Instead, they walked in through the front door and out to the rabbit warren of interconnected buildings at the back. They then spent fifteen minutes trying to find the Portakabin that held Gia's office with the aid of a hand-drawn map she had emailed them. When they finally arrived, they were still ten minutes early.

'How do you do it?' asked Frank stretching his arms above his head, as though hoping to flatten the curve of his stomach.

'What? Arrive early?' Cat smiled wryly. 'Long years of practice. Or of finding that my husband Charlie wouldn't talk to us if we didn't arrive on time.'

Gia's secretary showed them into her boss' office exactly on time.

Gia looked up from her papers and indicated the seats in front of the desk. The secretary shut the door quietly.

'Why do you think,' Gia asked, looking directly at Cat, 'Anastasia would want to kill my brother?'

'From what we've heard so far,' Cat replied, collapsing into a seat, 'money is the driving factor.'

Gia clasped her hands together and stared at her desk. Cat would have liked to babble on with explanations, but Frank had warned her that Gia liked long silent contemplation and would be unlikely to be swayed by anything she said. So, she sat on the hard seat trying not to fidget, examining the posters on the wall, including one of wild horses under a palm tree and another of nuns in short-sleeved tunics leaning over a trestle table. There was a sign on the table 'Little Girl Island'. One of the nuns was laughing at the camera. She wondered what Gia's project did and whether it might be short of money.

'Very well,' Gia said after several minutes. 'I will need a report, which should include details of current costs, every week and an interim report if anything of exceptional note arises. As an example of 'exceptional note' I mean something such as a fifth or perhaps sixth husband either alive or dead, other previously unknown children or particular expertise that might facilitate an unremarked death.'

She looked up from the desk and stared at Cat.

'Tonight, I would like to receive a detailed report from you on all the possible expenses. If you are uncertain of the amount, tell me and give an estimate with a maximum and a minimum. I also need to know your daily rate and any other possible costs.

'I will set up a bank account, to which only you and I will have access. In this will be a finite amount of money, which I will ascertain shortly. Once the money has gone, you will have to stop working. But I hope before that time to have your assurance on Anastasia's behaviour one way or another. If you have any questions send them by email, you have my personal one.'

She got up.

'Thank you. You have both been very helpful and I will be in touch with the contract shortly.'

As they walked down the corridor Frank said: 'Felt like being in the headmaster's office, hoping I wasn't going to get beaten, only the chairs were more uncomfortable.'

Cat smiled. 'I think this is the first time we've had a contract at the SeeMs Agency, feels like we are growing up.'

'So, grown-up kitten,' said Frank, 'you have your client, now what?'

Chapter 13

Cat flew to Aberdeen in a normal-size aircraft.

Once in Aberdeen, the passengers followed signs to the bowels of the airport, where only plane spotters and enthusiasts would willingly walk. Here there were no air bridges, no promise of champagne or coffee to ease your onward journey, only tarmac, pushback vans, sniffer dogs and cloisters leading the brave souls to the twin-engine shrimp that stood waiting to take them onward to Shetland.

Cat hesitated before climbing up the steps, clocking the windsock that stretched out horizontally across the runway. She reminded herself this was a much bigger plane than the Tiger Moth, and Stevie flew that daily without incident.

It would be worth it, she told herself, giving her bag to the attendant who muttered about size and weight. Cat had a single seat on the left-hand side.

'Lovely view,' said a cheerful man on the other side of the aisle. 'Probably one of the most exciting flights in the UK.'

Cat smiled, wondering what the word exciting meant here.

'I prefer it to flying out to the Scillies,' he added, 'best captains in Scotland, but then, of course they have to be ... the fog—'

Cat blanked out his voice and looked out the window. No fear of fog today, but the windsock did look rather active. Perhaps Shetland was sheltered. The words at least were similar.

As they taxied out the wings wobbled, and Cat's stomach lurched. Her cheerful neighbour cheered.

'I love listening to the changing engine note,' he said happily, 'don't you?'

'Yes,' said Cat weakly. 'So musical.'

He grinned at her.

'Some people say that engines know when they are over the sea, they like to tell the pilot.'

Cat bit her lip.

Never had she been so happy to taxi-in at an airport. No wonder some people kissed the tarmac when they arrived.

A rented Vauxhall Astra was waiting for her at the airport, the company helpfully texting the registration: ZE 50 BJJ.

Cat looked for the car. There was a rather dilapidated Vauxhall Astra near the terminal entrance, she checked the registration: ZE 50 BBJ. Yup, that was the one.

The driver's door was locked.

She stared at the unyielding Astra. Checked the registration again. Tried the door again. Her first interview might be with a locksmith instead of an oilman. She started to pull out her phone when a little voice in her brain suggested she try the other doors first.

On the passenger's side, the door opened. Phew. The

keys were in the sun visor as advertised but there was note
on the passenger seat:

'Don't use driver's door. Broken'

Hum, Cat muttered, clambering across to the driver's
seat, Stevie did say she got a very cheap deal.

Husband Number One, Johnny Holmes, had flown out
to the oil rigs from Scatsta Airport, on the north of the main
island. The manager of the parent company, Mr Smith, and
the PR man, Mr Outrage, agreed to meet Cat at 11 o'clock the
next morning at Scatsta.

Stevie booked her in at Busta House Hotel, close to the
interview airport.

Cat programmed her phone for Busta House Hotel.
Although it was only 46 miles, it was going to take her over
an hour. Didn't sound as though there was a motorway
going down the island.

Cat turned to Google Maps and, relieved to see the
cheap car started easily, drove out of the airport.

Leaving the airport, she felt a culture shock. The road
itself was well paved and fast, much better than the roads
down south, which were full of potholes. This ordinary
country highway wove through the hills, but there was one
staggering difference: there were no trees. No trees at all. Cat
had never considered what a treeless area would look like.
Now she knew.

The barren hills resembled the pictures sent back from
the moon; the distance of their landscape unbroken by the
usual towers of nature one took for granted. Even so, the
hills themselves had a stunning beauty, covered as they were
with a purple sheen of heather. The heather grew out of
peat that had lain there for so many millions of years, and
where the peat had been harvested, perhaps for the fire-

place instead of logs, there were great crevasses filled with brackish water edged with peat hags.

Down south, Cat thought, gardens lost their colour at this time of year, but here it seemed as though the colours were more vibrant and purer. Why had she not known this before?

A surprising amount of traffic was heading up towards Sullom Voe, which she now knew was the major oil terminal of The Shetland Islands. How, she wondered, could you have oil without wood? She wished she had studied geology at school, but it certainly hadn't been offered.

'How about Anastasia?' Cat thought, staring out at the magnificent undulations. How had she felt arriving here at seventeen years old? Was the young Spanish girl filled with awe and trepidation, comparing her own minisculity with those Herculean hills? Or was she so in love with her husband that she saw only cosy dreams?

Cat was herself married at nineteen. She could think of nothing but her Adonis, then. First love was so engrossing. How bewitched she had been, just married to the most perfect man in the world.

* * *

Cat had not been popular with boys when she was young. She was tall, lanky, silent. While her schoolmates smoothed out into sensual swans and made witty remarks, she remained the ugly duckling who quacked. While her schoolmates went out on dates, and upset their parents with louche behaviour, she got good marks at school and a place at university. Then, the holidays before she was to go up to Edinburgh, to read French and Spanish, her half-brother told her his best friend wanted to take her out on a date. She was eighteen and had never had dinner alone with a single man before.

'What will we talk about?' she asked, horrified. 'I don't know ...'

'Don't be silly, Catherine,' he said, 'He'll do all the talking.'

'OK,' she said, shrugging. Her fate accompli! 'How old is he?'

'Same as me, thirty-three. Don't worry. He's got a younger sister too. In fact, his sister is quite a good friend of mine. Don't fuck it up, Catherine OK.'

So, a week later Cat, wearing flat shoes, since that was usually necessary, and a simple dress, waited for Charlie.

Charlie had been a good thing. He was taller than her, lankier and he arrived in a sports car. Cat didn't know the type, but she could imagine the jealous looks of her school friends. He took her to Mirabel's, even higher on the school friends' jealousy rating, and he appeared to be interested in her school studies and her university place. No one had ever been interested in that before, even her mother found it a little unnecessary. But what particularly excited Charlie was her ability to speak fluent French, Dutch and Spanish. He admitted he had never been good at languages, but he really admired people who were.

'Odd combination,' he said, 'like knowing Welsh and Chinese.'

'Not really. Holland was part of the Spanish Empire from 1581 to 1714.'

This was Cat's stock response. Charlie was not the first person to query her language combination. The reality was her girl's boarding school in the 70s, in the distant country-side, far from lively civilisation, could attract few teachers of any calibre. However, they found a Dutch woman needing employment.

'And why not?' The headmistress explained to the parents, 'these girls need someone to marry them and the Continent is next door.'

French came from her mother who, like all French mothers, believed that theirs was the superior language – English just a modern adjunct constructed by American musicians. Cat went further, she loved the colour and sound of different languages, the ability to get inside another culture's soul and see the actions of its people harmonised by the abnormalities of the language. Linguistics became her passion.

'Oh,' said Charlie, apparently deeply impressed. 'How marvellous.'

Pleased by his interest, she started telling him English had a passive voice, while the Latin-based languages were reflexive and how that highlighted their differing cultural attitudes. Charlie called for the bill.

Taking her home after dinner, he asked if he could take her out again. She agreed. A few months later they got engaged, and the university place was cancelled: now deemed unnecessary by everyone.

Chapter 14

Busta House, Cat's hotel, was a bleak white building, with windows constructed to defend rather than let in light. Driving up the hill she saw herself surrounded by hordes of marauding Vikings, their desire for rape and pillage held back by the strength of this one citadel.

However, inside was unexpected comfort: warm radiators, Turkish carpets and a spread of sheltering sofas. She was just absorbing the contrast when a young man offered her a drink.

'Can I grab you a cup of tea?'

'I'd love one,' said Cat.

Perhaps modern Vikings fought over cups of tea for their clients. How much more pleasant to be a woman now than in the ninth century, when the fight did not result in a steaming cup of hot tea.

Sitting down, she picked up a pamphlet about the history of the house and found another mystery. The owners, the Gifford family, had a tragedy of their own. In 1748, the family lost four sons, killed in a storm. One son, however, had secretly married his orphaned cousin, Barbara Pitcairn, and they had a son. A secret revealed to his mother after his death. However, Lady Gifford, even while adopting the child, threw her kinswoman out of the house and sent her to live in Lerwick, a fourteen-hour horse ride from the family.

Barbara, banished from her child, died of a broken heart and returned to wreak revenge on her oppressors.

Hum, thought Cat. Would she die of a broken heart if separated from her children: the Throuple of Vanessa, Gloria and Victor, or her other daughter Caroline and the mad son-in-law? Unlikely, but she would love to be the revenging ghost who returned to roam the gardens. That bit sounded brilliant, she could imagine herself putting sun-loving plants in the shade and climbers up to all the bedrooms.

Would the young bride and her loving husband have stopped here on their way to Fetlar? What would Anastasia have made of that story?

CHAPTER 15
ABERDEEN 1987

Dear Mother and Father,

Here we are in Fetlar. I enclose pictures of the Laird's Palace which is beautiful. It is Classical. Built on models from Italy and France in 1825. I found people here whose parents and grandparents worked on the building, and consider it a unique piece of architecture.

You will be very pleased that I am learning to cook Scottish. The food here is completely different from home and perhaps (although I don't like to criticise) a little bland.

I have a friend here called Sarah, she is lovely, pretty in that fat British way with incredible skin. She is teaching me to cook and she can do everything including drive a boat, so we got out on trips all over the islands and make cooking fires on the beach. It is very exciting.

I am being a good wife and, God willing, I am a good daughter too as I will soon be able to tell you about a thrilling event happening in my life.

I miss you all very much and hope that when that happens, I will finally be allowed to come and visit you.

Besos, Ana

CHAPTER 16
SHETLAND 2018

The next morning, Cat drove to Scatsta Airport.

The airfield buildings were being renovated and scaffolding cluttered the route to the board-room. The receptionist led the way, climbing over poles, pipes and builders, while listening to Taylor Swift singing 'I Knew You were Trouble'.

Mr Smith and Mr Outrage were waiting for her, sitting in a low-ceilinged building on the edge of the runway.

'Amazing,' said Mr Outrage, after their introductions, 'someone looking into that old Holmes case now, after all this time.'

'Yes,' said Cat. *Oh no. Busted already?*

However, Mr Outrage was really just expressing his sense of frustration at having to spend so long looking through old records.

'I finally found this file on the event. It's paper of course, long before digital records, and it wouldn't have been worth digitising after all this time.'

He handed her a thick file. She raised her eyebrows.

'Yes,' he said, noting her surprise, 'they had to do a lot of in-depth work for the insurance company. Johnny Holmes took out a life insurance policy when he married, but it had a suicide clause, which meant they would not pay out in the event of suicide in the first twelve months. However, there were certain issues that made it pretty clear his death was an accident.'

Cat was intrigued. 'What sort of issues?'

Mr Outrage looked over at Mr Smith, who nodded.

'I don't know if you are aware of this, but platforms are dry. No alcohol.'

Cat was not surprised.

'No, I didn't.'

'It's for the safety of the men and the equipment. You can't have a load of drunks living out on the platforms and getting bored with all that high tech stuff around ... I'm sure you get my gist.'

'Yes.'

'I can tell you of incidents ...'

He stopped and looked at Mr Smith, who took up the story.

'The Piper Alpha disaster changed everything. In the 70s and early 80s, the oil world was one of madness, one of excess. The oil companies had found literally tons of oil and all they wanted was to get it out of the ground as quickly as possible ...'

'And they would pay huge money to get it,' continued Mr Outrage. 'I can't tell you enough ... some guys were earning £300, £400 a day in the 70s. A fortune: say £1,500, £2,000 now. They only worked between 120 and 150 days a year.'

'Think of that money back in the 70s, it's like a million a year or more now!'

'And they were crazy. Buy a Porsche one day, crash it and go back for another next day.'

'Wow,' said Cat. She had known nothing of this, down in her southern innocence.

'Honestly, in the 70s the support ships were like floating bars. They were run by the Italians and the French: men who like a drink with meals ... then it all changed in the 1980s, when they got Brits. The Italians could hold their drink, but the British couldn't. But they had to train up the Brits, even so, I mean it was Britain.'

'Legislation changed too,' continued Mr Smith. 'Too many drunks meant changes in the law, protection, safety, you understand and suddenly everywhere became dry ... except it wasn't really.'

The men were getting enthused with their stories. 'Kenny tells a good story,' Outrage told Smith. 'He was a radio operator on Alpha, the tubes were exactly the size of a bottle. So, he would send a request onshore asking for a tube replacement. Next flight he'd get a bottle of Courvoisier!'

'And the saturation divers, they were the worst.' Smith said not to be outdone.

'Absolutely. High as a kite, some of them.'

Outrage saw from Cat's furrowed brow that she was lost and added, 'Saturation divers are men who work in metal tubes under the sea, sometimes for as long as fifty-two days. They work at 1,000 feet under the sea. They have to equal the pressure, so they don't suffer from the bends. It's an odd profession and it creates some peculiar characters, but it is incredibly well paid.'

'Wow,' said Cat, imagining herself living in a metal box for almost two months. 'No wonder they took drugs.'

'True,' said Smith, 'but they knew which drugs to take and which to go easy with.'

'After a while, you mean,' cut in Outrage. 'In the beginning it was far crazier: drugs of all types were available, there were so many tales of idiots getting spaced out and going flying off the supply ships ...'

'Well,' said Smith, hastily returning to the point. 'Holmes was a drinker. The 70s had been his highlight. Easy money. Easy women. He was one of those who once back onshore got legless. So, once the 1980s started, the *powers that be* were watching him. They always checked his bags. He definitely could not have brought the booze up himself.'

Cat thought Mr Smith sounded rather defensive and wondered where this was going.

'Did he fall off the platform because he was drunk?'

'No, because he was fetching a bottle.'

Chapter 17

Cat stared at the men, amazed. Up until now she had presumed that he tripped or something, like the many incidents found by Stevie in *The New York Times*. Now it seemed he was doing something illegal and fell to his death.

'Why was there a bottle hidden under the rig?'

'Someone had placed a bottle of whisky under the platform jacket for him and the report decided that he was reaching under to get it, when he fell off the platform. It was still clasped in his hand when he was found.'

'Wow.'

'Quite, and that was even though they didn't find him for two weeks.'

'How did that happen? Didn't anyone miss him?'

Mr Smith and Mr Outrage again exchanged glances.

'Even though legislation and the like had changed things, well, see, it's not legislation that makes changes, it's culture. Rig culture, diver culture, pilot culture, you know,' said Outrage, rubbing his cheek as though checking his shaving.

'Things were considerably more relaxed than now. People went missing and no one noticed. Boats as well as helicopters went in and out from the rigs and platforms. The Brent platform was far offshore; the sea state could be very bad. At times the boats couldn't get there. You have to understand that although the helicopters came in and out when the weather was good enough, sometimes neither the boats nor the helicopters could get to the platform. The pilots had the Decca navigation system but that wasn't like today's GPS, it was pretty primitive. Often it was just down to compass and maps. Not easy when the visibility is down to a mile and the sea state is 5 to 6.'

'Sea state 5 to 6? Is that rough?' Cat asked, bemused by all this information.

'Yup, waves up to 6 metres. Very rough!'

Outrage paused and again glanced at Smith. 'And also, there were sometimes issues, you know, helicopters landing on the wrong rigs, wrong crews picked up. This was early in the days of the oil boom and in helicopter aviation. We were all learning a lot.'

Cat wriggled in the uncomfortable office chair. 'So nobody noticed he was missing?'

The pair exchanged further glances, then Outrage continued.

'It seems from the records that he may have been quite a difficult man. No one was found who knew him well. Except his wife of course, but she was back at their home in Fetlar. She reported him missing, but I guess it didn't get through to the powers that be until later.'

Cat lent forward. 'Are you saying no one noticed until ... until ... who found the body?'

'Well,' said Mr Smith, his voice defensive, 'records were

not as comprehensive then. No one could recall whether or not he had been on the flight off the rig.'

'So,' said Mr Outrage, 'people thought he'd probably gone on one of the boats, or a different helicopter, left early and then gone on a bender and would go home when he dried out.'

'I see,' said Cat. 'So who found the body and how?'

'Couple of divers. They're most likely not around anymore. Saturation divers are still in great demand and completely international: go all over the world for work. These ones might be in Angola, Saudi, or Brazil who knows.'

'Oh, is there anyone from that time who would remember Johnny Holmes?'

The two men looked at each other thoughtfully.

'Kenny Jamieson, maybe. He was working the radio operation on Brent at that time.'

'Yeah. He's still around. Retired to the Stakker Flets in Fetlar. Unusual, most of them go south when they retire.'

'That's coz most of them are southerners. From Glasgow and further south. Kenny was a local man.'

'Yeah. So, he's here. No mobile phone, but he has a landline. I sometimes have a beer with him, for old times' sake. If you like, I'll ring him.'

He checked his watch and pulled over his Ipad, getting up the ferry timetable. 'You'll have time to go up there this afternoon. The ferries are OK this time of year. Looks like … yup … I think there's one at 2 p.m. from Toft. That gets in at Gutcher at 2.20 p.m. then it'll take you twenty minutes, say thirty if you don't know the road to Ulsta, so you'll make the 2.50. It may go via Unst, but then on to Fetlar.'

He was murmuring as though talking to himself. Then said more loudly. 'You should be in Fetlar by 3.40 at the latest. Then it is just a short drive to the Stakker Flets where Kenny lives.'

'Thanks,' said the already lost Cat.

'The thing to remember is, leave enough time to get the ferry back. The Yell to Main Island ferries are pretty frequent but there aren't that many to and from Fetlar, so you'll need to check. Have I got your email ...? Ah yes ... here it is.'

He pressed send and a copy of the timetable arrived in her inbox.

'I don't suppose you'll be able to make head nor tail of it. Every guest I have looks in horror and gets on the wrong ferry, but ask the boys when you get off the ferry at Herman Ness, that's Fetlar, and they'll tell you when the next and last ones back are.'

'Thanks.'

Mr Outrage rang Kenny Jamieson and he agreed to see her that afternoon. He closed his phone cover and gave her Johnny Holmes' file.

'Don't miss the ferry back,' he said, rolling his eyes dramatically, 'you won't want to stay on the Northern Isles at night.'

As she walked away, she could hear them laughing.

Chapter 18

The ferry from Toft on to Gutcher was a surprisingly large vessel. Cat wondered if it was like that when Anastasia arrived in 1987. Or did they fly? Oilmen were obviously rich; perhaps they could afford to fly ... assuming there were internal planes then. She should have asked.

Once on the ferry, she got out of the car and stared at the water. Seagulls flew overhead while gannets dived for fish. Another tourist pointed out a pod of orcas following the boat.

'Unusual,' he told her. 'The Orcas are hunting seal. Rich pickings.'

Wow! This was so wonderful. So different. But again she wondered what it felt like to a seventeen-year-old Spanish girl? Did she love animals and birds too?

Cat drove across Yell and had another surprise. The hills around the roads were covered with sheep but had no barriers. Periodically there were cattle grids and sometimes the sheep strolled across the road. Did they know on drovers' roads sheep had right of way?

Again, there were no trees and instead a haze of purple heather stretching away into the distance. Undulating landscapes: when did hills become mountains? Was it a height requirement or something to do with cragginess?

After another ferry from Ulsta, she drove on to the island of Fetlar. Here the cattle grids had grass growing through them. Wandering Shetland ponies joined the sheep and even chickens ran across the road. The road was single-track with passing places and tall reflective poles lining the route. Was this to keep drivers on the road in snow? Or to show men, drunk on poteen, the way home?

Cat saw no cars and no people.

Cat drove slowly, looking for signs. One sign proclaimed: Airstrip. So, they could have flown. Most probably did. An oilman who liked a life of luxury would want to give his young bride the best.

Cat arrived at the Stakker Flets and, getting out of the car, was immediately struck by the other thing a young Spanish girl might find challenging: the cold biting wind. Even though it was a beautiful clear sunny day in August, it was cold and there was a pacey breeze cascading across the scree, blowing the leaves into fountains. What would it be like between November and February?

Kenny Jamieson was as delighted to see her as any hermit.

'Hello. You Cat? The Skinny Malinky Long Legs seed you were coming.'

'Ah? Paul Outrage?'

'Aye.'

For a moment he stood at the door, and she wondered if they might do the interview standing there on the doorstep like an unwanted canvasser, but he eventually led the way into the kitchen, where she felt the warmth of the Aga.

He sat down. After a moment, she pulled out the only other chair and did the same.

'Paul Outrage said you knew Anastasia and Johnny Holmes?'

'Aye.'

He looked back at his newspaper, slowly pushing it aside. His casement clock on the other side of the kitchen ticked loudly.

'It was a long time ago. Do you remember Anastasia?'

'Aye, I ken ha, the wee lassie. Wheesht like.'

'Did she,' asked Cat, 'speak English?'

Or understand the Scottish accent? She was finding it hard herself and yet she was a linguist.

'Johnny said yes, she couldsha' speak English.'

'Did she like it here?'

Kenny shrugged, as though liking or not was irrelevant.

'Did Johnny want a wife to cook and clean for him?'

Kenny shrugged again.

'I misremember why they merrit. He had nane but his earnings and she took the lot when she left. He no even had a huis ... he rented a Haa House in Finny.'

'Finny,' she repeated, thinking she could drive down there and have a coffee; there must surely be a café.

'My Sarie would ken more, but she is long gone.'

'Oh, I'm sorry, your wife?'

'No, me bairn.'

'Oh, no even sadder. So sad when a child dies before a parent.'

He laughed. 'Weel, might as well be but no doud, she lives in London nu, visits twice a year.'

Guessing that she wasn't going to get much out of the Trappist former oilman, Cat asked if she could talk to his daughter.

'Aye.'

'Do you have her number?'

'Aye.'

'Could we call her?'

'Aye.'

Cat gave him her phone and he called his daughter. She was at work, but she agreed to talk briefly to Cat.

'Hi,' she said, 'Da says you'd like a chat. And about Anastasia! Well, there's a name I've not heard for many a year. But I'd love to. Look I'm at work. I'm a nurse. But I'd really like a good chat about Ana. I'm in London now. I work down here and I'm not at all sure when I'll be back in Finny, but we could talk on the phone. Or are you a southerner? If so, do you ever get up to London?'

She paused for breath and Cat, reeling from the difference with her father, cut in hastily.

'Yes, yes, I'll come to London. I've got your phone number now so I'll text you and you can send me your address and when it would be convenient. Brilliant. Thank you.'

She looked over at Kenny Jamieson and found he'd gone back to his paper. He spoke without looking up.

'Gud. She spent time with the wee lassie.'

Chapter 19

Her interview having been shorter than expected, Cat drove over to Finny, which she now discovered was spelt Funzie.

Funzie had no café. Indeed, only a very few houses separated by roads and fields. What would the young girl have thought? Marooned here with no friends and the possibility of living here for the next seventy years. Did they even have roll-on roll-off ferries in those days? Or was it, as for the ghostly mother at Busta House, a fourteen-hour ride to Lerwick?

She returned to Houbie, where there was a shop and a café. The boy in the shop also ran the café and was the local postman. She asked him if he had heard of Johnny Holmes and his accident. He hadn't, but when she said it was on the Brent platform in 1987, he shrugged.

'Sorry, I was born in 1999. My nan said there were that many accidents on the platform that they learnt to keep mum.'

In the shop she bought a tea towel for Stevie and an apron for Miranda. The boy was delighted.

'They are so popular. Peter Coutes has only been drawing the Tammy Norrie, sorry Puffins, for two years and they've immediately become our best seller!'

After her coffee, she took the two ferries and went back to the main island, which she now discovered was called the Mainland. She wanted to visit Lerwick, where Frank had told her about the revolutionary museum and the art-gallery-come-film-theatre building but by the time she had got back to the Mainland it was past five and everything was closed. She drove back to Busta House. Clearly the pace of life here was not hurried, unless you were likely to miss a ferry.

And what did you do, if you missed a ferry? Contrary to the suggestions of her oilmen interviewees, the biggest danger seemed to be the likelihood of sharing a bed with one of the twitchers who filled the islands at this time of year.

Chapter 20

Cat's former life had not been hurried either. For most of the time, the children were away at school, Charlie was at work, she spent her days, her weeks, her years gardening, cleaning and cooking. She even toyed with daytime TV. Boredom forced her into reading job adverts.

The police were looking for volunteers with language skills. Her French and English fluency would never leave her, but had her Dutch and Spanish gone rusty?

She applied.

The police were amazed to find an English educated person who spoke four languages well.

After all her security checks were done, she started working there three days a week.

Now, although she was busier and less bored, she worried about Charlie. Always tired, he fell asleep every time he sat down. OK, he was fifteen years older than her, but still only in his late fifties.

Was he having an affair? There were unexplained deficits in their joint bank account. Presumably he thought she never looked at it, but she did constantly, dreaming of holidays abroad where she could use her languages and he would be impressed. Somewhat different from their normal home dynamic.

He often came home late from work, saying he had meetings. Absent minded, he would stare out of the window for long periods. Cat became increasingly alarmed.

One day, at the end of a long week with the police, she was just getting into her car when Charlie drove past, away from home. Feeling guilty (perhaps police work had turned her into a spy) she turned away from home too. She followed him, keeping her distance, never losing sight of the blue grey Audi.

He turned into an airfield, went unhesitatingly down narrower and narrower airport roads and finally stopped by a recently built brick house. Jumped out of the Audi and, using his own key, went inside.

His own key?

Cat was shaking so much she could hardly park her Golf, but she had the forethought to leave it far away from the house and walked back towards the ugly newly built box. Peeking in through the window she saw Charlie talking to a young woman, a very young woman, with mousey hair and slim build.

Just as Cat was about to burst into the house shouting abuse, she noticed something strange. The girl was paying Charlie money. It didn't seem a large amount of money and was being paid out in what looked like small notes and pound coins. Why? Could someone be paying Charlie for sex? *Really?* The fifty something bald beanpole paid for by a slim teenager.

Even his loving wife found that unlikely but her mind

buzzed with possibilities: had Charlie turned pimp? Lost his job and was compensating? *Charlie? Surely not?*

Cat hesitated, and at that moment Charlie picked up the money, turned and made to exit the house. Cat fled. Hiding behind her car as he drove past. He didn't even recognise the car. How odd was that?

Cat hung around the house, waiting to see whether the girl would come out.

She did.

Cat hadn't noticed, but there was a garage attached to the house. Without warning, the garage door swung open and a well-used Triumph Dolomite drove out. Cat ran to her car and followed the Dolomite. They didn't go far, just to a hangar on the other side of the airfield.

There, the girl opened the doors and pushed out an old biplane. She put wooden blocks under the wheels, did something inside the cockpit and flicking up some switches, hand-swung the machine. It started immediately.

The girl jumped into the cockpit, sat for some minutes, perhaps warming the engine. She did various things before jumping out, pulling away the wooden blocks, and jumping back into the machine. Then she taxied away onto the airfield. Cat stared out of her car window, now more mystified than worried.

What was going on? Why was this female pilot paying Charlie money? *Who was she?*

Cat drove home in a daze.

Charlie was home when she arrived. He was sitting on the sofa, staring out into the garden. He had a whisky by his side, but he'd hardly touched it.

'Charlie,' she started.

Charlie shook his head. 'Cat, darling. I need to tell you something.'

Cat froze. She had been convincing herself the girl with the pound coins was nothing serious, but now his voice made it quite clear something horrible was about to emerge.

She waited.

'Cat, darling,' he repeated, as though unable to bring out words that would definitely change both their lives forever.

'Go on,' she said.

'Would you like a whisky, Cat?'

'No. Just tell me.'

Charlie sighed. He brought his gaze back to his wife.

'I went to the doctor last week,' he said.

'Oh,' she said, feeling better, perhaps it was not so serious after all. Men were notoriously babyish about their health. Was that girl a doctor? But why would she be paying Charlie money.

'Yes. I had some tests.'

'What sort of tests?'

'Muscle, neurones, motor neurones.'

His eyes looked pleadingly at her, longing for her to understand. She didn't.

'And?' she asked, her voice still cheerful.

'I've got Motor neurone disease.'

'What is that?' asked Cat.

Chapter 21

That night, alone in her Busta House room, Cat read the file on Johnny Holmes. It would not have made enjoyable reading for his mother.

It seemed Johnny Holmes was a drunk, a slacker and a liar. The management only tolerated him because he was an extremely skillful engineer who could make engines work where other men failed. However, he had no friends and was generally avoided at all costs. The file said he was known for 'emotional outbursts'.

Two divers had found his body. The lead diver was called Marvin Poltro and he wrote the report attached. There was no second report; presumably the management did not think it necessary.

Attached was another lengthy dossier from the insurance assessor, querying the length of time taken to discover that Mr Holmes was missing. At the end the assessor concluded there was no satisfactory answer as to why Mr Holmes fell off the platform. Instead, he was forced to concede, it must be an accident, as there was no evidence that any of the other men on the Alpha platform had been with him when he looked for the whisky bottle. Moreover, the weather was so bad that evening, that no helicopters would have been able to get in or out. It was also unlikely that he had committed suicide as he had recently married. His wife had reported him missing.

The assessor then wrote a scathing paragraph about the way the management, police and company had investigated the accident, and added an addendum that they only appeared to have one diver's report, when it was known that divers may not work alone. Why was that?

The insurance assessor also seemed annoyed that the doctor's report seemed so slight, which was true; when she looked back to find it, realising she'd missed it the first time, she saw it was only a couple of lines giving the state of the body as 'grave wax' and the likely timeline of death: two weeks before.

The next day, she returned the file to the receptionist at Mr Outrage's office.

She booked a hotel in Lerwick. Leaving her car at the hotel, she walked through the town to the museum and art gallery, where she had discovered there was an exhibition about the Brent oilrig in the 1980s.

Walking through the town she felt its strength. This was a town built for purpose and yet there was a rugged beauty in the architecture. The Town Hall was a Victorian edifice made of sandstone with stained glass windows and ornate brickwork dominated by a clock tower. Some of the other buildings were grey and dour, and their hard lines appeared to be saying keep your distance. But the main street, which had cobbles and rose as you walked from west to east, had small quirky shops: A French café, 'C'est La Vie', Harry's with 20% off any 'Halo'. Vaila Fine Arts, left in the charge of an Afghan dog. A town of contrasts that yelled it would not be taken for granted. Were the inhabitants the same? Self-sufficient yet friendly? Independent? Unusual? And apparently halo wearing.

The art gallery had tried to combine this defiance and beauty. It was a light, modern building with blue-edged glass and the sweeping design of high waves at sea. She walked into the large reception, also the ticket office for the cinema and easily found the coffee shop. The café was in a tall space, a coffee bar on one side and a wooden staircase leading away to the upstairs. Magnificent windows let in oodles of light, so the place felt airy. It looked extremely new, and she doubted it was here in the 1980s when Anastasia lived here.

Cat bought a coffee and went upstairs to the exhibition. The photos were in chronological order, which made it easier, and she watched as the platforms grew before her eyes. The early years of helicopter travel, with scary looking machines with two propellers, front and back, and later more developed types. The different types of wet-weather gear the oilmen used and the differing equipment. Then there were some other photographs, much more scenic and totally unrelated to the utilitarian side of the platform. All in the 1980s section.

'Nice,' she breathed to herself. 'Someone had an eye for detail. These are good.'

She looked at the name of the photographer and her heart stopped for a long second: Anastasia Holmes.

Chapter 22

Finishing her coffee Cat went back for a refill. The barista was a young man with curly hair and sparkling eyes.

'The photos in the collection. Do you know how they were collated?'

He shook his head very much in the 'I only work here' manner.

But, as she continued to look hopeful, he added. 'You could ring. I've got a number.'

Cat took the number, secretly amused. She was old enough to find it funny that you were somewhere and ringing or emailing the people in the same space instead of visiting them. She wondered if a phone would ring on a neighbouring table.

The phone number took her through to reception, and the receptionist put her through to the curator. He didn't quite understand her question and asked why she didn't visit the gallery.

'I'm here,' Cat said, 'sitting in the coffee shop. I've just seen the exhibition and I wanted to ask you about one of the photographers.'

'Oh, right,' he said, there was a pause then he added. 'I'm here too. I'll come and find you.'

A few minutes later, a man in his mid-twenties with a flop of red hair approached her. 'Cat?'

'That's me.'

'Great. I'm Theo, the curator. Can I sit down?'

'Please. Can I get you a coffee?'

'I don't do caffeine, but a coke would be nice.'

Cat said fine. In her experience coke had more caffeine than coffee, but she wasn't going to argue.

Anastasia, it seemed, had donated the photographs to the pilot who took her out to the Alpha platform. It was her way of saying thank you. The pilot was Theo's father, and he had kept them for years. They were both delighted to be able to put them in the exhibition.

'We had the negatives and everything.'

'Did you contact her about the show?'

'We tried to, but even though I spent hours on the web I couldn't find her. I guess she remarried and had a different name. In the end, we thought it was so long ago it would be OK. And no money was changing hands.'

'I wonder,' said Cat thoughtfully, 'could I meet your father?'

The curator paused for long enough for Cat to wonder why.

'Look,' he said, 'I'll ring him and see if he's nearby. OK? He might be. He loves this space.'

'Thank you.'

Luckily, it seemed not only was Theo's dad nearby, he was also very happy to come over and chat, even when he knew it was about Anastasia.

As they waited for Theo's dad, Clement, to arrive Theo made polite conversation.

'Do you know much about helicopters?'

'I know what a Robinson R22 is, I had a flight in one. A trial lesson. It was special, changed my life!'

Theo smiled, twiddling with his phone. 'They're a bit small for us, out here. My dad used to fly a Bolkow 105 in the 1980s. They don't use those anymore.'

'Umm, I guess it's pretty windy up here,' she said, remembering her bumpy flight into Sumburgh.

'Phenomenally. Sometimes it is so windy they can't go up and down the stairs on the rigs. The S92 is the best in high winds.'

'S92? Is that a helicopter?'

'Sorry, yes, a Sikorsky.' He put his phone face down on the table. 'That's what my dad flies now. The oilies much prefer it, especially after the Puma crash.'

Cat was about to query the big-cat name when Clement bounced into the room, waving at various people he knew. He joined them at the table with a 'Hurrah'.

'Hello, Catherine is it? I'm Clement; my son says you are a friend of Anastasia's. How is she? What is she doing?'

He gave his hand to another passer-by. 'Hi Stewart, good to see you, how is Caro, great, fantastic.'

'Ailsa, good to see you? Robbie gone south? Back now? Great. Great.'

Theo laughed. 'Dad's a table surfer!'

Clement patted his son's shoulder affectionately.

'Sorry, Cat, that is Catherine ... is Cat OK? Great. Thanks. I've lived here all my life and I guess I know most of the island. On the Mainland, at least. Anyway, how is she? Our little Ana.'

Before leaving home, Cat, had discussed with Stevie and

Miranda what she should say when this question arose: *'I'm wondering if Anastasia murdered all four husbands, or just some of them?'* seemed a little blunt.

So she was prepared.

'I haven't seen her for years either,' said Cat, 'but I knew her when she was married to Perez, then we drifted apart. I was up here anyway, so I thought I'd try and find something that would lead me to her.'

'Well,' said Clement smiling, 'you are still way ahead of me. When I last saw her, she was a grieving widow ...'

'Yes, was that an accident do you think?'

'The company said so at the time. But for that you really need to ask the divers who found the body. I have their numbers if you'd like it? They work here from time to time, but it's not like it was in the 8os.'

'Please.' She took the numbers, which were mobile. Which country would she find herself ringing?

'Divers? How many men found the body?'

'Two. They aren't allowed to dive without a buddy.'

She nodded, watching his face, but he had turned to greet another passer-by. When he turned back, she went on.

'How did Anastasia manage to get those wonderful photos?'

'Yeah! They are brilliant, aren't they? Incredible to think that the utilitarian platforms we work on could be transformed in her pictures to look like elegant palaces, landscapes, works of art. And that she did it with the technology of the late 1980s. She had real talent and stamina.'

'How did she get out to the rigs? I thought women were not allowed.'

He grimaced and paused before continuing.

'It's true, they weren't. But she kept asking me. She really wanted to see the rigs, to take photographs. I felt sorry for her. Johnny was away all the time. Her only friend was Sarah, who was only fourteen. '

'Kenny Jamieson's daughter?'

'Yup. Lovely girl. Grown for her age, but still a child. She comes back a few times a year to see her da. You'd think he'd be lonely, but he's a loner. Must have been hard for her growing up, with only him for company and mother long dead. I expect she thought of Ana as a real boon, and then she left too. Poor kid. No wonder she went south.'

'How did you meet Anastasia?'

'With Sarah. She came down every week from Fetlar to go to Anderson ... the senior school,' he added, seeing Cat's blank look.

'They only have a junior school on Fetlar, and that only if there are enough kids. From eleven on they make their way down here on the ferries. They stay over all week – it's a border – and go home at weekends. Since Sarie was in school all week she introduced me to Anastasia, so the girl would have someone to talk to when Johnny was away on the rigs.'

'Was he OK about that?' Cat asked.

It was impossible to avoid the fact that Clement was both handsome and charming. Not the sort of person a husband might like his new bride to spend time with.

Clement laughed. 'If he'd known, he'd 've killed me, but he was either on the platform, one of the support boats or drunk up in Fetlar. He had no idea what his wife did while he was away, nor did he care. He bought her to be his cook and cleaner!'

Clement's voice grew terse.

'Bought her?'

'I'm joking of course, but it certainly felt that way. She was seventeen. He was nearly forty. I gathered she was the youngest of many and her parents were elderly and wanted a good match for her. They can't have done much research. Johnny wouldn't be a good match for a Tammie Norrie, let alone a girl.'

'Tammie Norrie?'

'Puffin. It's an old Norse word.'

'Wow. So, she got to know you and persuaded you to take her out to the rigs. Was she already a photographer?'

'Yup. She showed me some photos of her life in Spain. Very different. Beaches. Sunlit villages of white adobe. Parties, horses even. There could not be a greater contrast to her life with Johnny the Brave!'

Cat noted the sarcasm with a smile.

'So, the photos were a way of quelling her loneliness?'

'Guess so. I flew the 105, the Bolkow, then. I was still a rookie, just arrived from instructing. That's how I built my hours. I went down to Aberdeen for that. It's OK Aberdeen, but I'd not want to spend my life there. I wasn't ex-military like most of the guys, who went straight onto the Chinook, and, when that crashed in 1986, on to the S61, the Sea King, and much later the S92, the Sikorsky, that is.'

'Is that what the oil men flew out in?'

'Aye, I mostly brought in supplies, tools and the like, whatever was needed, sometimes, if it was a small bunch, I flew the guys in. Sometimes when a surveyor or whatever needed me, I'd just have one guy for the whole day. That was the most fun. A guy might say: there's a good chef in Alpha for lunch and then a good one on Charlie for dinner, so we'd go from one to the other. I suppose they did some work between meals! The powers that be were pretty OK with me. I'd been up here all my life and I ken all the weather patterns. Shetland weather can catch a man and wring him dry, but I was used to it and the companies liked that.'

'Mr Outrage said things changed a lot between the 70s and 80s. Did that make it better for you?'

Clement's smile showed wry amusement. 'Weather is still weather, and we still have some of the worst up here. But you were asking about flying Ana in. It may be hard for you to understand in today's world of checks and more checks, but things were much more relaxed then. If you wanted to take a friend along, as long as he didn't cause trouble, that was OK.'

'But no women,' said Cat.

'Well, you know Ana, she's skinny as a boy and as adventurous. Or she was then. We put her hair under a cap, gave her a jump suit ... not even all the oilies wore those anyway. No one fussed about safety suits in those days. And while I was doing my things, she took photos.'

'How often did you take her in?'

'Three times.'

'Was that before or after Holmes was killed?'

'Twice before. Once after. But don't forget we didn't know he was dead. We just thought he'd disappeared. And people did go off on benders. Johnny more than most. He wasn't what you'd call a woman's man. I was frankly amazed when he got married. I couldn't see how he could have found someone to marry him. Especially not a sweetheart like Ana.'

'The oilmen were well paid, weren't they?'

'Yes, for sure,' he said, but the puzzled look on his face made Cat realise he saw no connection between Ana and marrying for money.

* * *

After Cat had left, Clement turned to his son. 'That woman has never met Anastasia, I'm certain of it.'

'How do you know?'

'Call it informed instinct or anything you like, but think about your mother and sisters. If they were looking for an old friend they'd talk about them, all the things they knew about them ... she didn't say one thing about Ana. Not even that she has flecks of different colour in her eyes.'

'But,' said his son, 'maybe she is just so used to it, she no longer thinks it remarkable. Or perhaps she wore contact lenses. Cat admitted she didn't know her very well.'

'Maybe,' said Clement. 'Why was she up here? She didn't mention it. Would you really journey all the way to Shetland looking for a friend? One you'd drifted away from? Possibly, she's looking for her for another reason. And I doubt it's a lottery windfall! Why don't you see what you can find out about Mrs Cat on the internet?'

'OK, Dad' said Theo, his eyes watching his father thoughtfully.

* * *

That night Cat sent Stevie and Miranda an email:

'Lots of interesting developments here:

1. Anastasia could and did get on to the rig where her husband was working. So, opportunity was there.
2. JH does not sound like a loving husband! So, looks like there was also motive.
3. Oil rig culture 70s/80s sounds like wild west
4. Met a man called Clement, who also had motive and opportunity. Can you (Stevie) find anything

about him? He's a pilot, and has a son called Theo (mid-20s) who is the curator of the art gallery, if that helps. He was flying in the late 1980s so possibly fifty plus age.

5. Clement, the pilot, gave me the mobile numbers of the two divers who found JH's body. I rang them, but they both live down south, so we need to visit them once I'm back.

6. On the way home I'm going to visit Sarah, who was a friend of Anastasia's when she was on the island and lives in London.

7. Tired now, going to bed. See you tomorrow.

The report she sent Gia contained the same facts, but without point 5 or 6 and set out in a much more formal manner. She also gave a list of the cost so far, broadly the same as the estimate.

Chapter 23

Stevie was sitting quietly at the computer when Miranda bounced into the room. She nearly tripped over an elderly dog sitting by the table.

'What the? Where did this old girl come from?' She bent down to stroke the curls of the black and white spaniel. 'Beautiful girl.'

Stevie nodded. 'Yes. I just fetched her from the police pound. They found a whole lot of dogs at an encampment up on the Downs. Sent me photos and the only one I knew was ours was this old girl. She belongs to Mr Samura at the edge of the square. Know who I mean?'

'Yes, of course. Chatty old boy, wife died a few years ago, dog was the love of his life since then. Got nicked about a week or so ago. Does he know you've found it?'

'Err ... Not yet. I was about to ring ...'

Miranda looked up sharply at Stevie hearing the lack of enthusiasm in her voice. Clearly Stevie was going through one of her 'non-people' days.

'Shall I take her round to him for you?'

'Would you mind?'

Miranda laughed. 'Not at all, happy to. Come on dog ... what's her name?'

Stevie looked it up. 'Silver Dollar.'

Miranda grinned. 'Hey ho Silver, let's leave Stevie to her friend Terry Terminal.'

And girl and dog bounced out of the room.

Stevie returned to getting information about Carlos Perez, Anastasia's second husband.

Miranda danced through the square, greeting people and chatting. It took her a quarter of an hour to arrive at Mr Samura's house, by which time he already knew she was coming and was at the door to meet her.

'Come in, come in,' he said. 'I've got the tea on.'

He patted the dog lovingly.

'Thank you so much, Miranda. I missed Silver so much. I can't understand why anyone took her. She useless for breeding, we had her 'done' years ago and she ain't a pretty young pup.'

'Yes, no,' said Miranda, 'I think they just take anything, randomly and hope some will resell.'

They walked into his living room talking and soon Mr Samura was asking Miranda about the agency and what they were doing now.

She hesitated for a moment, but thought it would be OK to give him the outline of what they were doing.

'We're investigating a murder case. Possible husband killer on the loose.'

Samura laughed. 'Don't tell me. I know the woman ... you mean Anastasia. Used to live in the big house on the hill with Tom Drayton. Draytons wanted to believe she killed him, but really he died of a heart attack. She and Pete hated each other from the get-go. Then she got half their money. What a hullaballoo that was!'

He laughed.

Miranda kicked herself. Of course, such a notorious local case, everyone would know of it, just not the nub.

'Did you know her?'

Miranda didn't think he would, no one really seemed to *know* her only *know of* her.

'Yes, we were on a charity together, volunteers.'

'A charity.' Miranda moued. This brought out another unexpected aspect of the woman. 'What sort of charity?'

'Well, you probably don't know this, but many years ago I used to be a doctor. I retired twenty years ago and what does a retired doctor do? Goes and volunteers for a medical charity.'

'Awesome.'

'Yes, it was related to infertility ... in humans that is, not animals.' He laughed. 'With your work you might think I was referring to dogs.'

Miranda half laughed reflectively. 'Yes, no, maybe.'

'Anyway, Anastasia and I were both there to give advice on fundraising, and, in my case on any related medical issues. She was a clever woman and raised lots of money. I suppose she had lots of rich friends, but she was generous herself too. Gave big donations of her money as well as her time. She knew a lot about chemicals. I was surprised at her knowledge. She was fun to be on a charity with. But I could see what got Pete's goat, she was pretty strong-willed. You went her way or no way, as you young people say nowadays. She didn't pull her punches.'

'Yes, no. When you say she knew a lot about chemicals ... what exactly?'

He nodded. 'Just what I say. When I mentioned, say, sildenafil citrate she knew I was talking about Viagra. We could discuss the selective inhibitors without my needing to explain anything. Unusual in a non-medical person. But I suppose she did it for the fundraising. If you want to sell medicines you need to know about them in detail.'

'Right. Do you know anything else about her?'

'Only that she was an excellent photographer. She had an exhibition of her work in aid of the charity and we raised a large sum of money.'

'Awesome.'

'Yes. I was sorry when she left. I think the atmosphere round here got to her after Tom died. Pete was so antagonistic, not that you can blame him, losing half your business isn't much fun. But anyway, she rented out her house and moved off somewhere. I've heard she lives in London now, but I don't know if that's true.'

Chapter 24

As she walked back to the office, Miranda mused on the difference between the local reaction to her arrival and that of Anastasia.

Phillip and Miranda's arrival had been met with such enthusiasm that Phillip wondered if they'd confused him for a celebrity. Flowers were left on the doorstep. People came round with offers of help while the removal men were still unpacking the lorry. Miranda's eldest, Jane, was a teenager then, and Felix just a baby. It seemed their presence reduced the average age of the village sufficiently to protect it from becoming a retirement haven.

Like Anastasia, Miranda was an outsider. Like Miranda she had children, although Miranda's accompanied her. But the difference was that Miranda's husband was still alive. Was that the issue?

Neither Cat nor Stevie had been part of the Welcome to Owly Vale Party, however Blinkey had arrived with a bottle of goat's milk for the baby, and Caroline, Cat's daughter, had come round with a bottle of wine.

Caroline and her wine stayed on long after the others

had left. She offered to help with the baby, but after she put the nappy on upside down, Miranda redid it and let Caroline drink and talk while she rocked Felix to sleep.

'My parents never understood me,' said Caroline. 'After I ran away from school ...'

'You ran away from school? Why?'

Miranda was mostly self-taught. She longed for more formal education. Running away from school sounded like educational suicide.

'They didn't understand me ... they compared me with my twin sister. Just because Vanessa got a scholarship to Oxford, they thought I was stupid. But when I ran away, they thought I was wicked.'

Miranda bit her lip, trying to quell the rush of emotional longing for teaching as well as learning.

'My mother followed me all the way to Peckham. At least my father let me live my own life. And then there's my grandmother ... a real religious nut. She disapproves of everything we do.'

Miranda, forced to leave school at sixteen to help her mother in the shop and pay for her younger siblings, put her arm around the young girl and listened to her woes. The mother of children sympathised with the girl but the rebel inside longed to meet both Caroline's devilish sister and her heartless mother. She was so pleased they had moved here, this village seemed to offer a lot of inspiration and fun.

* * *

A few weeks later, she met the heartless mother. Miranda, worried that Cat might not like her daughter's friendship with her unknown neighbour, suggested Caroline bring her mother over. Cat had been delighted. Caroline less enthralled.

'My family spoil everything,' she told Miranda. 'They'll be trying to poison me in your eyes.'

'Come on, Caroline,' said Miranda gently pinching her arm, 'that's not possible. We are friends. Friends don't just start disliking each other because of their parents. Trust me.'

'OK!'

Cat, invited for a quiet coffee with her daughter's new friend and neighbour, had cased her six-foot X-ray body in Tiger trousers and four-inch red stilettos. She sailed into the house like a mother defending her cubs but whatever safeguarding scheme she might have planned seemed to fizzle out when she saw Miranda. Visibly comparing her own Monday morning body with Miranda's Friday afternoon fiasco, a friendly smile slowly suffused her face. Laughing, she put out her hand saying in her deep voice. 'Hi, I'm Cat.'

Then Stevie arrived and Cat, turning, apparently in shock, asked her if she was Charlie's illegitimate child. Miranda would never forget Caroline's excruciated shriek: 'Oh Mum!'

But even she could not have imagined that soon the three of them would soon be running SeeMs Detective Agency looking for lost dogs.

Chapter 25

The next morning, Cat took the plane to Aberdeen and then flew to Gatwick, from where she took a train into London. She was meeting Sarah at her home in Central London.

Sarah lived in an ex-council flat in Fulham, close to Eel Brook Common. She worked as a nurse in the Chelsea and Westminster and was on earlies.

'Come over after 5 p.m.' She had texted Cat. 'I'm on the first floor. Bells outside. No names. Push 12.'

Cat took the tube to Fulham Broadway and walked up Harwood Road, through Kempson Road and across the common.

She passed a teenager texting and was suddenly struck by a memory so painful it pinned her to the spot.

* * *

In 1995, Caroline, Cat's eldest daughter, then fourteen, ran away from boarding school. She left a message with a friend that read:

I am not just Vanessa's twin. I am a person in my own right. So I'm taking my right and going off to London. Don't try and find me. EVER!

After four days, the police found her in a squat in Peckham. The police said they could not go in and told Caroline's parents it was up to them now. Charlie refused to fetch his daughter.

'We've given her everything,' he told Cat. 'If she'd rather be a pauper in Peckham, let her.'

So, Cat went alone. She'd only been to London a few times in her life, so she took several maps with her for reference. These included a hand-drawn one from the police for the area her daughter was in.

Getting off at Victoria she looked for the train to Peckham. There was a sign to the underground, so she followed it. Anthony, the social worker, had sent a message via the police to take the overground, but a quick inspection of the map showed that the underground included an overground. Presumably that was what he meant.

It wasn't.

Having gone as far as Parsons Green, only to discover her mistake, she returned to Victoria, and asked a porter. Finally found the real overground. Even then she went two stops in the wrong direction.

By the time she got to Peckham Rye it was dusk. As she left the station, she saw a man sitting in a box. She stared at him.

'Spare some change, love.'

She battled with herself. She should. She could afford it. But would he spend it all on alcohol? Would that be worse for him? What should she do? She was so unused to making her own decisions. Usually, Charlie told her what to do.

As she moved away, she saw another young man quite

openly injecting himself with a syringe. What? Why? How come ... what was this place? How could this be happening in wealthy London?

As she walked through the streets of Peckham, she felt numb. There were beautiful Georgian and Victorian houses, but peeling paint, rotten and crumbling bricks had downgraded their loveliness. Washing was drying on once elegiac pillars. A burnt-out car full of rubbish had been driven on to the pavement and left, surrounded by broken glass. What was her daughter doing in this part of London? Or was all London the same?

She followed the hand-drawn map from the station and walked across Warwick Park. Why had the police sent her through a park, in the dark?

Then suddenly, out of the haze, an enormous figure approached her. She was a tall woman herself, but he seemed to fill the air around them. He was huge. Her mouth went dry. Her heart was suddenly throbbing in her ribcage. She clasped her bag to her chest.

My God! A drug dealer! Keep calm Cat. He isn't interested in you. Keep going. Keep going! Remember, if asked you have no money. Or, just give it to him and run? Eyes on the ground. Keep walking. Don't make eye contact.

'Excuse me,' he said.

What? What does he want?

Her mouth went dry. Keep going. Ignore him. Remember, this is for Caroline. Or is this it? Will my life end here on the cold grass of a Peckham Park, covered in cigarette papers and empty syringes? Breathe Cat. A hysterical giggle made its way up to her mouth.

'Excuse me,' he said again, 'are you Cat?'

Cat? That must be some kind of code. Are you Cat? Are you a buyer? The irony of such a thing steadied her. Too far to run. OK, she must speak. In films people often reasoned with their attackers.

'I'm Judo trained!' she yelled, her voice louder than intended.

The man, who had been looking concerned, smiled. He looked slightly amused.

Her fear turned to fury. She stopped dead.

'How dare you laugh at me?'

He stopped smiling and looked sad, nodding slightly. The look on his face unfathomable in her nervous state.

'I'm Caroline's social worker,' he said. 'Who did you think I was?'

Cat felt cold. Her body started shivering as though understanding what he said before her mind caught up. Slowly she assimilated his words. Her name was Cat. He knew her name. He was a social worker, not a drug dealer. Her fear turned to shame. Because he was tall and Black, she had assumed the worst. She was the very embodiment of the person she warned her daughters against: the hypocritical liberal. Shame and fear mingled to make her angry.

'Sorry. OK. I assumed. I did assume! It is true. But so did you! I was fucking terrified. Do you have any idea what it is like being a woman alone in a park at night when a big man comes towards you? Do you?'

She was trembling so much she wondered if her knees would hold.

He stopped laughing, put out his hand. His eyes rueful.

'No. I'm sorry. I didn't think of that. I came out to make sure you got to us safely. Sorry. I'm Anthony.'

She took his hand and it felt like a lifeline. She held it tight to prevent herself falling and her shaking transmitted itself: his hand began shaking too.

'Me too. Thank you, Anthony. I am so, so sorry.'

* * *

'Excuse me, are you OK?'

A woman was looking at her with concern. 'Only you've been standing in the middle of the path for ten minutes.'

'Sorry,' said Cat, 'I was thinking. So sorry.'

She hurried on towards Parthenia Road.

Chapter 26

Sarah's building was at the end of the street. While all the other houses were Victorian and had ornate trim work with gingerbread cutouts and spindle work, small testaments to the success of an empire, Sarah's building, an ex-council block of flats, was a long concrete slab of Stalingrad appearance with energy-saving windows. There was a twin opposite, and both reminded the world that 1960s architecture was there to serve not to exult.

She pushed number 12 and with a grating, metallic sound the door swung open. In front of her were heavy concrete steps, leading to the two upper floors, and a smell of cooked cabbage.

Sarah opened the door of her flat and greeted her effusively. A small woman she was slightly overweight, but with twinkling eyes, full of zest for life.

'Hello, hello, so glad you made it OK. It isn't the easiest place to find. What would you like? Tea? Coffee? Something cold? I've got elderflower, orange juice and I may have some apple juice if you'd like it.'

Cat said tea would be lovely. Sarah ushered her to a seat

on the balcony and danced off into the kitchen to make the tea.

Inside the flat, it was completely different from the external architecture. The rooms were much bigger than she expected, and the long windows let in a lot of light. There was a small balcony over the shared garden. Someone had decorated the rooms with magnolia paint, putting a light frieze at the top, there were flower-print curtains and painted furniture, making the flat feel homely and welcoming.

She went out onto the balcony and a few moments later, Sarah joined her with a crowded tray.

'I forgot to ask if you like milk or lemon or sugar and some biscuits. So I brought them all.'

They sat on comfortable deck chairs in the still-warm sun, their view of the garden somewhat obscured by a large tree.

'How did you meet Anastasia?' Cat asked, although she was pretty sure everyone on such a small island knew everyone else.

Sarah sighed. 'On the day they came back from Spain. Johnny brought her over. He asked my da, "your bairn cook proper food?"' She dropped her voice and imitated an Englishman trying to speak with a Scottish accent, her eyes twinkling.

'Like my da he wasn't much of a talker. My da said yes and so Johnny turned to me. "Teach her to cook proper and I'll give ye a tenner." And he left.

'So, Ana, we all called Anastasia Ana, stayed with us until she could cook. At first, she was a nightmare. She was a party girl. Johnny told her he owned Brough Lodge and she thought she was going to be the Lady of the Manor.'

'Brough Lodge?'

'A huge property on Fetlar. It was, probably still is, owned by the Nicholson family. It's a ruin now but then it was still big and brave, with towers, turrets and you'd want to live and die there. Johnny showed Ana's parents photos of it. They thought Ana was going back to a *Big Huise*, but instead he rented a *Haa Huise*, and the landlord lived in England!'

'What? He pretended he was the laird?'

'Yeah. I don't know all the details. Just when we went past Brough Lodge she told me, Holmes said it was his, and her family believed him.'

'Wow. So he deceived her from the start.'

'Yup. I'm not sure she even knew he was an oily. Holmes was an Incomer, one of those who decided to settle in Shetland. He didn't like people. He chose to settle on Fetlar because it was one of the least populated islands. Basically, I was the only one even close to her age and I was fourteen at the time, still at school in Lerwick. I came home at weekends and then, if he was at work, Ana and I would play. I had made a shelter on the beach, with protection from the wind and we would meet there. I think she often went there when I was at school.'

Sarah offered Cat a homemade shortbread.

'Anyway. She arrived being only able to cook Spanish, and not much of that, and Johnny didn't like it. He wouldn't take her back until she could do his reestit mutton tattie soup with bannocks, tea and tabnabs, black pudding and porridge and the like. She didn't want to go back to him, so she was hell to teach.'

'What was she like?'

'Like a child. You know, I had just me Da, no mudder and I learnt to do everything. I could cook, clean, sew, take out the boats, feed the chickens and roo the sheep.'

'Roo?'

'Shear by hand. It's an old practice, not many do it nu, but we did then. Ana never learnt but Johnny no had sheep. Anyway, Ana couldn't do anything except sing and dance, she was good in the ceildhs.'

'Kay-le?'

'Ceildh. Entertainment. Dancing, singing, playing instruments. A get together.'

Cat nodded deciding she could look it up on Google: if she could work out how to spell it.

'Eventually, Holmes came for her. He'd come back onshore and he wanted his woman. She was away for the ten days he was onshore, and when she came back she was quieter and did everything immediately. He'd been beating her. I work with abused women now and looking back I recognise the signs. I didn't know then. Then, I was just glad she wanted to learn.'

'Didn't her family contact her at all, when she was in Fetlar?'

'No. People didn't so much, back in the day. Phones were bad and you had to book a call via the 'change' in Lerwick. Travel was expensive. No email and stuff. We just got by. Looking back, I sometimes wonder how we survived. Then, other times, I think it was better. We were more resilient. You should see some of the kids I work with now. Can't do naught and get exhausted. We did everything. We had to. When I arrived as a nurse, you did what you were bid: "Starch your uniform properly, girl!" We even wore the awful hats you had to fold yourself, and a clean one every day. Now, they question every order. It drives me potty.'

She bit into the shortbread, staring into the tree.

'So, Holmes was offshore ten days, onshore ten days? What did she do when he was away?' Cat prompted her.

Sarah looked back at Cat. 'We played! Out on the wooden boat, secluded beaches. Cooking on fire pits, using the fish we had caught. I was fourteen and although she was hell to teach, she was wicked to be with. Clever. Witty. At first, I was the leader, she the follower. Don't get me wrong. It was great. We had fun, got up to mischief. My da never complained. He liked that I had a friend, but Ana's husband ... he went wild at us sometimes. And, you know, we weren't doing anything bad, just silly.'

She smiled at the memory.

'I used to love going to her croft when Johnny was away. They had a fridge that talked to you.'

She imitated the pop-pop singing noise of a fridge about to expire.

'And a toilet that sounded like the Orkney Ferry leaving harbour every time you flushed.'

She put her hands to her mouth like a loudspeaker and trumpeted loudly.

'Looking back, I guess Johnny paid very little rent and the landlord couldn't be bothered to fix anything, but at the time it made us laugh.'

She half smiled at Cat. 'You know, one time we borrowed a boat and went up to Unst from Fetlar. It was a rib, so it was fine, a big sturdy boat but drivable by one. Then, Ana said she'd never seen the lighthouse at Muckle Flugga. It was a long way to walk and all through the Bonxie fields, (sorry Skuas) so I said we'd motor up. I checked the fuel. I wasn't an idiot. We had enough. But I hadna realised how strong the tides were up there ...'

'You got into difficulty?'

'Yeah! We were lucky, a herring boat saw us and towed us in but Johnny was there when we got in. He went ballistic!'

She stopped and made a face.

'I just went home, and my da was cross, I was gated but naught else, he was more worried than angry. And relieved. But Johnny ...' she stopped, as though finding it hard to speak. 'Well, he beat her again ... and then,' she took a deep breath. 'And then he raped her.'

Chapter 27

Cat, her arms automatically crossed over her body, stared at the girl in shock.

'He raped his wife, for what, for wanting to see a lighthouse?'

'Umm.' Sarah drank some tea. 'She said later he was like a man possessed. She fought back. There were reasons why she fought so hard. He didn't care. Of course, they'd had sex before, she expected it and, even when she was no longer enamoured, she was compliant. But this ... this was savage.'

She stopped. Tears slipped edgily out of her eyes.

'I'm sorry. I know I work with this all the time, but sometimes, often, it gets to me.'

She breathed deeply and Cat wondered about the break. Was she leaving something out?

'After he beat her, he tied her to the bed. He went drinking in the hall. It was a Saturday; they always had a social on a Saturday. When he came back, he raped her again ...'

Cat leant over and squeezed Sarah's arm. 'Oh, my God, I'm sorry.'

'Yeah! It changed me too, as well as her. That was when I decided to become a nurse, and to work with abused women.'

She stopped for a moment and stared at the large tree.

'You know, wife beating wasn't rare at that time on the islands. And, as I said, he'd hit her before but I think this was worse than anything. The first time she was just quiet but this time she had a simmering anger. You change, anyway, with our type of island life, if you come from outside.'

She paused again, thinking.

'I grew up with it. So, I knew you had to do things or die, but she came from a different place. She was an innocent young girl from Spain, soft like. As I said, she liked music and dancing. But after this she toughened up quickly. She took control.'

'How long was this before he fell off the rig?'

'Probably only a couple of weeks. You can see why we weren't very upset.'

'Indeed'

'How did she get the pictures of the oil rigs? The photos?'

'Oh those!' She laughed. 'You saw the photos?'

'Yes, they're in the exhibition. At the museum. They are brilliant.'

'Did you meet Clement?'

'Yes.'

Sarah looked at her enigmatically. 'How come?'

'I was in the café and saw the photos. I asked about them and they directed me to Theo, who told me about his dad, who then came over.'

Sarah sighed. 'Well, if you've met Clement then you have your answer. He's a great, great guy Clement. One of the kindest people in the world! Everybody's friend. He loves people. He'd do anything for anybody.'

Her eyes grew soft, and she smiled.

'Ana desperately wanted to go over to the rigs. She wanted to see what it was all about. But, you know, everything was so sexist in those days. No woman allowed. Honestly. But Clement was different. He'd just got married. Had Char, that's Theo's elder sister, on the way. He wanted everyone to be happy.'

She drank some tea.

'He was taking a risk. If they'd been found out, had an accident or something he'd have lost everything: his job, his licence ... well, even his life. But when you're young, you take risks. You don't think of the consequences and Clement believed in his own skill. Honestly, I can no say enough what a kind man he was and is, and Theo too. The whole family is bonnie.'

'Nice,' said Cat, 'very nice.'

'Yes,' said Sarah, smiling at Cat, but again looking slightly cautious.

'They didn't tell Johnny. He'd have gone wild. I think she went in a couple of times. I thought she was trying to find a career as a photographer. To get some money, so she could get away from Johnny.'

She stopped and again seemed fascinated by the large tree.

'What about her parents?' Cat asked.

Sarah sighed. 'They were alive, but very old. I'm not sure they would have thought beating your wife, or even raping her was much to get excited about. They were a bit old school. You know, it wasn't even illegal to rape your wife until 1992!'

'1992? Is that right?

'It's right. Basically, in the 8os you were free to rape your wife and get away with it!'

She shook her head silently.

'Did you meet them? Ana's parents?'

'Yes, after Johnny's body was found, her parents came up to help her with everything. As I said, she was a bit child-like, I think they thought she wouldn't manage alone, and she was still only eighteen. They were very protective. They spoke English but with a strong accent, which was funny, because her English was better than mine.'

'Spanish accent?' Cat asked.

'I guess.'

'What did you think of Holmes, before the abuse I mean?'

Sarah wrinkled her nose. 'He was always creepy. My da liked him, as far as he liked anyone, brought him home sometimes, but I never felt OK with him. I always made sure Da was there; I was never alone with him. I didn't trust him. You have an instinct for that kind of thing when ...'

She left the time blank and Cat filled the silence.

'I wonder,' said Cat. 'Do you have any photos of Ana?'

Sarah thought.

'I might have. If I do it will be from the old Instamatic. Do you remember them? Dreadful photos, but that was all we had. I'll have a look.'

Sarah, who was clearly much better organised than Cat, found her photo and an old diary in ten minutes. The photo was so hazy it was impossible to see details. A very young girl stood by a boat, looking at the camera. Cat had no idea if she was smiling or scowling, the photo was that bad.

The diary had a very old phone number and even better an address in Marbella.

'Thanks,' said Cat. 'I guess the number's changed, if it's

anything like here, but the address is good. Most likely the house is still there.'

Cat took a picture of the address on her phone.

'If you find her ... say hi from me. I'd like to see her again. See how she grew up. Maybe she'd like to see how I grew too.'

CHAPTER 28
JEREZ 1993

Dear Mother and Father,

Mateo was born on *martes*. Already full of the heroic spirit of Mars! Carlos and I are so happy to have given birth safely after that incident in Fetlar. That is over now and I look forward to a long and happy life with my new family.

Carlos says Mateo is the 'real deal'. Carlos loves the USA; lots of American expressions. *Carlos* is the real deal. I cannot understand how I was so taken in by Johnny Holmes, if I had met Carlos before, Johnny would not have deceived me.

Without Carlos my life would be misery itself.

Carlos says, if you would like to come and live with us on the vineyard you would be most welcome. There are lots of houses on the estate and he would love to have you all nearby. Do say yes, it would be the best thing ever if you come here.

I so look forward to seeing you when you come to visit next week.

Besos, Ana

Chapter 29

After talking to Sarah in London, Cat took the train back to Petersfield. Stevie met her at the station, longing to hear the news.

'Her first husband seems a bit of a shit,' said Cat, 'you can hardly blame her for killing him. How about the others? Any idea?'

'Well, the second husband had a heart attack in bed with his mistress, she was crushed, injured, when he died. Her name was Teresa Garcia, and she got compensation from the family.'

'What? How is that possible?'

'He was rather large, and the mistress was rather small. '

'No! You're having me on! But I meant ... did he have insurance? Can you get ... what? Sex insurance? Perhaps if your mistress works for you, you can say it was injury while on active duty.'

Stevie snorted.

'No idea. I'll look it up. Truth stranger than fiction, perhaps?'

'Sad that he had a mistress,' said Cat. 'Doesn't sound as

though the second marriage was much good either.'

'No.'

As they drove back to the village, Stevie said. 'I've found something else. There's a Spanish professional photographer called Anastasia Marin ... I know everything we've heard so far leans towards our Anastasia using Rodriguez, her maiden name, but do you think she might occasionally use another name? Or perhaps the name of the husband we haven't found yet?'

'Possibly,' said Cat. 'Once, helping Frank with the children's books, I was told that if you write about different subjects, you should use different names, to prevent confusion. It might be true if she's doing a different type of photography. More conceptual or something. Does she look like Anastasia in the wedding photos? Should be easy to spot her.'

Stevie laughed. 'You were right about conceptual. You should see the artist's photos, there're lots including loads of her, but all distorted. Her blurb says she's a "... conceptual artist who likes to make you think the way you breathe." Anyway, she's having an exhibition in London in a few days' time. We might as well go. Fun to have a day in London: even if it's the wrong Anastasia. I've got a friend in the art world. He'll arrange for us to go to the private view.'

'Stevie,' said Cat, 'you have friends everywhere!'

'So would you if you'd been flying businessmen since you were twenty, instead of marrying them.'

'Love you too!'

* * *

Stevie dropped her at home and refused to come in, saying she wanted to chat to her mother's carer before she went to bed as she was leaving for Heathrow very early in the morning.

Frank was sitting in the kitchen, flicking through a children's book Cat had promised to translate. The dogs heaved themselves up and strolled over to welcome her.

'Hello, world traveller,' said Frank.

'Hello darling, do I detect a touch of peeve?'

Frank laughed. He wasn't good at expressing his emotions, but Cat saw through him, as she had from the moment they met.

'Sorry. It's just we need to get this book to the printer. I'm off next week for an Italian trip with Angelo and I'd like to think it was being printed as I sell it, not months afterwards.'

She kissed him. 'I'm completely yours, for at least the rest of today.'

'OK. Funny girl. From now until 7 a.m. you mean.'

He showed her his watch face, which beamed up the news it was midnight.

'Oh, sorry. I didn't realise it was so late. Would you like a drink before bed?'

Frank laughed and blew her a kiss.

'Incorrigible!'

He went to fetch a couple of glasses.

'Caroline's pictures are here,' he said, his head inside the fridge. 'They're brilliant, as ever. She said she and Lagertha would like to come and stay next weekend, apparently Rupert's away with some chums playing golf.'

'That's great. We can all do a lot of work on the books before you leave, if Lagertha will allow us.'

Frank snorted. 'I'm going to end up calling that baby Lager, you see.'

'You do realise Lagertha was a Viking queen, don't you? Be rude to her and you'll probably lose your nose!'

Frank laughed, bringing her a glass of wine. 'Is that what Vikings did? Chop off your nose?'

'No, but babies often do!'

'Lovely Larger languishes lonely by the Liffey,' Frank sang, blowing her a kiss.

Cat pouted. 'Caroline hides a lot of pain. When I went with Anthony ...'

'Caroline's social worker?'

'Yes. When I went into the squat where Caroline was living ... if you can call it that ... I was horrified. Two or three bed sharing: one in while the other worked and vice versa. Filth everywhere. Beetles. One bathroom. One tiny kitchen. And when I said I was shocked, Caroline was furious with me for being shocked. She said:

'These are real people, Mum. Not everyone has privileges."

Cat felt tears forming in her eyes. She shook them away.

'I can't help comparing my life with Anastasia's as we know it,' Cat said. 'We both have children, dead husbands, speak many languages. We have a lot in common.'

Frank gave her a shoulder hug. 'And a lot of differences. Unless you are planning to poison my wine! Incidentally, I don't know if Stevie told you, but Miranda discovered Anastasia used to work for a local infertility charity. Raised a lot of money for them.'

'Did she. That gives a very caring side to her nature,' said Cat sleepily. 'Could she be a sort of Dr Jekyll and Mr Hyde figure, do you think?'

'Interesting idea,' said Frank, 'who would be a Black Widow's split personality? Bluebeard?'

'No,' said Cat, 'a white knight, without the K!'

'Or,' said Frank, 'with too many K-isses.'

'Ha ha, go back to publishing,' she said, kissing him.

Chapter 30

Anastasia Marin was a tall woman, but considerably wider than the Anastasia in the wedding photos. The long blonde curly hair that cascaded around her face gave her the look of a Valkyrie, moreso as she was wearing a tin hat with horns.

'Klaus darling,' she said, as Cat was introduced to her. 'Mrs Catherine is a linguist, so you'll be able to fascinate her with stories about my work. Take her away, darling.'

Klaus obeyed. Cat hoped no one was expecting her to speak German, but Klaus seemed perfectly happy to talk in English.

'So, Mrs Catherine, which photos are you most interested in?'

'Do you have anything from the 1980s? I'm particularly interested in Shetland.'

Klaus gave a shout of joy. 'That will delight my beloved. However, she tells me she was not alive in the 1980s, so I suppose I have to believe her.'

'Ah,' thought Cat, 'well that answers that question then!'

. . .

Having been greeted effusively by Anastasia, Stevie and her companion went to chat to their mutual friends, leaving Miranda alone.

Miranda wandered around, wondering who to talk to. Around her, conversation was taking place in Spanish and German, but she could not hear anyone speaking English. Miranda was monolingual and found all this chatter intimidating. Unlike Cat's French mother, Miranda's Polish father had not wanted her to learn his mother tongue. 'How can you integrate?' he asked her, 'if you babble away in *Grypsowanie* like a thief?'

Even worse, it was one of those rare evenings in August when London was hot in the evening and, although the gallery had air conditioning, the crush of people inside made the atmosphere hot and sticky. A bead of sweat ran down Miranda's nose and she wondered if she was going through premature menopause. It was rare in women in their late thirties, but not unheard of. Might explain why her weight was creeping up again, in spite of all the dieting.

She turned and looked at some rather appealing photographs of children, pretending to be unconcerned by the lack of companions. The barista approached her with a bottle of champagne, and she smiled invitingly at him. She might not have conversation but at least she had booze and good stuff at that.

She ogled a rather handsome young man who was speaking Spanish to a pretty girl. The girl turned her back, but the young man looked her way.

'Hello,' he said in English. 'I have a feeling you are not a Spanish speaker?'

He gave her the most heart-churning smile and, for the first time in her life, she wished she were a linguist.

'No,' she said, fiddling with her wedding ring. 'I'm afraid I'm like a lot of English people, useless at languages.'

'But that is so heartening. I detest having to speak Spanish with those who mangle the language, I would so much prefer to speak English and improve my own poor quality. But look, your glass is empty.'

He made a slight gesture and the barista appeared at their side with a full bottle and several delicious canapés. Her new friend took the bottle, indicating they would keep it with them.

'Tell me what you are doing here, at this great occasion, my Mafalda?'

'Mafalda? Close, my name is Miranda.'

'Miranda, but that is a Spanish name. It means 'worthy of admiration' and indeed you are. I thought you were the sassy Mafalda but now I see you are both sassy and worthy of admiration.'

Miranda blushed. 'Most people just scream: *Do the Miranda!*'

She lifted her arms to demonstrate and nearly took out the barista, who jumped back hastily.

He laughed. 'I am not so banal.'

'So, mi Miranda, let me introduce myself,' he took her hand, 'I am just a poor Nicholas. A dull seeker of world intelligence from Argentina. And you? Are you looking for photos or love? For entrancement or power?'

Miranda giggled and, conveniently forgetting about Phillip and the children, murmured she was always enchanted by beauty whether it be in men or pictures.

Nicholas roared delightedly. 'Mafalda indeed! Then I must assuredly introduce you to my stepmother at some future time. She is a connoisseur of both. Luckily, she is not here tonight, or she would certainly wrest you away from me, instead I shall try and entertain you to an equal style.'

'Is your stepmother a photographer?'

'She is indeed, and she has a most splendid exhibition coming up, and you are invited.' He paused. 'By me.'

Miranda laughed.

'You see, you think I jest but give me your card and I will arrange the invitations.'

He looked so deeply into Miranda's eyes she forgot she was a detective.

'Oh, we'd all love to,' she said, again deciding not to mention she had a husband and three children. 'That is Cat and Stevie, my friends, and me, I'll send you an email, reminding you, or would you prefer I contacted you via LinkedIn?'

He gave her his phone.

'I am Nicholas Romero. Give me your LinkedIn contact. We will be business friends. My business is to admire, yours to be admired, My Miranda'

It seemed only minutes before Stevie came up to them.

'Oh, there you are. Cat's gone to get the car.'

'Ah, this is my friend Stevie, Nicholas, she flies a Tiger Moth.'

Nicholas looked deeply into Stevie's eyes.

'Wow! How wonderful. How clever.'

'Not really,' said Stevie, as starchy as a Victorian aunt. 'It's training.'

She pinched Miranda's arm. 'Come on Miri, Cat will be waiting.'

'Bye, bye Nicholas,' said Miranda smiling softly at her new friend, 'I look forward to our next meeting.'

'No more champagne for you,' hissed Stevie. 'You flirt.'

Miranda gave a final wave and blew Nicholas a kiss. Then Stevie dragged her out to the car.

'It's all business, Stevie, I'm just doing my bit.'

Stevie sighed and pushed Miranda into the car, locking the door before Miranda could nip out the other side and return to the party.

'But wasn't he just so gorgeous, that handsome Argentinian.'

'I prefer them fatter,' said Cat, 'more reliable.'

'He was a creep,' said Stevie.

Chapter 31

The phone number for Anastasia's parents no longer worked. Cat looked up the address above Marbella on Google Maps and showed Stevie a villa with a pool, white walls and a view of the sea, albeit from some distance up the hill.

'Not a bad looking place. They must have had some money,' said Stevie.

'Possibly. Spain wasn't expensive in the seventies and eighties,' said Cat. 'Quite the opposite! I remember going on a riding holiday in Orgiva with Charlie in the late 70s and we hardly spent a penny, even though living like princes.'

'It does explain why she was called Anastasia,' Stevie said.

'What do you mean?'

'Marbella, it's full of Russians, it even has a Russian film festival. I took some clients down there one year, must have been about six years ago. It was when I was still doing the medium twin flying.'

'Rodriguez doesn't sound very Russian.'

'No, but does Harrington sound French? Or Saxe-Coburg and Gotha sound English?'

'You mean people anglicise or *españolizar* their names?

'Precisely my dear Watson!'

'Ha, ha.'

'And we have no idea how long the Rodriguez family were living in Spain. Could have been escapees from Jewish pogroms under Peter the Great, or more recent escapees from the Soviet Union, or even just liked a friend's name ... do you think it matters?'

'Could, I guess,' said Stevie, turning back to the computer. 'Finding the family story often gives an insight into the person.'

* * *

Indeed it does, thought Cat, playing with her phone.

Once Charlie had explained that Motor neurone disease has a long slow progression into immobility and death, Cat didn't feel capable of asking for details about the girl in the biplane. However, the girl and the house on the airfield nagged at her constantly. *Who? How? Why?*

A few weeks later, Cat and her daughter, Caroline, were invited to visit Miranda. Miranda was then a recent arrival in the village and Caroline had fallen upon her in delight. She was only a couple of years older than Caroline, but in maturity she was at least ten years ahead and had a cuddly open warmth that Caroline felt her parents lacked. Caroline spent most of her holidays dropping over at Miranda's house and telling her all her problems.

One day, Miranda invited Cat to visit her too. Cat, already stressed by Charlie's illness and the unexplained house on the airfield, was suspicious. What reason could the neighbour have for inviting her friend's mother round? It stank of trouble. She dressed for danger and accompanied her shocked and silent daughter around to the friend's house.

It seemed another villager also decided to drop in. When Cat and Caroline arrived, Cat was confronted with a neighbour she barely knew and a woman she immediately recognised as the sandy-haired biplane pilot who had given Charlie money. She gasped. So this was the trick? The girl!

'Oh?' she growled, putting herself between Caroline and the interloper.

'Hello,' said Stevie in a friendly voice, 'you must be Cat, I'm Stevie.'

And, Cat spat: 'Are you Charlie's daughter?'

'Mum!' said Caroline, her eyes showing her worst fears had been realised: her mum had gone crazy.

'What?' asked Stevie clearly puzzled.

Only Miranda laughed. 'No, she's Blinkey's daughter. You know, lives over the other side of the village.'

'Oh,' said Cat, 'the runaway?'

'MUM!'

* * *

Stevie turned back from the computer.

'Penny for your thoughts?'

Cat smiled. 'I was thinking about Russians?'

'Anastasia and Russians?'

'Yes. What do you normally think of when the term Russian comes up?' asked Cat.

'The Antonov? Or the Mil series?' said Stevie.

'What?'

'The AN-225 is the largest plane in the world ... particularly during Cold War times Russians built for size. The Mil helicopters are the most numerous helicopters in the world, more of them were built than ...'

Cat shook her head.

'OK, maybe, but most people would think of Russian mafia, the Novichok poisonings in Salisbury, that sort of thing.'

Stevie stared at her computer screen. 'Hum, I see your point, but are you suggesting that Anastasia's dying husbands might all be related to some mafia plot?'

'I'm putting it out there for discussion.'

'OK, it is possible. But I had assumed that as Anastasia's name had a royal,

rather than a modern, connection. Her family were probably White Russians, if they are Russian at all.'

Cat nodded. 'It was just a thought.'

'OK, well I'll have a search for any possible connection on the web, while you get hold of the divers who found Johnny Holmes' body.'

'It's a deal!'

Chapter 32

The divers who found Johnny Holmes' body were currently in the UK. Marvin Poltro, writer of the report, lived in Redhill, but was busy until next week. His fellow diver, Billy Holecroft, however, was free and keen to meet Cat.

'Come and find me,' he emailed, 'I love answering questions. I'm one of those guys who fill in questionnaires and surveys. Canvassers queue up at my door. Pollsters know my name.'

Cat drove over to Portsmouth early in the morning and parked outside Billy's three-bedroom Edwardian terrace house in Copnor. A wicket gate led to a front garden full of toys. Cat tripped over a red and blue tractor, parked next to a faded tricycle and sitting on scattered bits of Lego.

After rubbing her sore toe, she went up a couple of shallow steps and lifted the fox doorknocker. It crashed down with a thundering noise and she hastily backed away from the door. Was it her fault if he had a knocker rather than a bell, and it leapt out of her hand?

A clean-shaven thickset man with curly salt and pepper

hair flung the door open. He was wearing a dressing gown and holding a bottle of beer in one hand.

'You're nice,' he said waving the beer at her and ushering her back up the steps. 'Married?'

'I'm a widow,' said Cat, pausing on the first step, 'and I live with a boyfriend.'

'Widow 'eh! I expect my bitch wishes she'd been a widow, then she'd have got the lot, not just half.'

Amused by this unexpected greeting, Cat relaxed and followed him into the sitting room where a low table was covered with bottles of beer, some open, some closed. An opener had fallen onto the floor and was half buried in the thick carpet.

'Want one?'

'What, err oh, no thanks.' Cat stared at the table, hoping he would not think her standoffish. 'I'm driving and, err, 10 a.m.'s a bit early for me.'

Billy shrugged, dropped down onto the sofa, finished the bottle in his hand and picked up another.

'More for me, then! My bitch left me when I was away slogging my guts out underwater in Saudi. She took the kids too. I had to fight to get them back. She said I was never home. Those were the least fun days.'

He sighed and drank again. One foot danced on the floor making little patterns in the thick carpet.

'I could tell you stories about suicides and blame games then, but you want to talk about Johnny Holmes, don't you?'

'Yes, please.'

Cat perched on an armchair at right angles to the sofa. Billy threw out his feet, so they were touching hers. He grinned.

'He was a drunk. And he had no reason to be. His missus wasn't like mine screwing all the local lads when his back was turned. She was a cutie, and innocent like. You can see it. She had a virginal way of looking around her, though obviously she wasn't.'

He laughed dirtily rather than unkindly. 'What was her name?'

'Anastasia,' said Cat. 'When did you meet her?'

'Ana-as-tasia. Yup. That's it. 'Eh? Oh, Clement brought her over to the platform a couple of times. Not many people knew that, but I liked Clement. He was genuine. He wouldn't sleep with another man's wife. You could trust him. Unlike most of the lads up there. Bastards.'

'How many people knew she'd visited the rigs?'

'Only me, and Clement of course. We were friends. I showed her around when she took her photos. She did lovely ones. Wonderful talent that lady. What happened to her?'

'She remarried. A Spaniard.'

'Good girl. Get her away from that diving community. It stinks. You can't trust another fellow in it. My bitch of a wife married another diver!'

'Tell me about Johnny? How did he come to fall off the rig?'

'He was an idiot. He wanted someone to hide a bottle of whisky for him under the platform jacket.'

'Jacket?' asked Cat, imagining the platform dressed up for a meeting.

Billy sniggered. 'Sorry, you call it the platform, I call it the platform jacket, technical term!'

Cat wasn't sure if she understood any better.

'Johnny persuaded Clement to bring it in. Ana hid it for him under the platform. Of course, Johnny didn't know it was Ana with Clement or he'd have gone crazy. Drunken bastard was the most jealous man I've ever known.'

Cat was shocked. 'Clement brought in the whisky?'

'Yes, didn't he tell you? I suppose he felt guilty. Thought it was his fault, though it wasn't, was it? How was he to know that stupid bastard would fall off the platform getting it? I like to imagine the scenario sometimes. Johnny snuffling around under the platform, hoping no one would see him, grabs the whisky and loses his balance, but he's not letting go of that bottle whatever, so rather than grab something and save himself he plunges fifty feet into the sea. Stupid sod!'

'Can you remember which day it happened? The date?'

Billy thought about it. 'November, wasn't it, the thirteenth? We went back onshore on the fourteenth, the day Johnny should have gone home.'

'Clement said he was still holding the bottle when you found him.'

Billy looked slightly surprised.

'He was holding the bottle all right, but I didn't find him, that was Marvin. Marvin Poltro. Lives in Redhill. His bitch of a wife left him too. We sometimes have a drink together. He's the one what taught me not to take tramadol mixed with any alcohol as it can have consequences. Guys used to take them to make them drunk quicker, but it makes you woozy. Better, he said, to mix cider and beer, then you get very drunk without the sleepy stage. Dangerous on the rigs!'

'Are you saying Johnny wasn't the only one who got booze in on the rigs?'

Billy took a swig of his beer.

'That was in the 70s, really. The stories I could tell! Probably no one would believe me. The support ships were floating bars. Run by Ities and Frogs what can you expect? That lot can't last a day without sipping the sup. By the 80s, management was getting fly. They were checking us. Makes you laugh, really. Checked us for booze on the way in, but on the way out they didn't even know who was leaving!'

'Like Johnny?'

'Stupid bastard. He did sometimes go by boat, sometimes on the Sea King.

Sometimes he even took a lift with Clement without telling anyone. He liked to leave them guessing.'

'Why?'

Billy laughed. 'They're not girls, these guys, they like to break rules. Like stealing your fucking wife.'

Chapter 33

Mateo Perez Rodriguez lived outside Jerez. The family vineyard had an excellent website, which impressed Stevie. Someone professional and imaginative set this one up, and, unusually, checked the spelling and grammar. As well as their own vineyard, the Perez family had interests in other companies and were advising one in New Zealand and another in Chile. Successful as sherry makers for many years, Mateo's father Carlos was the one who brought the company into the modern era.

Carlos Perez saw that sherry had had its day. He moved into wine production earlier than any of his competitors. He and Mateo, already interested in the family business from a very early age, had invited some talented young winemakers to join them, and they were now one of the best vineyards in Spain.

The Perez vineyard's first attempt at wine making had been sparkling wine, and although Carlos did manage to bring two- or three-years' growth to the table, it quickly became obvious his still wine tasted better and sold in much greater numbers.

* * *

'He died intestate,' Stevie told Cat. 'I looked for the will and found a lot of interesting stuff there.'

'You can look for wills online?' Cat was shocked. Was her three pennyworths, divided between her three children, online to be examined and pulled apart?

'You can find most things,' said Stevie amused, 'and especially things that aren't there that should be. There's deduction for you, Sherlock!'

'Oh! And?'

'Since Carlos died without a will everything passed to his wife, Anastasia. It seems, though, that although she nominally owns the vineyard and land, Mateo runs it, is the MD and everything. His sister is a director, as is his mother.'

'Can you find her will too?'

'Actually, I did.'

'Oh God Stevie, you're making me feel sick. I'm not from this digital age where everything is known. Is anything secret these days?'

'Not much.'

'Go on, then.'

'Two days after she married her third husband, Anastasia made a will ensuring that everything was left to her two children in the event of her death. Of course, as it happened, he died before her. I've got his name now, but I haven't done much on him yet.'

'So, she made a will leaving everything to her children? I wonder? Did she think he might kill her? Was she insured? That's an odd twist, and different from the fourth husband.'

'Yes, but we already knew that Tom Drayton died intestate and she fought his brother for half of the company and won. She is some feisty lady!'

Cat felt a splurge of admiration. She didn't want Anastasia to have killed any of her husbands, whatever the reason. However, she reminded herself, detectives must be impartial at all times.

Social media had given Stevie lots of information about Anastasia's family, but it was mostly from friends. From Anastasia herself there was no online trail.

'No surprise there,' said Cat. 'She's only a few years younger than me, and I certainly don't do any of that social media time wasting!'

'But,' said Stevie, 'what about her photography? Instragram is a perfect place for that, or LinkedIn, perhaps more her demographic.'

Cat sighed, ignoring Stevie's problem. 'Caroline and her daughter are coming for the weekend and Frank is still hassling me to help translate his latest book. It would be easier if I just email Mateo rather than go visiting in the south of Spain.'

'Easier, yes but,' said Stevie, 'much less reliable. You are going to be asking this guy about his father's death, possibly his father's murder and perhaps perpetrated by his mother. You need to watch his body language when you ask questions. Why don't you pose as a wine journalist, you can mug up the information on the internet, and then go and interview him?'

'Well, I could. A subsidiary of the company I used to translate for owns a wine journal, *Corkscrew Magazine*, but do many wine journalists ask if your mother killed your father?'

Stevie laughed. 'You'll find a way. Think laterally.

Outside the box!'

'Outside the coffin! OK, get me a flight, perhaps I can finish the book on the flights there and back.'

Chapter 34

Jerez was easier and cheaper to get to than Shetland. Ryanair still had a direct flight to the city and the flights were frequent. Cat hired a car at the airport. She did the paperwork, wishing she had asked Stevie to book it online. Miranda, of course, would have taken a taxi, keen to chat up the driver, even though her linguistic skills were zero. And what would Stevie have done? She'd have taken the bus. Pointless to waste money on a taxi or a car, when you are young, strong and the bus is available. No wonder they worked so well together.

Cat found the car, which had none of the Shetland eccentrics, and drove into Jerez, where she was staying in a small hotel near the Plaza de Arenal.

Walking down the Calle Guarnidos she was assaulted by a waft of garlic, forcing on her a memory so strong she collapsed on a chair outside a bar. That smell!

She was in a small Spanish town; she had been translating non-stop for three days and nights and she was exhausted. She went back to her hotel, sat on the terrace and ordered a glass of wine.

The camarero who brought the glass looked at her sympathetically.

'A beautiful woman should not be so sad,' he said, 'look inside, what you see will make you laugh.'

Cat walked into the hotel and saw two horses standing in front of the ballroom door. For a moment she thought they were stuffed, then the closer horse threw up his head, earning a rebuke from the rider. Her eyes walked up the horse to the rider's legs, which were sheathed in leather, with knee protectors. As her eyes travelled further up his body, she saw he was holding a polo stick, gloves, a helmet and on all of them was embossed in gold lettering ROMERO.

'It is an engagement party,' said the polo player looking down on her. His face impassive: horses in a ballroom were clearly a day-to-day event in his life.

'And they will play polo? In the ballroom?'

The player gave a grimace.

'Of course not. It is too slippery.'

* * *

'*Algo para beber*? Anything to drink?' asked the waiter, returning her to the present.

She ordered a glass of wine from the Perez vineyard. Good to know the taste of what you are about to investigate.

The next morning, she drove over to the Perez Bodegas. The vineyard was set into the hillside and she passed through vines climbing up behind the slope and on as far as she could see. Brick walls delineated the roadside edge of the property. She drove through recently painted gates, down a neat drive with colourful borders. At the end was the

Perez mansion, a white hacienda with a tower at one side, its stucco glinting in the strong southern sun.

There were a few cars in the courtyard and each one was parked next to a yew tree, as though hoping to get some shade from the intense heat. She parked her car next to the only remaining free yew.

Inside, the clamshell entrance was cool and shady and there was a large reception desk, reminding Cat that as well as making wine, the bodegas did on-request vineyard tours. A man behind the desk smiled and welcomed her in English.

She answered in English. 'I've come to see Señor Perez, my name is Catherine Harrington. I'm from *Corkscrew Magazine*. I made an appointment.'

He eyed her slightly dubiously; perhaps she didn't look like a wine journalist. *Were they all overweight men with red noses?*

'Take a seat, Señora, I will see if he is free. Would you like some water, a coffee?'

She accepted some water and walked around examining the photographs in the lobby while waiting for Mateo to arrive. All the photographs were by Anastasia Rodriguez and showed an artistic side to winemaking that Cat had not previously considered.

Cat felt Mateo enter, his presence louder than his steps. *Did he creep up on his work force in the same manner?* A tall young man with black curls and a military bearing: someone who would be followed to death by devoted troops. At his side a dog that looked like a Jack Russell on stilts. Mateo held out his hand smiling, but he too gave off a vague scent of suspicion.

She bent down to pat the dog and he smiled.

'What type of dog is this?'

'He is a Ratonero Bodeguero Andaluz. They were bred from your English Jack Russells to protect the bodegas from rats. We call him Costner.'

She laughed. 'After Kevin in *The Bodyguard*?'

His eyes lit up. 'You are quick.'

She smiled.

'Very nice to meet you, Mrs Harrington. Please, come into the boardroom.'

As he led the way to the back of the building, Cat realised with a shock, that she was about to ask this young man to give her information that might lead to his mother being convicted of murdering his father. She should be careful, thank Heavens so many people knew where she was.

The boardroom was big enough to house an army of grape-pickers; perhaps this was where they had pre-picking briefings. The vast teak table could easily have held a hundred flowing baskets and still have room for the workers. Running down one side of the room a picture window gave a clear view of the vines, but the glass was tinted to prevent the harsh light blinding the occupants.

'Thank you,' she said, sitting down on the chair he pulled out for her.

The dog strolled over to his bed near the window. She opened her bag and got out a copy of *Corkscrew Magazine*, pushing it over to Mateo.

'We use this room for wine tours,' Mateo said, sitting at the head of the table and automatically opening and flipping through the pages of the magazine.

'I can imagine. The view is beautiful. Do you mind if I take photos later? *Corkscrew Magazine* likes its journalists to get the ambiance as well as the answers.'

'Of course. Ramon will give you a tour, and perhaps you would like some lunch afterwards.'

'Thank you. That is very kind.'

He smiled, his eyes drooping. 'After your tour, Ramon will bring you to my office.'

'Tell me how,' said Cat, getting out her notebook, 'your father came to discover that sherry was no longer the drink of choice.'

Mateo rocked back in his chair, stretching his arms up and resting them on his head.

'My father was a well-travelled man, and he enjoyed culture, history, food, he was an Epicurean philosopher. He understood why fortified wines were so successful in their day, and how much the British nation increased their use.'

He inclined his head slightly at her.

'He spent time in London in the late 60s and early 70s, he was a young man about town.' He smiled at her. 'He was offered sherry in clubs, in homes and in restaurants, but even then, it was really the older generation who liked sherry. Amongst the young it was increasingly rare.'

Mateo looked out the long window, sighing softly as though seeing his father tending the grapes.

'When he returned to London in the 1980s, he saw that much less sherry was being drunk and he anticipated the future. He returned home and started to plan. He was a unique man. My mother, sister and I were lucky in having known him.'

Cat went on to ask about the Palomino grape and how flexible it was in changing its use from sherry to wine, especially as the company went through a champagne stage. She had found the knowledge on the internet and was rather proud of her research. Certainly, Mateo had a strange look on his face when she asked about the use of Palomino in champagne, and she congratulated herself on the question.

However, after that the interview seemed to go wrong

and although Cat asked several leading questions, she never found herself in a position to ask the questions she really wanted answered.

Then Mateo was getting up saying. 'Well, I imagine that has covered everything. Ramon will show you the vineyard and I will see you at lunch.'

Whistling the dog, he was gone.

Cat wondered if Ramon would be able to answer any questions on the family. However, it seemed that Ramon had only been at the bodegas for six months and was still learning the information himself.

Mateo met her for lunch. They sat outside in the court-yard, on a small table with vines brushing their shoulders as though curious about what they were drinking. The dog had another basket in the shade.

Mateo ate very little, but Cat revelled in the Jerez kidneys, calamari and langoustine. She tucked in heartily, asking several cooking questions, which Mateo answered himself, although he said everything was prepared by the chef. When the pudding came and it was Tocino de Cielo, Cat's tastebuds did a little dance of joy.

'This is fabulous, gorgeous,' she said. 'Absolutely divine, so light and yet so creamy ... just heavenly.'

Mateo smiled. 'It's a house specialty. In the past, vine-yards used to use a lot of egg whites to clarify the wines, as, of course you know, and this pudding is made entirely from the yolks, of which there were many left.'

Cat was enjoying the taste too much to notice the slightly ironic tone in his voice.

'Have you been a wine writer long?' he continued. 'I can imagine it being a dream come true for many wine experts.'

'No,' Cat replied honestly, 'I've written on a range of

subjects from helicopters to babies. I'm just a hack! I go where I'm needed.'

Mateo softened and began to look less suspicious. 'I see, perhaps that explains it.' He raised an eyebrow.

'Explains what?'

'We have been talking about why my father decided against sparkling wine, because the Palomino grape is not successful other than in fermentation and yet you keep referring to champagne. I have never met anyone in the wine industry who did not know that champagne is only made in that area of France and that anywhere else the creation is known as sparkling wine.'

'Bother,' thought Cat, she assumed that her brilliant knowledge of the Palomino grape was rather a good question, now she realised she'd mucked up on the basics! Of course, everyone knew you should not refer to sparkling wine as champagne, unless you were Russian!

'Ah,' said Cat, 'I think I had better come clean.'

'Please.'

He looked at her, waiting. She tried not to feel intimidated.

'I work for an insurance company Miftip, they employ me on various matters. In this instance, I am on a life insurance case.'

She pushed over a card.

'I see,' he said, picking up the card. 'You won't object if I check this claim?'

'Go ahead,' she said smiling, although she had butterflies in her stomach.

He called the receptionist and, giving him the Miftip card, asked him to verify her credentials, then turned to her to continue their conversation.

'Tell me about your mother,' said Cat, nibbling a piece of

chocolate that had accompanied the coffee. 'Is she involved in the wine making process?'

'No,' said Mateo, pursing his lips. 'She owns the vineyard and she and my sister are very interested in the process, and, of course, in tasting and drinking the product, but they have other deeper interests. The vineyard was totally my father's family and it was embedded into the blood of us Perezes. He tended the vines with his own hands, and he taught me to do the same. The vines work for us because they see how closely we love them. We understand the thinking of the plant world.' He stopped and gave a little laugh. 'You might say that my father was one of the first to see the importance of working with nature and not against it. He had vision. It is true he could sometimes be a little high handed with those who did not have his gift, but he was completely honest through and through. He saw very early on that if we treat the environment well, it will work with us ... now *gentes* are aware, but then he was an outcast, a rebel. Someone who wanted to be different.'

Mateo's lips tightened, and he looked out of the window, silent for a moment. 'His death devastated us all ...'

'Yes. I am sorry. I'm sure your mother was heartbroken.'

Mateo turned and looked at her with a direct glance that almost frightened her.

'Mrs Harrington,' he said and he changed into Spanish. 'You are a widow.'

How does he know that? Cat was surprised.

He was continuing. 'Your husband was much older, no? Knew what was best for you, no? A trifle patrician, no?'

She stared at him.

'Did you kill him?'

How did this happen? Who is interviewing whom?

'Of course not! I was heartbroken,' she said.

He nodded curtly and Cat felt as though she was in a small sailing boat and the helm had suddenly been taken by a much more expert sailor.

'You know how much death hurts. How much it destroys, not just in the immediate but also in the long term. I do my little bit for the vineyard but I lack the brilliance, the *estaz* of my father. I miss him so much.'

'I understand,' she replied in Spanish.

The receptionist returned and said a few discreet words to Mateo, who turned back to her, and smiled. He continued in English, as though they had never had the more intimate moment. 'Forgive me for checking, but I have to be so careful.'

'Of course.'

'Your firm acknowledged the detection.'

She smiled back. Thank God for Frank, who had set up her alibi with some colleagues. They were all very worried about Angelo and keen to help.

'Please explain exactly how this life insurance request relates to the Perez Bodegas.'

Cat nodded.

'At present' she said, 'we are dealing with a life insurance beneficiary who is related to your late stepfather.'

Mateo's head jerked up from the magazine, and the look he gave Cat would have caused a more nervous woman to jump up and start packing her things. The room was filled with silent tension. The dog moved in his basket and gave a slight moan.

Then, just as suddenly, Mateo gave a hard bark of laughter. 'Nicholas Romero! That stupid, stupid *sanguijuela*.'

He picked an imaginary bloodsucker from his arm.

'I will tell you,' he said in Spanish, 'what you want to know. We will speak in Spanish. But you are, as you English say, barking up the wrong tree. Nicholas Romero wants to believe my mother killed my father and his father too.' He snorted.

'My mother loved my father too much. She was as devastated as my sister and me. We are all very close and I would know if she had murdered him. I might not tell you but I would know and the family would deal with it in their own way. But I know she did not. She should have killed that species, that hombre who was briefly my stepfather but she did not either. My mother is not a killer.'

Cat said nothing. Her heart was beating so fast she felt breathless, realising just how deeply she had insulted this stranger and how amazingly well he was behaving. She slipped into Spanish and tried to explain the unexplainable.

Mateo put up his hand and she felt his power swell over her like a wave.

'You are unusual, Mrs Cat. You speak very good Spanish even for a French woman, but why do you think my mother is a killer?'

How did he know that?

'I'm only half French,' said Cat.

He looked at her and then, unexpectedly, amusement flooded into his eyes.

'Mrs Cat, please, ask me your questions but try not to mention that lowlife Nicholas Romero.'

Cat started by asking what Anastasia's children knew about Johnny Holmes. As they were born after he died, their input would be entirely via their mother or grandparents, but nonetheless, she felt there could be some insight here.

'Mr Holmes was,' said Mateo, 'as you English say, posh with dosh. He arrived in Marbella in a Mercedes. My grandparents were not to know that a Mercedes could be bought for nothing, they thought he was a millionaire. They said he was spreading money like butter. When he splashed the cash they were totally taken in. He claimed to own a large property in The Shetland Islands. He told my grandparents all sorts of tales about land clearances in the past, crofting and how his ancestors had behaved cleverly while others had failed. They believed everything. They thought he was a Scottish laird. My grandmother thought it sounded like Russia. They should've known to be suspicious but they weren't. He was clearly taken with my mother and they were married three weeks after meeting.

'They had their honeymoon there in Marbella and then he took her to his ancestral home, only it was actually a hired croft in one of the least populated islands, called Fetlar.'

'But she was so young?' said Cat. 'Why did she have to marry?'

Mateo grimaced. 'My grandparents were immigrants from Russia, they had six children. She was the last and they were getting old. My grandfather was sixty-three when she was born, my grandmother forty-seven, so he was already eighty and she sixty-four. They wanted her off their hands, and Holmes seemed like a prince from Heaven. He was rich, a Scottish laird with an island and they thought she would have a lovely life. Instead, he was a drunk, an oilman and an abuser. After he died, they discovered everything about him, but before ... they thought God had provided!'

'After he died,' said Cat, 'what happened?'

'They flew out to Shetland. There was some investigation, although very little. Everyone saw he was dead. It seemed obvious what had happened and there was little to be done. My grandparents were appalled about their part in the action. They thought it was their fault, and actually it was.'

He pushed the magazine absent-mindedly. 'My mother came home. She went back to living with my grandparents and went back to school.'

'How did she meet your father?'

'My grandfather came to a wine tasting. He was a polymath, interested in everything. He and my father became friends, and when he took my father home and introduced him to my mother, they fell in love, immediately. They were both brilliant, beautiful people with the same sense of humour.'

Mateo looked out of the window.

'We had a lovely home life. My parents taught us to debate, to speak in many languages. They gave us an excellent start in life.'

'But your father took a mistress?'

Cat hoped she wasn't being too direct.

'Well yes,' Mateo said, 'but after my mother disappeared.'

'Your mother disappeared?'

'Yes, and no, we knew where she was, but she was so interested in her photography that she neglected my father ... and, *lo siento mucho*, but my father was a *man*! Can you blame him?'

'You're saying he took a wifelet?' asked Cat. 'Someone of no importance? Did your mother see it that way?'

The boy laughed. 'English joke? I like it. She was my mother's maid, Teresa. It was a shame she was under him when he died. She can never work again, but she has been compensated.'

Mateo shrugged at this bit of collateral damage.

'There was an autopsy. My father, who loved his food and drink, was sadly overweight and always so active, died of a heart attack. Even earlier, when he approached sixty, my mother had told him to slow down, now he was in his late sixties. Men, we always think we are still twenty, but as you get older you slow down, only my father didn't. If anything, he did more. He had to be busy. It cost him his life.'

'After your father died? Your mother married again?'

'Yes,' said Mateo, 'to him, the funny Argentinean. The polo man. That's what we called him at home, the Poloman: a man with a hole in him. When my father took a mistress, my mother had to have a lover. They always competed with one another. It was like a game to them both. Romero meant nothing to her. It was just her way of showing my father she was attractive too.'

'Romero had been married before?'

'Yes, the poor girl. She fell into the sea, off a yacht. Some people say he threw her off, others say she jumped. I don't think she jumped; I'm told she was a devout Catholic. Romero was such a playboy. His wife had the money and he just spent it all. I don't think he did a day's work, the *coño*. And then his stupid son, Nicholas Romero, who is a playboy just like his father, but without even the talent for games!'

'You didn't admire your stepfather?'

'He was what you English would call a piece of posh totty! He had the money but no way the class.'

'Um,' said Cat, 'more likely he'd be called nouveau riche!'

'But that is French thievery!' He laughed. 'And then that fool Romero fell off his horse playing polo ... silly idiot. What kind of man does that?'

Mateo snorted.

'He was so proud of being my mother's lover. Before every game he would swig down a glass of my father's failed sparkling wine crop, adulterated with brandy and bitters and toast my father. Then he would smash the glass, before going off to play. On the occasion he died, he did that as usual, but maybe this time it was just one glass too many. He got woozy on a fast chukka; fell off his horse and his opponent's horse trampled on him. He was dead before he arrived at hospital. Good riddance to a piece of jaded rubbish, as you English say.'

Chapter 35

When Cat returned home she was ecstatic. 'He told me everything I wanted to know. It was fantastic.'

'Indeed,' said Stevie. 'Like Miranda.'

Cat looked at her sharply. 'What do you mean?'

'Do you know both he and his sister have Mensa ratings?'

'I didn't but so?'

'I wonder if he told you everything, he wanted you to know? Like Miranda does in the pub, laughing and joking with them, buying them drinks, letting them all think she's a fool, while getting all the information she wants?'

Cat pouted. 'Having a Mensa rating doesn't mean you can control people. Lots of people with Mensa ratings have problems with daily living.'

'But clearly not Mateo, who runs an extremely successful business.'

'Yes,' Cat felt once again like a schoolgirl. 'He may have told me what he wanted me to know, but it was also what I wanted to know.'

'Good.'

As Cat gritted her teeth, Miranda danced into the office.

'OK, what goes girls? Shall we have a pow wow? Fill me in with what you have discovered?'

'Good idea,' said Cat, 'a lot has happened, and I need to send Gia an update. 'So. What about this:

'Husband one: Johnny Holmes, big time deceiver, falls off rig either in an accident or pushed. Ana has motive and opportunity.

Husband two: Carlos Perez, autocrat but loves his wife, however, has a mistress. Heart attack. Carlos had recently seen a doctor, carried nitrate pills and a spray for his angina. Ana no opportunity or motive.'

'Oh,' said Miranda, 'don't you think having a mistress is a motive?'

'Maybe, OK, possible motive.'

Husband three: Romero ... do we have a first name?'

'Not so far,' said Miranda, 'but since we know there was a son, we can call him Father Romero.'

Cat raised her eyebrows. 'OK. But sometimes it shows that you weren't brought up in the church.'

Miranda made a face.

Cat continued. 'Husband four: Tom Drayton, builder, died of heart attack. Ana got half his business. Motive and opportunity.'

'On the other hand,' said Miranda, 'we have now discovered that Ana raised lots of money for charity and although Pete Drayton hated her, others in the local area thought she was wonderful.'

'She's certainly proving a complicated character,' said Cat. 'Not an easy person to make assumptions about.'

'And,' said Miranda, 'we have no proof either way!'

Chapter 36

Miranda was manning the office and brushing the dog. Stevie had taken Blinkey to the memory clinic for a series of tests.

'In case,' Stevie said to Miranda, 'they discover she is normal, and we are the dotty ones.'

And Cat was on her way to interview the main diver, Marvin, who had agreed to meet her in his house in Redhill. So, Miranda was a bit surprised when the office phone rang and a voice asked:

'You waiting for Marvin?'

'Er ... sort of,' said Miranda, feeling like Felix; that was his standard answer to most things perplexing. 'Can I help?'

'He's not coming,' said the voice, 'he's shy.'

Miranda stared at the wall, watching a fly crawling towards a spider's web. 'One of our agents, Cat, is on her way to his house,' she said. 'She'll be with him soon. Sorry but, er, who are you?'

'I'm his mum,' said the voice, 'look I am sorry. Can you stop your Cat coming?'

'Yes, yes, of course,' said Miranda. The woman sounded

unhappy, and Miranda felt her heart jolt in sympathy. 'Are you OK? Can I help at all?'

There was a silence and then the woman said, 'Yes, maybe. It's the social, see. Since she took the kids away, they've made his life hell.'

'Oh, dear,' said Miranda, 'how awful. I do understand. They can be very difficult. Who was it took the kids away? Social workers?'

'No. Her. Marvin's Mrs. It was all a mistake but he supported his mum, and who wouldn't? You'd support your mum, wouldn't you? If she made a small mistake?'

'I would,' said Miranda, 'I'd always support my mum.'

She could hear Marvin's mother starting to cry on the other end of the phone. 'He's a good boy,' she said. 'He'd never hurt a fly. The black eye wasn't him, I told them that, she tripped, hit her face on the edge of a chair. He's never been violent. Never! Not even when his father hit him.'

After Miranda's father fell under a train her mother had to fight to keep the children. Luckily, Miranda's mother was from Yorkshire and she wasn't letting any Clapham do-gooder stop her keeping the kids. But Miranda, then sixteen, remembered the battle.

'I'll stop Cat coming over,' said Miranda, 'but if you'd like me to help in any other way, I'd be glad to. Would you like to talk?'

'Thank you. I'd just like to sit a bit and listen to you. Tell me about your agency, it would make me feel better.'

Miranda sent a text to Cat.

'Marvin busy. Mother rang. Can you come back to the office ASAP?'

'There are three of us in the agency,' said Miranda to Marvin's mother, 'Cat, Stevie and me. I'm the office dumbo, you know there is always one, the idiot who gets it all wrong, that's me ...'

From the other end of the phone Miranda heard a watery laugh. 'Go on, love, you sound like my sort of girl.'

'Well,' said Miranda, 'there was this big dog, see, whose name was Stanley Albino Caruthers Kirk, known as Zac for short ...'

Miranda had just put down the phone when Cat got back. Cat was no longer a cool cougar but a hot spitting domestic feline.

'First of all, I was behind a Golf driver who thought her car was a horsebox and needed to be driven in the middle of the road. Then, I had just got past her when I got your phone call, so I turn round and find myself joining a steam engine party ...'

'YMMV,' muttered Miranda unsympathetically.

Cat, who anyway had no idea what YMMV meant, was continuing, '... there can't be that many steam engines in the world, why were they all in Sussex this morning? And all coming in this direction.'

'I've been talking to Marvin's mother.'

'Oh. Any good?'

'Well, maybe. She says Marvin and Billy were diving together when they found Johnny's body. She says he never dives alone.'

'Oh, great! The opposite of what Billy said. Then, we still need to talk to Marvin. Did she happen to mention who left the bottle for Johnny or when?'

Miranda shook her head. Was Cat going to blame her for not getting information when she hadn't shared the question?

'His mum had heard of Anastasia,' said Miranda quickly, 'Marvin went to her wedding.'

Cat stared at her. 'What? He went to her wedding! How come?'

Miranda felt rather pleased with herself. This had been Cat's interview and she'd cracked it already. 'Apparently he knew Tom Drayton. They were friends.'

'How come?'

'Mum didn't know. Just said he went to the wedding, which was unusual because he don't socialise much.'

'Hum,' said Cat, 'we really need to meet Marvin in the flesh. Something is going on there.'

Chapter 37

Isabella Perez, Anastasia's daughter by her second husband Carlos, lived in Paris, where she was studying linguistics at the Sorbonne, but she was in London for an exhibition on the Therapeutic Power of Language. She agreed to meet Cat in a club just off Berkeley Square.

They arrived at same moment. As Cat opened the door, Isabella walked straight in almost brushing Cat aside. She was a tall Goth, with long blonde ringlets. *Would she, prefer to speak Spanish or English? Would they kiss two or three times?* These cultural niceties were so difficult to get right. There was so much room for embarrassment.

'Good morning,' said Isabella, briefly giving Cat her hand, before turning, striding up the reception stairs, through the sitting room, and out the French windows.

Cat followed meekly out into the courtyard. Isabella had already sat down at a table standing apart from the others and was motioning to the waiter that they would drink coffee.

'Patrician!' said Isabella as Cat sat beside her. '*That* is the word that describes my father.'

'Hum,' thought Cat.

'My mother loved her photography and in the beginning he supported her, but, *vaya*, when she started to do well, to make money out of her work ... then he wanted to curb her ... to prevent her flying!'

Her hands demonstrated how the birds of photography were suppressed.

'So, she flew away. Her parents had died. She had some little money of her own ... she didn't need him any longer ...'

'Why didn't they divorce?' Cat asked.

'Divorce?' said Isabella in an astounded voice. 'Out of the question. What humiliation!'

She paused for a moment, looking at Cat with a shocked face as though she had said something appallingly filthy.

'Besides,' she added in a calmer voice, 'she loved him. We may find that odd, but she did. My brother and I,' the girl sighed, and pulled at one of her ringlets. 'We suggested she took a lover, to make Dad jealous. She took Romero but it didn't work, and then she got stuck with that fool. Luckily, he was such a fool he killed himself, and that spared her a life of humiliation.'

Cat digested the information that her children had suggested the lover.

'How did your mother meet Romero?' asked Cat, putting down the coffee which was too hot to drink.

'I was a friend of his son, Nicholas. Nicholas has charm but nothing underneath it. I didn't see that at first. I just saw the fascination, the handsome man, the animal attraction. Only after I had introduced him to my mother did I see his shallowness, his ...'

She spread her hands making a noise with her lips. 'I

give you an example: *coño*! His father was having physio-
therapy in Hospital Alemán, a private hospital in BA. *Eso*,
we go to pick him up, to take him home. Nicholas is in
the waiting room and he starts to chat up the technician:
"Oh, he says, you are Mafalda ..." she giggles like a fool,
and then he is on her, chatting, smoothing ...*vaya*!
Sickening.'

'Mafalda?'

'She's a heroine in Argentina. A cartoon heroine! Only
Nicholas would use a cartoon woman as his reality. In
Argentina they all know her. She was a young girl, sassy,
strong, funny ... maybe if the Belgian Tintin was a girl ... *eso*!
It was his perpetual pick-up line. He used it on me too! I was
very young, else I would not have been attracted to such a
species.'

She spat. Cat hoped no one would notice. Spitting was
frowned on in London.

'When we left the hospital, he says to me: "Ha you don't
know who that is, do you?" Like he has just earned a prize.
"That is Maria Arinez," he says. The way you would say that
is Madonna. When I say, who? he laughs.'

Isabella spread her hands and dropped her chin, giving
a fine impression of a Russian doll.

'Then, the way he says: "Only the daughter of one of the
most powerful mafia families of the 1980s." As if that was
like meeting Christ. I laughed then. I was not even alive in
the 1980s and he thinks I should want to idolise the gang-
land *niñas*!"

She spat again and Cat got an urgent desire to get up and
step over it, hide it from view. She hoped this was a very
international club.

'Nicholas introduced my mother to his father. *Vaya*!
What a mistake! But that would be his humour. He would

date the daughter, while his father would date the mother. All that gives you an idea of Nicholas Romero.'

Cat said nothing. Two out of the three husbands so far appeared to be pretty poor choices.

Isabella continued. 'Then, the day after my mother married his father, he dumped me for Maria Arinez. And he told me by text! That is the kind of guy Nicholas Romero is.'

She picked up her coffee cup and for a moment Cat tensed, lest she throw it to the ground in anger. However, she put it back in its saucer and twiddled with her ringlets again.

'So,' asked Cat, 'did you get to know Romero the father at all?'

Isabella shook her head. '*Mal Bicho*! No. I avoid the son, I avoid the father.'

'Your brother said your mother went back to school after Johnny Holmes died.'

'*Eso*, she went to university.'

'University? Could she? I mean ... did she have any schooling?'

Isabella spread her arms. Cat was beginning to see why she had chosen a table as far from the others as possible.

'My mother was clever. My grandfather had some contacts. My mother did not disappoint.'

'Oh?' Cat asked Isabella. 'What did she do?'

'She had always wanted to study but her family could not afford it. She had older brothers who needed educating, so she got very little. Now that she had the insurance money from Holmes' death, she could pay for herself. She was clever, no qualification but they understood her position and they let her in.'

'I meant, err ... What did she study? Photography?'

'No, chemistry. Apparently, it was always an interest and

it did include the chemicals necessary to do her own photo-graph processing.'

'Wow. Did she get a degree?'

'*Vaya*, for sure. She got a first. She continued to study and did a PhD in causes and treatment for infertility while we were growing up. My mother is an exceptional woman.'

'How did your mother meet your father?'

'He met her parents at the Russian embassy.'

'Why?'

'You mean why Russia?'

'Yes, why were they at the Russian Embassy?'

'They were Russian. Our grandmother's family was White Russian. Hence Anastasia. Mama's name was my grandmother's choice. Grandmother's family escaped from St Petersburg in 1916. Our grandfather's extended family was already here, I mean in Spain. He and his parents went first to Ecuador and then joined his extended family in the 1920s. The life of an immigrant can be ... is ... varied! They still spoke Russian at home. Both grandparents were alive when we were very little but they were very old, they died in the late 1990s.'

'I see. And why was your father there? At the embassy?'

'He was interested in Russian champagne. They call it champagne there, although it is sparkling wine, a sort of Russian arrogance, I suppose. It was just becoming popular in Spain then. He had an idea they might do it instead of sherry. You know it worked well in UK vineyards. He started talking to my grandfather about it. My grandfather was a polymath; he could talk on any subject. He was born in Kaliningrad Oblast in 1903. He was a Volga German.'

She glanced at Cat to see if that meant anything to her, then explained. 'Volga Germans are ethnic Germans who live on the Volga River in Russia, mostly in the Saratov area of Eastern Russia. They grow up speaking two languages. But in the Second World War the Russians considered them collaborators and they had to flee or be interned. So his family fled. They moved to Ecuador. Living in South America and then later in Spain, he soon acquired more languages. In some ways he was my inspiration. He died at 107 years old and still had, as you English say 'all his marbles'. He was crap with people, and so strict with us children he frightened me, but with facts and linguistics he was an ace.'

Her face softened from an angry Russian doll to a gentle rag one.

'My grandparents brought my father home and he met my mother and fell in love. Both my parents were interesting and beautiful, clever, witty. My father would make my mother laugh even when she was angry. And sometimes she was very angry. Passionate.'

Chapter 38

When Cat got home, Frank was deboning a chicken, closely watched by the two dogs, telling them they would not want to be fatter as it would make them less attractive to lady dogs, and getting very little response. His glasses had slipped down his nose. *Did he remember his joke that their first encounter had been a meeting of cold minds over hot readers?*

At first, he was concentrating too hard to notice her, then, as her shadow fell over him, he looked up, and his face was transformed with joy.

'Welcome home super-sleuth.'

'You've got a rapt audience.'

He laughed. 'Rather like the one when I used to tell jokes on stage. It is only later I find they are either asleep or have actually died.'

She laughed. 'Lucky I saved you from that fate, and brought you back into the life of publishing deadlines! Did you miss me?'

'Always.'

Over a green Thai chicken curry that Frank had created

from scratch, Cat told him about attempting to visit Marvin, and that his mother had said Billy was his dive buddy, while Billy had denied it.

'There's probably a very simple answer,' said Frank.

'Such as?'

'You aren't allowed to dive alone, right? It is dangerous. You might lose your job. So, if you did, would you tell your mother? If she's anything like my mother she'd tell her best friend, who would tell her daughter who would tell her best friend. All in the greatest confidence, of course.'

Cat looked at him thoughtfully. 'I see your point.'

'Ask some other divers. Do they ever dive alone? Bet I know what the answer is! Don't forget you are talking of an era when we didn't always do what we were told, because there wasn't always someone with a camera recording it.'

* * *

Was there someone recording her first meeting with Frank? If so, they would have rolled their eyes like Miranda.

Four years ago, Cat had yet again been translating in Spain, but a little imp in her brain was longing for something different. Something more challenging ... and ... sometimes she was forced to admit to herself that she was lonely. On her way to the bar, she saw a sign.

Comic Ingles Actuando 7 p.m. ¡Esta Noche!

Underneath:

English Joker Performs Tonight!

It was exactly 7 p.m.

Why not? She entered the auditorium. Empty. She was the audience.

Probably she was too early. After years of working in

Spain she realised she was the exception. She sat in the front row.

A minute later, it went dark and the comic, a pudgy middle-aged man, walked on accompanied by two Labradors. Did they perform too?

'*Buenas noches y bienvenido,*' he said in Liverpudlianos Spanish. 'And now, the best of English jokes.'

He proceeded to tell a stream of jokes that were popular when Cat was at school, all in a smooth Liver-Bird accent. Cat laughed.

The stage went silent. The performer walked forward, peered through the lights, staring at her. Gave a little wave. Returned to complete his brief. She laughed again. Could she be the only person who had ever sat in the audience?

When the lights went on, Cat clapped and the comic moved forward, staring down at her. This time he gave a small bow. Then, he and the dogs retreated behind a curtain.

She went into the dining room, which had just opened, and was flicking through the menu, wondering what to eat this time, when she felt a presence hovering above her. The comic was standing, without dogs, by the empty place at her table.

'*Es posible* ...' he started in the same schoolboy Spanish he learnt in Liverpool, '*si yo yo yo ... puedo.*'

Cat broke into giggles, soon tears were dripping down her cheeks and she was unable to control her breathing. Breathlessly she indicated the empty chair.

'I was only going to ask to borrow your glasses,' said Frank in an offended voice. 'I seem to have left mine upstairs.'

'Sorry,' said Cat, coughing to pacify her laughter and giving him her glasses.

He twirled them in his hands, still standing above the empty chair.

'You were funny tonight,' she said. 'I haven't heard those jokes for twenty years!'

He slipped into the chair and put the readers on. His face was wider than hers so they sat balanced dangerously on the tip of his nose.

'The Spanish are very complimentary about my accent,' he said huffily.

'They probably don't have many Liverpudlianos here,' she said grinning. 'I love it.'

He glanced sideways at her without moving his head. His nose twitched.

'Do you ... er ... usually have ... er ... bigger audiences?'

'No, I had a couple of drunks one evening, and another time a man who thought it was a strip show.'

He played with his nose.

'If I order a bottle of wine,' she asked, 'would you have a glass or two?'

'Yes, please.'

'And the dogs?' asked Cat.

'No, they're teetotal.'

'What? Oh!' she laughed again.

'My assistants. They help with the tricks.'

Cat shook her head. 'Have you always done this? Told jokes?'

'Not professionally, I used to be a publisher.'

He squished his nose again.

'Oh, what happened?'

'I published the wrong books. Didn't sell. Once publishing was a game of two haves: those that *have* it and those that *have* made it, but it has evolved. Now everyone wants to make money, whether they have it or not.'

His nose was by now completely flat to his face.

Cat laughed. 'So, now a new career?'

'Yes, publishers with a history of failure are not much in demand. Comics have a better shelf life.'

'Really,' said Cat putting her elbows on the table and looking at the man at her side, 'and yet I may well have a job for you. Foreign languages are a passion of mine, and they are so badly taught in Britain. My elder daughter and I are thinking about starting a business writing children's language books. With her drawings and my stories, we could change all that. But I need someone who knows about marketing.'

'Really,' said Frank, 'I think I'd rather be a detective than start publishing again. Not that there is much difference. In publishing you are inundated with people who write criminally and you try and save one or two. In PI work you are inundated by right criminals and you catch one or two.'

Cat didn't laugh, her mind elsewhere. A detective agency? Now that would be something different.

That night she dreamt of Spanish detectives with squashed noses in Liverpool.

Chapter 39

Cat arrived at the Hall in response to an anxious call from Stevie. The pilot was pacing up and down, dressed in her uniform, her little bag by the door.

'You OK?'

'Worried. Not only has the carer not turned up, and I have to go flying, but Miranda has started an email correspondence with that sexy Argentinian we met at the art gallery.'

'How do you know?'

Stevie's eyes soared towards the ceiling, refusing to meet Cat's look. 'Is it my fault if you girls insist on using my computer and then don't shut down properly?'

Cat laughed. 'OK, so you are keeping tabs on us. Just don't tell Phillip, we'll never hear the end of it. I expect Miri's infatuation will blow over in time, you know what she is like with her enthusiasms.'

'Maybe, but she *is* emotional, falls in love. Remember the guy with the big dog ... luckily he was uninterested!'

'But' said Cat, 'underneath that flirty exterior she's very

moral. She would never leave her children. Remember how she looked after her mother when her father died, even though she was forced to leave school. She has a strong sense of duty. It could well be that she intuits he has some bearing on the Anastasia case.'

Stevie bit her lip. 'I hope you are right.'

Cat took her arm.

'Don't worry about your mother, I'll take her home. She can entertain Lager while we work. Your mum thinks my house is her house anyway; she'll probably start rearranging the flowers. We'll get on to Miranda's naughtiness when you get back. I'll stop her running off with a puppy and children in tow. Just go and fly. Save the world for womankind.'

'Thank you,' said Stevie, grabbing her small suitcase. 'Thank you so much, Cat. It is so wonderful to have you nearby.'

* * *

Cat watched her go. Their first meeting had been so odd, that it would not have been surprising if Stevie regarded her with some suspicion, but she didn't. Instead, she had immediately explained the mystery of her connection with Charlie.

When Stevie's father said he did not want her to be a pilot she left his house, deciding to move in with her only friend: her Tiger Moth.

The Tiger Moth was hangared at a nearby airfield. There she slept in her car, washing in the outside tap, and sneaking into various bathrooms on the industrial estate whenever she could.

For the last ten years, the airfield had been the go-to place for car boot sales. The previous year an entrepreneur,

Clive Creamer, seeing aviation on the rise, bought it, converting it back to an airfield with an onsite industrial estate. Next to the industrial estate, he built a housing estate with a spattering of affordable lots, thus getting substantial tax benefits from the government. The ordinary houses he sold to his friends; a brilliant investment opportunity he told them.

One of these friends was Cat's husband Charlie.

Charlie and Clive had been friends for many years. They worked together, drank together and often discussed private worries. Clive's latest worry was Stevie.

Charlie came over to Clive's office on the airfield, in response to an anguished call from his friend. They sat in the boardroom with glasses of beer and Clive explained his latest problem.

'I've got a girl,' said Clive.

Charlie raised his eyebrows. This was unlike Clive and Charlie felt a touch of surprise, his friend had been 'business first' for so long he doubted there was an emotional side.

'No, not like that,' snapped Clive. 'I don't have time for misbehaving, besides everything is in my wife's name. No, about three weeks ago this girl parked her car here on the airfield, up by the Tiger Moth hangar, and is living in it. Security see her sleeping here at night. It worries me. She must be a runaway.'

'And,' said Charlie, with the quickness that endeared him to his friends, 'you want me to go and talk to her?'

'Would you? Your girls are about the same age. You understand kids. I don't.'

Half an hour later, Charlie tapped on Stevie's car window.

'Hello.'

Stevie said, hello, winding down her window a small crack and peering out at the strange man.

He crouched stiffly down beside the window and Stevie registered his unusual height. That struck a memory. This very tall man lived in her parent's village: she used to see him swinging over to the village shop to get his newspaper Saturday and Sunday mornings.

The thought nearly made her wind the widow back up. Had he been sent to fetch her home, and on to secretarial college?

'I'm Charlie Harrington,' said Charlie. 'I own one of the properties on the airfield.'

'Oh?' said Stevie her voice humming.

'Yes.'

Hearing the suspicion in her voice, Charlie realised he'd better get to the point quickly or lose the girl entirely.

'Yes. I have daughters too, and one ran away from school. Is that what you've done?'

Relieved, Stevie realised he didn't recognise her.

'No. I'm too old for school. I'm eighteen.'

'Are you? You look younger. If you haven't run away from school, why are you living in a car?'

'I'm looking for a job.'

Charlie bit his tongue, trying not to smile. 'How?'

'How what?'

'How is living in a car helping you search for a job?'

'I'm waiting for the manager of the factory to get back from holiday. The guys there said they needed workers and I could apply when he got back.'

'Did they! What skills do you have for the factory manager?'

'I'm a very good engineer, and I can fly.'

Charlie ignored the fact that few factories needed pilots.

He didn't laugh, instead he felt an unexpected rush of sympathy for this silly girl. Was she Blinkey's daughter? There had been a lot of talk about the girl in the pub. She was unusual and villagers like gossip. The gossip was that she had run away.

'Do you have any licences? Pilots and engineers need licences.'

'I want to train for my licence while I work in the factory. Other guys have done it that way.'

'OK,' said Charlie, pulling at his right ear. Who were these well-meaning guys offering her unfounded hope? 'Well, the manager won't even consider you if you are living in a car.'

'Oh yes he will,' said Stevie gripping the steering wheel in front of her. 'Don't worry, I'll convince him. I don't smell like a tramp.'

Charlie noticed the girl had a very determined chin. His sympathy was replaced by a surge of admiration.

'OK,' he said, surprising himself. 'I can help you. I have an empty property on the airfield. Houses are better for being lived in; you can live there as long as you pay the bills. I'll charge you a small amount of rent. I'll lend you the money to get started and you can stay there until you start earning, then you will have to start paying me back. Is it a deal?'

'Yes.' Stevie was delighted. 'Thank you.'

It never crossed Stevie's mind that Charlie might have any ulterior motive, however Charlie was perfectly aware that everyone else in the world, including his wife, would.

'Good, but this is our secret, OK?'

'Great,' said Stevie: that would prevent her parents finding out, at least in the short term. Later, of course, they would be overjoyed.

* * *

Cat shook her head. It was odd that Charlie, who was so tough with his own daughters, could be so kind to Stevie, who had no connection with him at all. Is it easier to be generous to strangers, than to your own family? Sometimes it would seem it was! She'd better go and fetch Blinkey, give her the good news she was coming to stay for ten days.

Chapter 40

When Caroline and Lagertha arrived in the Nissan Leaf (having stopped to charge the battery twice on the way) Cat was still out, but Frank had just arrived back from shopping and was taking things out of the Volvo. Caroline parked neatly at one side of the drive to make room for others.

'Hey, Frank.'

'Caroline, great to see you. Do you want some help with Lager ... er ...the baby?'

She looked at him through narrowed eyes.

'No, I'm fine,' she said.

Caroline liked Frank. She knew her sister Vanessa had no patience with his stream of jokes and refusal to take life seriously, but she liked the fact that he adored their mother. And she was so glad Cat no longer went round wearing short skirts and flirting, the way she did after Dad died. So embarrassing for her children.

'Mum out searching for miscreants?'

'No, she's popped over to see if Blinkey is OK. Apparently, the carer was late arriving and Stevie had to go flying.'

'Uh oh. Does that mean we'll get Blinkey over here? Last time she went off for a swim in the river at midnight and we had to go and find her.'

'Not sure,' said Frank, his mind on what he was going to cook tonight.

'Weird!' Caroline continued slightly louder, 'I hope she's OK with children.'

Frank nodded. 'Bound to be.'

Caroline sighed. Was there a man in the world who listened when not paid to do so?

They took the shopping and the baby inside. Caroline went upstairs to inspect where Lagertha was sleeping, while Frank put the shopping away.

Upstairs, Caroline spotted signs that her nephew, the baby Charlie, had been staying recently: toys and clothes left behind in drawers and cupboards. She felt a splurge of jealousy that she tried to quell. Of course, there was no reason why the little family shouldn't visit their mother too, but it just seemed every time she did something, Vanessa, the younger twin, had done it first.

Lagertha was asleep. Caroline put her into the cot and put the baby monitor on the chest of drawers, next to one of Charlie's toys. She tested it a couple of times, but it seemed to be working OK. She'd leave the door open anyway, just in case.

'Have the little family been visiting?' she asked Frank, as she arrived back into the kitchen.

'Yes, last weekend. Just Victor and Gloria and, of course, Charlie. Vanessa was on a business trip.'

'Oh,' Caroline wasn't sure if she was relieved Vanessa wasn't there or annoyed that she was doing so well at work that they sent her on business trips.

'Yes, they've bought a Tesla. Fantastic. I went out with

Victor and he let me drive it, amazing power those electric cars have and range. Victor demonstrated the effect of the radio on the power though and ...'

'Really,' said Caroline smiling through gritted teeth, 'would you like to have a go at my Leaf? I believe it is actually more efficient than a Tesla even if it doesn't have the range.'

Frank gulped. 'Yes, please, that would be super.'

Much to Frank's relief, Cat and Stevie's mother arrived, making all the noise that usually accompanied Blinkey.

'Hello darlings, ah! There you are. You're the pretty daughter, so much easier than your sister, the clever one. And Hello Francis, how are you? Still telling awful jokes and not getting paid?'

Cat hugged Caroline, who was defo wondering why she had come for the weekend.

'Oh, darling, I'm so glad you are here. We can get the books finished and sent to the printer. I just loved your pictures ... brilliant ideas ... it *is* your pictures that sell the books, not my writing ... I wish my bit was as good as yours.'

'Thanks, Mum, how's the Mystery Detection going? Found any mysterious fly tippers yet?'

'Now, Caroline, there was something I wanted to ask you about that.'

'Yeees,' said Caroline, her muscles tensing. *Why did Mother always ruin everything?* 'What exactly?'

'Are you still in touch with your social worker?'

'Anthony! You know I am, Mum.'

'Great. I wanted to ask him a couple of things, do you think he'd mind?'

'If you are going to ask him to spy on his clients, or give you information then yes, I think he'd mind very much.'

'No, this is something else. It's just a point of principle, why something might have happened. One of my cases.'

Caroline twisted her mouth for several seconds, finally she said: 'OK, I'm meeting him again Wednesday week. You can come.'

'Thanks, darling. What time are you meeting him?'

'I'm meeting him at 3 p.m. but you can come at ten past. I need to warn him that Macavity the Mystery Cat is coming!'

'Eliot.'

'What? You mean Andrew Lloyd Webber!'

Chapter 41

'Are you my daughter?' Blinkey asked Largertha at breakfast. 'You've got my eyes.'

Caroline jumped up protectively but Cat put her hand on her daughter's arm, shaking her head gently.

'Your daughter's an airline pilot,' Cat told Blinkey in a kind voice. 'She's flying at the moment.'

Blinkey stared at her, then back at the baby.

'No, she's too young. One day maybe. You know,' she added, still talking to Largertha, 'your aunt lives in a throuple.'

Caroline stared at the old woman. How could Blinkey, who hardly knew the time of day, know a word like throuple? Did old women become parrots? Who had been talking? Was it Stevie and Miranda? Did they laugh at her behind her back? Did they say, you know Caroline; she's the dull one, dropped out of school and married the first man who asked? Her sister Vanessa is a lesbian and lives in a throuple with her lover Gloria, and her brother, Victor, whom she hates. Isn't that wonderful? Unique. What a character!

'Have some more coffee, Blinkey,' said Cat.

Honestly, thought Caroline, her mother was embarrassed by her daughter's set up. Hated to talk about it. How could someone who freaked out when her husband died and became a Cougar Cat judge her daughter? What was wrong with this family?

'You know,' said Blinkey, still addressing Largertha. 'I killed my husband.'

Cat bustled over with milk.

'Look at the weather Blinkey, isn't it a lovely day?'

'Really,' broke in Frank. 'How? What weapons did you use?'

Cat gave her boyfriend a look that should have made him roll over like a puppy. He blew her a kiss.

'I was very clever,' said Blinkey, 'most women poison their husbands, but I thought it would be more fun to do something different.'

'Do most women kill their husbands?' asked Frank, jumping up and down in his seat. 'Thanks Heavens I'm a boyfriend.'

'Yes, usually during sex or just after. Like that insect ... you know the one. With the big legs ... pounces like this ...'

She jumped her claw onto Lager's nearest arm. The little girl laughed and her mother shot up again.

'Did you smother him with a pillow,' asked Frank, his eyes shining.

Blinkey picked up a saucer, filled it with milk and gave it to the little girl.

'Certainly not! Nothing so amateur. I put a black widow in his bed, once the deed was done the spider left to have her babies and I was free. I wasn't even there, so they couldn't blame me.'

Caroline bit her cheek. Why the hell didn't she stay at

home this weekend? Why did she even think she needed to visit her family? She could feel an anxiety attack coming on and breathed deeply, forcing her shoulders to relax. Thank God she was meeting Anthony next week. Only the thought of his sensible counsel kept her going.

'How did her husband die?' she whispered to her mother.

'Car accident,' said Cat, 'he was still driving in his late eighties and lost control of the car, hit a tree and broke his neck. Unlikely there was a black widow on board, don't worry!'

'She picks things up Mum. She probably knows who did it! Why don't you use her in your team?'

Chapter 42

When Cat took Blinkey home ten days later, Stevie was reading a book on principles of flight, but she clearly wasn't concentrating, as she looked up relieved when Cat deposited Blinkey in her chair.

'What's up?' asked Cat. 'Miranda up to tricks?'

'How did you know?'

'She's Miranda!'

'Well, a couple of days ago a parcel arrived for her, redirected here because she was out. The gardener took it in and put it in water.'

'Put it in water? What was it? A bomb?'

'Ha ha. It was flowers of course. White oleanders.'

'Gosh? Don't tell me Phillip has come over romantic, suddenly.'

Stevie made a face. 'Come over subtle perhaps! Anyway, he's far too busy breaking his heart over you!'

Cat raised an eyebrow. 'That is lust not heartbreak, but since Frank arrived he's been much more circumspect. Anyway, the flowers, who from?'

'Her flirt at the art gallery?'

'Indeed.'

'Interesting choice of flowers, white oleander?'

'Do you know what they are?' Stevie asked.

'Yes, beautiful evergreens, white flowers come out in summer. What's his name, by the way this flirt?'

'Nicholas Romero,' said Stevie blandly.

'What!' said Cat. 'Son of husband number three? How come we missed that connection? We should have clocked that at the Vernissage.'

'We should,' said Stevie, 'but Miri was just looking into his beautiful eyes and not thinking about her detective work. Just in case there are lots of Romeros, I checked it on one of the polo sites. Our Poloman did indeed have a son called Nicholas. And there's more. And clearly this time *you* haven't clicked: white oleanders are deadly poisonous flowers!'

'I think I did know that. But is it relevant? Are you saying you think Nicholas Romero knew that when he sent them to Miranda?'

'Do you ever go to the flicks, Grandmamma? To fil-ems?'

Cat stuck her tongue out and muttered, 'Bébé. Sometimes. Are you going to tell me there is a film about a wife who poisons her husband using oleander flowers?'

'I am. And for your information it came out in 2002 and had Michelle Pfeiffer in the leading role, as the poisoning wife and mother.'

'Hum! While I might think that was rather apt, are you actually suggesting that Nicholas sent oleander flowers to Miri to indicate he thinks his stepmother killed his father?' Cat shook her head. 'I mean ... does he even know she is a detective?'

'If you were having an email correspondence with Miri, you'd find out pretty quickly, don't you think?'

'OK, I'll give you that one. Have you given her the flowers, by the way?'

'Yes.'

'What did she say?'

'Well, at first she thought it must be Phillip. Then she looked inside at the card and said it *was* Phillip, but with that look on her face that we both recognise!'

'Ah, time to visit Mother Miri, I think.'

* * *

Miranda opened the door looking guilty. Cat wondered how she could be a detective with such a transparent face.

'Hello my darlings. Come in. I'm just putting the children to bed. Cat, will you read them a story in Spanish?'

Cat raised her eyebrows. 'Happy to, but do they want it?'

Miranda's son, Felix, called down from upstairs: 'Cat, Cat! Come and read me a story.'

'OK.'

When she went up the wooden stairs, she found the puppy sitting on his bed.

'Is he allowed up here?'

'Sort of,' said Felix grinning. 'He likes a story too. He loves Spanish stories.'

'OK, but he's got to go downstairs afterwards.'

'OK.'

'So which one do you want?'

'*El Perro y El Cordero.*'

'*Muy buen,* nice accent.'

'Gracias.' Felix giggled. 'Cat, Mum told me about your magic glasses.'

'Magic glasses?'

'The glasses that let you see in the dark. When you found that big dog.'

'The stolen dog?'

'What the woman with the flying carpet gave you to find the lost dog.'

'Oh! The night vision goggles the emergency helicopter pilot lent us.'

Felix looked at her. 'That's what I said. Can I have some? Can I have a go?'

Cat laughed. 'OK. How about you write me a story that I can translate for other children, and I'll take you on a trip with NVGs? Deal?'

'You bet!'

'High five.'

'High five.'

When Felix and his sister Peta were asleep, Cat came downstairs to find Stevie and Miranda watching a DVD: *White Oleander*.

Miranda was holding a glass of wine. Stevie held a cup of tea.

'I thought we might get some clues,' said Stevie. 'I've been telling Miranda what Anastasia's daughter told you about Nicholas Romero. About his Mafalda pick-up line.'

Cat glanced at Miranda and saw she was looking a bit deflated.

'I'm sorry. I guess I thought he was rather fun. How was I to know he was looking for a patsy detective?'

She took an unhappy gulp of wine.

'Cheer up,' said Cat, 'we don't yet know he intended his flowers to be clues. It might be a coincidence.'

'Huh!' Miranda said. 'Come on! Who sends a girl oleanders? Hardly roses are they?'

Cat smiled at her. 'I think it is time to go to a photography exhibition. Have we all been invited?'

'Yup,' said Miranda listlessly, 'it's next week. There's a Vernissage the evening before it opens.'

'Great. Chin up, Miranda,' said Stevie, 'he may not be the new flirt anymore, but there will be champagne.'

Cat wrinkled her nose. 'Don't encourage her!'

However, the next day Miranda called Cat while she was working on her French translation.

'Nicholas has invited us all to dinner tonight. Can you come?'

Guessing from her tone she would go anyway, Cat said yes.

When she rang Stevie, the girl said she was willing but only if Cat went too.

'I'm not going to chaperone Miri and that creep,' she said. 'You realise she is much more likely to burn in hell than your children.'

'You been talking to my mother?' asked Cat. 'I know she thinks the thouple haven't a hope of making purgatory, but Miri hasn't done anything wrong. Anyway, luckily for Phillip, we'll be there to protect her. Although, I think she may have gone off him now.'

'Maybe.'

Before they left for dinner, Stevie looked up the Romero house on Google.

'Why are you doing that?' asked Cat, waiting to give her a lift.

'Habit. I tend to look up people and places when I meet them. I thought we might find something interesting. Sometimes you do, sometimes you don't.'

'OK, so what have you found?'

'Well, the house is set in 1,000 acres and has its own chapel.'

'Its own chapel?'

'Yes, apparently it used to be a billiard room, but after the dissolution of the monasteries it was changed into a private chapel.'

'While still pretending to be nothing but a sports room? Clever,' said Cat. 'Amazing how often religion pops up in unexpected places. How old is this house?'

'The oldest part, including the chapel cum billiard room, is from 1340.'

'Wow,' said Cat, 'does Nicholas like history? Could he be very religious?'

'Guess so,' said Stevie, 'we don't know anything about him, apart from my gut instinct that he's a creep.'

Cat ignored that. 'What's the place called?'

'Bunyou Manor, it's a bit outside Buriton, which has easy access to Cowdray, in case anyone fancies a game of polo.'

'Ha. I can't imagine Nicholas is much of a fan of polo these days,' said Cat.

Chapter 43

When the girls arrived at Bunyou Manor it was clear Nicholas Romero had started drinking without them. He threw his arms around Miranda in welcome. Kissing her passionately on the lips. To their surprise the hall was decorated with bunches of oleander flowers.

'Welcome, welcome my Mafalda and friends. Welcome to my humble abode, much-loved travellers from afar. Come in and grace my tabernacle with your elegant feet.'

Stevie and Cat exchanged glances, but Miranda danced in, unabashed.

'What a lovely house. It has a really masculine feel. I love the alluring scent of sandalwood.'

'Yes, it was my father's. He held polo parties here. My stepmother gave it back to me.'

'How kind of her,' said Cat, examining an eloquently elongated statue of a polo horse in full flight, with its owner falling out of his stirrups. There was a crucifix draped around the horse's neck and a funeral urn under the table. *Why was it not in the chapel?*

'How – kind – of – her!' said Nicholas, his words cutting into her thoughts like little angry wasps.

She turned towards him. His face had gone black; in it his eyes appeared like flashing pinballs, his hands clenched.

'How kind of the thief to return the swag! How kind of the killer to leave the body! How kind of her indeed.'

All three girls were paralysed, staring at the exploding man, his body stiff in fury. They tensed instinctively, ready for the moment when they needed to defend themselves. Spontaneously, their bodies swayed together.

Nicholas threw out his left arm as though to hit some unseen object and Miranda came back to life. Tentatively she reached out and stroked the unmoving arm.

'Must be so difficult for you. Are there lots and lots of memories here?'

Nicholas breathed out; slowly his face lost its blackness and his charming smile returned.

'Yes, you are right. Whenever my father was in England, we came down here. It has some of my loveliest memories. *She* never came here! Preferred the flat in London. She would have ruined the place.'

He laughed, the sound incongruous from his taut body and slowly he unclenched his fists. Cat noticed how long and elegant his fingers were, how clean his nails. These were not a workman's hands.

'But first, champagne, then we will go into the film room. I have a fascinating show for you.'

'Do you think it's *White Oleander*?' whispered Stevie, 'if so, we can save him the time.'

Cat grinned, her body relaxing. 'Let's wait and see.'

'Just a second,' said Stevie. 'Nicholas, would you mind if I used your bathroom?'

Nicholas inclined his head, his charming smile once again creasing his countenance.

'No, of course not. I'll not make you use the boys' room. For girls, up the stairs, second on the right.'

They carried their champagne flutes into a slightly darkened room, following Nicholas with a magnum and more glasses on a tray. That it had not always been a film room was clear from the long windows and the fireplace at the end, but the long curtains were pulled and a screen was in place above the grate.

Stevie rejoined them a few moments later, took a glass from the tray and when they were all seated, Nicholas started the video. As they watched, his enlarged face came into view on the screen.

'This,' his voice said to the camera, 'is an example of my brilliant father's polo skills. We are at Hurlingham, outside Buenos Aires, and he is playing for the Triple Crown.'

Nicholas stopped the video and said to the girls. 'It's a promotion. He loved doing the Argentine season, but the English season was too dull. He needed a new rich English woman to employ him.'

Raising his eyebrows, giggling at his own naughtiness, he pushed the button and the video recommenced with a long view down a tree-filled drive to the polo field.

'Hurlingham,' said Nicholas's voice-over, 'was named after the British club in London and was set up in 1888 by Anglo-Argentines. It has five polo pitches and stabling for three hundred horses.'

The scene then moved to Daddy Romero, who was walking down the drive towards the polo ponies with a tall beautiful woman wearing a Min Agostini day dress and black cape, with stiletto boots and a Dior headscarf.

Nicholas stopped the video again.

'My father and stepmother, *An-ass-tay-zia*.'

In Nicholas's voice the name sounded like a curse.

The video continued and Cat watched the couple walking together towards the polo stalls. There was none of the loving playfulness of the newly married. Instead, their body language suggested one was an employee, and although Romero waved his arms around and walked with a swagger, sometimes punctuating his words with short repetitive hand movements, there was an underlying deference in the way he bent his head towards his wife. Anastasia's body, in contrast, appeared to be walking alone, unconnected to the play-acting on her left.

The couple approached the paddock. The camera swept over the ponies and the grooms frantically plaiting their manes and tails. Romero reached for a champagne bottle and handed his wife a glass. Nicholas's stepmother seemed to stiffen, her body bending away from the extended hand. As they watched she backed away, thrusting her hands behind her body, apparently refusing to touch the glass her husband held out to her.

She stumbled backwards and nearly fell, then turned to the camera. She said something to Nicholas in an inaudible voice, her face contorted with pain. Turning again she walked out of the screen and Cat found herself sagging with relief, empathising with the other woman's pain.

Nicholas stopped the video again.

'She's now going to the grandstand to watch the game,' he said, a repressed giggle in his voice. He pressed the start button again and the girls exchanged uncomfortable glances.

On screen, Romero filled the glass to the brim, toasted

his departing wife and said in a loud voice that seemed to fill the film room:

'To Carlos, may he rot in hell along with his shitty and totally adultery-ated champagne!'

And he downed the contents in one wild sweep, throwing the glass into a tree away from the paddock where it smashed with kaleidoscopic effect. He jumped, waving his arms flamboyantly, onto his pony and galloped out onto the pitch.

Nicholas stopped the video again.

'What you are about to see contains violent images,' he intoned like a newsreader. He started the video again.

The chukka began. Romero was riding wildly, his body dancing over his saddle. He thrust his horse towards the ball just as another horse filled the screen. For several seconds both men battled over the ball, their polo sticks clashing with a harsh sound. Then the defeated opponent's horse pulled away. However, instead of hitting the ball with his extended stick, Romero plunged after the disappearing horse. Falling to the ground with the thud of a heavy sack. His own horse reared up in surprise, the reins pulling the man back so his body rose in an arc, before smashing back onto the ground. His horse thundered away, but the man lay still while another horse rode over the prone body, his rider unable to prevent the inevitable.

The video swept over to the grandstand, where Anastasia could be seen jumping over the rails and running towards the man on the ground narrowly avoiding colliding with a couple of horses. In just a few seconds the polo ground became chaotic: riders jumping off their horses, horses grouping together and stampeding back and forth with a strange swaying momentum. Grooms appeared on screen, running after the loose horses. Spectators jumped the barriers and hastened towards the downed man.

Nicholas alone remained calm. He did not drop his phone but kept filming. Only when an ambulance pulled up did he stop.

After a break, the video continued with Romero being loaded into an ambulance by two paramedics. Anastasia jumped in beside him. The doors were closed and the ambulance thundered away.

The video was turned off and the girls sat in silence.

'So,' said Nicholas, pouring a large flagon of champagne cocktail for himself. 'So, you see the end of my glorious father and the enriching of my glorious stepmother. We must drink to Anastasia; may she live forever!'

He gulped down his champagne and threw the glass into the fireplace so hard it shattered, showering the hearth and some of the nearby carpet in pieces of crystal. All three girls stared silently at the broken pieces.

Miranda was the first to recover.

'Was that the Perez Sparkling wine?' she asked.

'No, that, like my father, is gone forever. This was Dom Pérignon.'

'Oh,' said Stevie. 'What a waste.'

He turned to her in drunken delight. 'What a waste indeed. He was an athlete, a sportsman, a gentleman, a wonderful dramatic and brilliant individual. His tales were amazing, his character sublime. Men like him are lauded and rightly so, his polo game was second to none and even his handicap did not really reflect his brilliance on a horse. Gone. All gone.'

He threw himself in a chair and began to sob.

Even Miranda was somewhat bemused by the fast

change of events and did not move. Nicholas jumped up again.

'But we shall avenge him, shall we not?'

He grabbed a stick from the log pile and drew a circle like a fencer.

'A *pointé*,' he yelled. 'You detectives. You know my stepmother is a murderer. You know she did him in, just as she killed all the others before him. You must stop her before she kills again.'

And he fell on his knees in front of Miranda.

'Miri, darling, I implore you. Save my father's soul.'

'Oh,' said Miranda, avoiding Cat's eyes. Even without looking she knew that Cat was on the verge of giggling.

'Oh! But we don't know that your stepmother did anything wrong. She looks very much appalled by his death, as much as you were. The way she ran across the field, she looked anxious.'

'Hah!' he said, throwing himself again on the armchair. '*Que actriz!* Who was the last person to touch his glass? Who was a chemist? Who would have known where to get poisons and how to administer them? Who but Anastasia?'

'Actually,' said Stevie, 'the groom was the last person to touch the glass. She passed it to your father. Your stepmother didn't touch it at all. And the police report says that, as far as they could tell from the fragments found where your father threw the glass, it contained nothing but sparkling wine and brandy.'

'Hah! The police! I ask you? What do the police know? Who are the police? Lackeys? In the pockets of big money! You think the Argentinean police are like your British bobbies, drinking tea and fighting for justice. No. This is Argentina. We make our own laws depending on who is in power at the time. Money is the law in Argentina.'

The girls said nothing. Although Stevie had lots of friends in the UK police, none of them had discussed the Argentinian police, so she could not tell if this was true or merely the drunken rambling of a man who had lost all his inheritance to his stepmother. Stevie looked wistfully at a computer slightly concealed under a blackout curtain.

Chapter 44

Stevie flew the Boeing 777 out of Heathrow en route to Buenos Aires. After two days in the capital, she would fly on to Santiago and, after a two-day layover, back via San Paulo and Rio. This was one of her favourite trips and this time she had arranged to meet up with Vanessa, who was on an international legal course, in BA.

The early morning sun was glistening on the waves far beneath them, as they approached the South American coast. The tall mountains ahead shone white and blue. Stevie sighed in pure delight. She was so blessed to have become an airline pilot: it was just the best job in the world.

Not surprisingly, since only 1.42% of all captains are female, the captain was a man, and one Stevie had not flown with before. She was the hands-on pilot this leg and as they crossed the coast her captain asked.

'What made you become a pilot, Stevie?'

Stevie sighed. 'I always wanted to, but I had to fight my parents. I think they thought I would be discriminated against. You know less than 5% of airline pilots are women.'

The captain smiled. 'Really? Sometimes it feels like 95%! Were you discriminated against?'

'Occasionally, but I've had loads of help from both men and women. Especially a friend's husband, who gave me a loan. Now she and I, and another girl have a detective agency.'

The captain raised his eyebrows. 'Fuck a duck. A detective agency? How do you combine that with flying?'

'Oh, I only do the internet research. I can do it from anywhere.'

The captain made a noise but was distracted by a call from ATC. When he turned back to Stevie he said, 'I'll bet there's a few on this flight could do with being investigated. Did you see that shifty looking man with the bald head and tattoos? I bet he's up to no good. That young bird with him looks like someone else's wife to me. Shall I broadcast that there's a detective on board and see if he runs for the toilets?'

Stevie smiled politely. She looked at the instruments and ran through the pre-landing checks, while the captain tried on the false ears he had bought for his youngest son.

While the captain detailed a few more weaknesses of crew members who needed investigation, Stevie wondered if he'd read the recent report that many airlines were desperate to recruit women pilots as statistics showed they were more reliable, concentrated better than men and had a much better safety record.

It really was a beautiful day up here at 40,000 feet.

Chapter 45

Stevie returned on Friday. Cat waited until she had been back a day before going over to visit her. She found her on the strip having just pushed the Tiger Moth into the hangar.

'Haven't you had enough flying? Come home and straight out in the Moth?'

Stevie chortled. 'Never, Cat. Anyway, the Tiger is my relaxation. But I've got some interesting news.'

'Great.'

The girls walked back together and through the French windows into the library, where Blinkey was dozing in her chair. They went through to the kitchen, and Cat started to make coffee.

Stevie took the milk out of the cat's basket and replaced it in the fridge.

'Did you know Vanessa had been to Argentina?'

'Who? Vanessa my daughter? When? Now?'

'No, last week. She went for a conference on international law.'

Cat snorted. 'Whoever tells their mother anything?'

Stevie smiled. 'Meow, Cat! I met her at her hotel. Ironically her firm had chosen Hotel London.'

'Really,' said Cat, imagining the girls having drinks and laughter together on a sun-baked terrace and trying to ignore that jealous knot in her stomach. 'Did you have fun?'

'Yes, lovely. But that's not why I'm telling you about it. I got some information.'

'About the case or about my daughter?'

Stevie frowned. 'About the case, of course.'

'Go on.'

Stevie grinned wickedly, noticing her friend's envious look. 'Well, we were having a drink in Hotel London, on the balcony, the sun was just setting and the whole sky was pink. I was stretching like a cat after a long day's flying when Vanessa's phone goes off. She answers and, making a face at me, goes out to find somewhere quieter.

'So, I was sitting, daydreaming and I hear a couple behind me talking. He's much older than his companion and the two are very loving, so I'm thinking, "Typical! older man with younger mistress". Obviously I've been spending too much time with cynical captains!

'Anyway, I listen to the conversation and it soon became clear that the man is a lawyer. Then I hear the name Romero. As you can imagine, I'm really listening then. Maybe it is a common name, but, as we know, it is also the name of Anastasia's third husband. Could I really be listening to someone talking about our case?'

'Do you understand Spanish?' asked Cat sceptically.

'They were talking in English. I believe a lot of Argentineans are bilingual.'

Stevie smiled sweetly. Cat bit her lip.

'So, I'm listening intently but they change the subject and talk away about this and that. So annoying. However, then I get a lucky break. Someone comes up to his table and asks him something and the lawyer reaches into his wallet and gets his card.

I thought, bother, I cannot see the card from here, or I'd get his name, but then I see he accidentally pulled out two cards and one has fallen under their table. Now I only have to wait until they leave to nip in and get his card, before someone else picks it up.'

Cat laughed. 'Don't tell me, you had to stay there all night!'

Stevie smiled. 'All in the course of the investigation. Anyway, Vanessa eventually comes back to the table. But, to do so she has to pass the lawyer's table. And what does she do? She stoops and says to the lawyer. "Oh excuse me, you seem to have dropped a card."

'I could have killed her.

'She sits down beside me and says, "What's up? You look like I just stabbed your Dad."

'I lean over whisper what happened and she roars with laughter. She jumps up.

"Come."

'I sit tight. You know how embarrassing she can be when she's got the wind of something. Back she goes to the lawyer's table and she says in Spanish:

"Señor Charleston, could I present my friend Stevie?"

'It seems that Señor Charleston had been giving a presentation at the conference.

'So, we join him and his daughter.

'At the conference they had been talking about wills. Pretty ironic! Vanessa had so little interest in helping us last time I asked her about it. Anyway, the short story is we spent all evening there chatting to Señor Charleston and his daughter and during the course of the evening it came out that Father Romero died intestate.

'Three of Anastasia's husbands could not be bothered to make a will. Isn't that extraordinary?'

'Not really,' said Cat, 'so many people put it off, thinking it doesn't matter because their family will get it anyway. People don't envisage the complexity ... Charlie and I did, but only when he got MND, before that we just assumed it would be OK. That everything would go to the other one ...'

'It seems,' said Stevie cutting through Cat, 'that Romero had an original will and probably didn't realise that when you marry that becomes null and void. Lots of people don't realise. Actually, I didn't know it either. And, after all, they had only been married a few months, how many people bother?'

'Anastasia did,' Cat pointed out. 'Two days after the wedding.'

'The exception that proves the rule. But the interesting thing is that in his previous will, the will which was made null and void by his marriage to Anastasia, he left everything to his son Nicholas.'

'Ah.'

'The same son who showed us that video. Coincidence, was it, that he happened to make a video that day, and not on any other?'

Cat wrinkled her brow. 'I don't understand. What do you mean? If Nicholas knew that his father hadn't made a will, wouldn't he have suggested he make one?'

'Possibly. I just wondered why he made a video that day. From what Mateo Perez told you, Romero had been doing that drinking and insulting Carlos thing for some time. Why make a video that day? The day he fell off his horse and died.'

Cat stared at her, while her coffee grew cold.

'Are you suggesting that Nicholas made the video that day because he knew his father was going to die that very day?'

'It's a possibility.'

'But that means he would have had to kill him himself, or be in league with Anastasia, which doesn't seem very likely. But why would he kill his father when he knew Anastasia would benefit from the lack of a will?'

'Does Nicholas strike you as someone who listens to other people?'

'No, not in the least.'

'Does he strike you as someone who might have made a will himself? Or is he the sort of guy who acts first and thinks second?'

'The latter.'

'Then I'm thinking he had no idea that his father's marriage to Anastasia made the will void. Rather that he thought it was necessary to get rid of his father before he made a will leaving everything to Anastasia.'

'Wow.'

'And then. Having discovered that she got the goods, he wanted to implicate her in the crime so she would get nothing and he would benefit after all.'

'But would the will then be valid?'

'No, but with Anastasia out of the way Romero only had one living relative: Nicholas.'

'Gosh!' said Cat. 'But do you think Nicholas has the brains to commit a murder? He seemed much more shouty and less thinky, to me.'

'True. Perhaps he had a more capable ally,' suggested Stevie.

'Maybe. Although that begs the question: who? And

then: the crime itself. How would he or they, if he had an ally, have done it?'

'Well,' said Stevie, 'Vanessa and I discussed this in some depth. She suggested that since Romero was a sportsman, and getting elderly, the chances are he had a variety of aches and pains. What do you do when you have aches and pains?'

'I don't know, acupuncture?'

'No, come on Cat, you take drugs – painkillers.'

'Oh I see,' said Cat.

Stevie continued. 'And then, drink alcohol on top of the painkillers and you get woozy.'

'Interesting,' said Cat, thoughtfully. 'But I don't see how you can implicate Nicholas in this?'

'I went up to his bathroom before the video.'

'Oh yes, I remember.'

'He has enough tramadol up there to sink a battleship.'

'Why?'

'Who knows? He also had a stash of Viagra, hundreds of paracetamol, ibuprofen and lots more I didn't recognise.'

'Really! Perhaps he's a hypochondriac,' said Cat.

'He is the one suggesting his father was poisoned. No one else even thought about it, everyone thought it was an accident.'

'Good point.'

'Of course,' said Stevie. 'That had been his father's house, so the drugs could be his or his fathers.'

'Another good point. Did his father have an autopsy?'

'No.'

'No? Why not?'

'Interesting isn't it,' said Stevie. 'I asked the lawyer about the law on autopsies in Argentina and it seems the law requires one in all sudden deaths. That would surely include this one?'

'And yet it was not done.'

'He told me that in some places in Argentina the family can request, for religious reasons, an autopsy is not performed.'

'Oh, what religion was Romero?' asked Cat. 'He's unlikely to be a Jehovah's Witness.'

'You'd think Catholic, given the chapel.'

'Indeed,' said Cat. 'Which reminds me. Did you notice there was a funeral urn in the house?'

'Was there? Where?'

'In the drawing room. Of course, it might have been empty. If there were ashes in it, it should have been in the chapel.'

'Interesting,' said Stevie thoughtfully. 'I'll see if I can find out what happened to Romero's body.'

Chapter 46

After Marvin's ambivalence about meeting Cat, the women were surprised to get a call from Billy about him.

'Hello beautiful,' he said, 'Billy here. Now, I've got young Marvin here and he's happy to meet you, but only if you come to my house and only as long as I'm there too. I'm happy to play along if you are. What you think?'

Cat agreed. Miranda suggested she should join.

'I'm better at chatting to people than you,' she said, annoying Cat. 'You're OK with mad Mensa wine professors in funny languages, but I'm just better at talking to normal people.'

To Cat's further irritation, Stevie agreed, although her comment: 'Yes, Miranda's much more their type,' annoyed Miranda too, so that both girls were furious and Stevie fled to the safety of the uncritical internet.

Miranda said she had an earlier appointment in Portsmouth, so she'd meet Cat at Billy's house and Cat could drive her home.

Cat arrived at Billy's house early, not thinking of

watching the house like a TV detective, but because she was always early for appointments. As she sat in the car waiting for the allotted time, the door opened and a young woman and two children around twelve years old came out. They were swiftly followed by Billy, his fist raised and behind him another man, who was attempting to hold his arm.

Cat couldn't hear what was said, but it was clear that there was a very angry interchange going on. Then the young woman stormed off down the street, dragging the children with her, stopping at a rather dilapidated Ford Cortina and driving away at speed. Cat noted down the registration, WAR 923 more by habit more than thought.

Cat thought she'd better leave it a few minutes before going into the house, hoping everything would have calmed down. There were clearly better days for her interview. She wondered whether to wait for Miranda, who was obviously going to be late, as usual.

As Cat approached the house, she heard loud music. She knocked on the door, which, to her amazement, was opened by Miranda wearing a very short skirt and extremely revealing top.

'Come in, 'fraid I got here before you, so the boys invited me in. Could be his ex-wife got the wrong idea too!'

Cat was horrified, but Miranda was enjoying herself.

'There was a bit of a hullabaloo,' she said, leading the way into the sitting room, her voice holding a giggle.

The boys were sitting on the settee drinking beers, there were quite a few empties in front of them and Cat noticed that Miranda had a beer in her hand.

'Hello beautiful,' yelled Billy over the music. 'Come and join us ... Miranda just made my day. Now the old bitch thinks I'm spending all her alimony on gorgeous sexy girls. It's a great day.'

And he swigged down a rush of beer and leered at Miranda, who giggled appreciatively.

'To my new friend Miranda, may she cause lots of trouble in the world!'

The other man in the room put out his left hand to Cat, keeping his right hand over his ear. 'Hello, I'm Marvin. Come and talk to me where we can hear each other.'

With relief Cat followed him into the kitchen, leaving Miranda to booze away with Billy.

In the kitchen Marvin made some tea. 'I'm sorry about Billy and his ex-wife. My split wasn't as angry, but she got the kids, which was bad.'

His eyes momentarily filled with tears, and he coughed. 'Sorry. It wasn't fair. Fathers do *not* get equal rights, but I know you don't want to hear that. You want to talk about Johnny Holmes.'

He breathed deeply.

'I gather you talked to my mum.'

'Yes.'

'Look, what I'm going to tell you must never get to her ears, OK.'

'Sure.'

'She worries about me. I'm still working and she thinks every day I take a risk or two. She doesn't understand. Things are bad for her too. She wanted grandparent's rights and she didn't get them either. It's not fair. She's had problems of her own in the past and my ex-wife brought them up in the hearing. The social were against her too. She's devastated. She loved those kids and she'd never do anything to hurt them.'

Cat nodded. 'I'm sorry.'

Marvin sighed.

'What do you want to know?'

'You found Johnny Holmes' body, right.'

'Yup. He was grave wax!'

'What?'

'Sorry, it's what we called it. The skin turns all kind of soft and soapy and greenish black. It was covered in blisters and part had been eaten away by crabs and things. Especially the eyes, they always go for the eyes. It's bloody cold in the North Sea. It keeps a body intact for a long time, the fish benefit and the crustaceans. Put me off seafood forever.'

'I can see it might. Which day did you find him?'

'Twenty-seventh November, that day is etched on my mind. I went up the next day, so if only it had been one day later, I'd have missed it.'

Cat drank her tea.

'So,' she said, 'in spite of that state, he was still holding the bottle when you found him.'

Marvin swirled his tea around his cup. Some of it spilt over the lip and he watched it drip down the side onto the kitchen counter. Cat resisted the urge to jump up and get a cloth and waited.

'No. I just said that for the report. I discussed it with Billy in case he was asked too, we were meant to be in the sub together, so we could coordinate our stories. In fact, they only wanted one report.'

'The sub?'

'Yes, sorry, I'm a saturation diver, we go so far down we have to use a mini sub. Lots of things went wrong with them back in the day, even after Wildrake.'

Cat was going to ask about Wildrake but thought she'd look on Google. *Might distract him.* In fact, he elucidated. 'Nasty accident that one, diver killed and did they learn?'

He paused.

'Did they?'

He shrugged. 'No, of course not. Anyway, what was I saying? Oh, yeah. Actually, it was on a long piece of tape.'

'The bottle?' Cat interjected.

'Yes. The tape was attached to the bottle and had got caught around him. I imagine the bottle must have been hanging from the tape; perhaps the tape got stuck as he pulled it up and he overbalanced and fell. Somehow it all got caught around him. It was dug into the perishing flesh when I found him.' He shuddered slightly. 'It isn't the first time I've found a body, but I really don't like it. We put the arms out, you know the machine has collecting arms, to bring him in like, and bits came off ... well you know ... as I said it was grave wax.'

'So, Anastasia attached the bottle to the tape and dangled it under the platform?'

'Is that what Clement said?'

'He said Johnny was clutching it, Billy suggested he might have toppled over reaching for it.'

'Oh, did he? OK. Well, I wasn't there on 12 November, I was down in the support boat, so I guess better to ask Billy.'

'The 12th? I thought Clement took Ana in on the 13th?'

'Oh, is that what he said? I thought Clement took Ana to Alpha on the 12th, then was working on Charlie on the 13th and they all went back onshore on the 14th but who knows? It was a long time ago. What does Clement say?'

Cat said nothing. When she met Clement, she hadn't known about this potential timeline issue but the way he smiled, looking straight at her as though underlining his point, made her pretty sure he was telling a lie. *Why?*

'Why was Billy on the platform, if you were in the support boat?'

Marvin grimaced. 'Cooking.'

'Cooking?'

'New chef on Alpha, he wanted to try him out. He's keen on food, is Billy. And booze, as you can see.'

Cat sucked her teeth. 'Your mother says you were at Anastasia's wedding. How did that come about?'

Marvin gave a twisted smile. 'Oh, that. I shouldn't have told her. I just wanted her to think I had some friends. She gets so worried. I was a gatecrasher really. Mark, he's one of the Drayton crowd, was chatting to me in the pub, said he was off to a wedding and did I want to come? So I went along. Frigging amazing! Must have cost an arm and a leg that one ... and then she goes and snaffles half the business as well. Makes you pretty much vomit doesn't it? What a cunt, 'scuse my French.'

'Just one more question, a little personal I'm afraid. Why did you agree to meet us this time but only with Billy?'

Marvin stared at her. 'That was Billy's idea. He suggested I came here.'

'Oh,' said Cat.

Once again, she got the feeling someone was lying. *Was it Marvin or Billy?* And why? What would Clement say about timing? Were they all trying to protect Anastasia in some way?

Chapter 47

Eventually, Cat poured Miranda into the car and they started the drive home.

Miranda was unusually quiet for a long time. Then she said.

'That guy you met in Lerwick. Was his name Clement?'

'Yeah.'

'Apparently he was an amazing pilot.' Her voice slurred around the Z.

'Oh,' said Cat abruptly, annoyed with Miranda for getting so pissed. 'Really, so what? Billy was his friend; he would say that.'

'Yes.'

They drove a bit further in silence. Miranda looked out the window.

She said, 'Apparently he flew in all sorts of terrible weather, known for it.'

'And?'

'Sometimes, even when he was going to one platform, he had to divert to another for bad weather. On more than one occasion he diverted to Alpha rather than Charlie, or Bravo rather than Delta. They used a Decca navigation system in those days, but it wasn't very reliable.'

Cat was listening now. 'Yes?'

'He would take risks that other pilots wouldn't,' said Miranda.

'Yes?'

'The night Johnny died was some of the worst weather ever. No helicopters could have got to the rig that night. Billy remembers it. He was on the rig. They didn't even come up from below. The weather was that bad.'

'Oh.'

'And yet one landed there.'

'Go on,' said Cat.

'It was the Bolkow. Billy heard it only because he was in the toilet, which was by the steps to the platform.'

'Was Clement the only Bolkow pilot?'

'No, but the other one was away in Unst that night, with his family.'

'Go on.'

'Apparently it landed. Didn't even shut down. Waited a bit until the weather cleared enough to go on, and then left. He doubted the pilot even got out; the weather was that awful.'

'Why did he tell you that?'

'I'm a good interviewer,' said Miranda. Then adding with a giggle. 'Or he was drunk and wanted to get it off his chest.'

'We don't actually know which night Johnny fell off the rig. No one missed him and they just assumed it was his last night on shift, 13 November but it could have been the night before. And now even the day Clement took Ana in is under dispute, Marvin says the 12th, Billy says the 13th.'

'Drunks usually tell the truth,' said Miranda, 'I'd put my money on Billy.'

'Maybe,' said Cat, 'you have more experience there than me.'

'Ooh, Catie!'

'After all,' said Cat, 'thinking from Johnny's point of view, he would want his booze ASAP. So if they landed on the 12th, he'd have looked for it on the 12th?'

'But, if Billy heard the helicopter landing on 13 November. It looks like Clement came in two days in a row.'

'Well,' said Cat. 'That's not surprising, since it was his job.'

'Except,' Miranda pointed out, 'the weather was so bad that night, that it seems crazy he was there. My only thought was perhaps he diverted from somewhere else. We need to look at the logs.'

'Logs?'

'Logbooks, pilots and planes have logbooks, you know that from Stevie. She's always scribbling away in her logbook.'

Cat told Miranda what Marvin had told her about the tape.

'Well, that makes sense. I was wondering how Anastasia had managed to secure the bottle under the platform. Putting it there nipperty-quick, at that, so no one saw her. Think of the vibration in an area where helicopters land and take off. How long would a bottle stay there without breaking or falling off into the sea? But a bottle on a tape, where you just sling it over the side, and run the tape back and secure it to something solid makes much more sense. She could even have pretended it was something to do with her photography.'

'Yes,' said Cat, 'but what we are looking at is still a mystery. Even if Ana, pretending to be Clement, leaves a bottle for Johnny, that doesn't make her a murderer. Even if

Clement lands on the platform on the night Johnny falls ... a night we haven't yet established as the same night, and then takes off again ... well that still doesn't mean he pushed Johnny off the platform.'

'No,' said Miranda, 'but things are not looking good for your Clement.'

'Maybe,' said Cat, 'but he gave me the divers' telephone numbers. Why would he do that if he thought they would incriminate him?'

'We are not all chess players!' said Miranda tartly.

'Meaning what?'

'We don't all look many steps ahead. Besides,' added Miranda, 'even if he pushed Johnny off, he's not the one marrying Angelo. If he did kill Johnny, he did it because Johnny was a wife beater, a liar and an abuser, and he wanted to protect Ana. Would our client, Gia, care about that?'

'Hum. That is not the point. If he did, it is still murder. And if he did it for Anastasia, she is still responsible.'

'Rubbish,' said Miranda, shutting her eyes and going to sleep.

'Stevie was right,' thought Cat, Miranda was better at getting information from people than her, and right now things were not looking good for Clement. Her instinct told her Clement was not a killer, but she knew that instinct was a poor substitute for facts.

Chapter 48

When they told Stevie the results of their interview with Billy and Marvin, Cat said, 'I think I'd better go and see Clement again.'

'Huh?' Miranda scoffed, 'and ask him if he killed Johnny perhaps?'

Cat wrinkled her nose.

'How's your hangover, Clever Dick! I was thinking of asking about his diversions to other platforms and to see if we can ascertain if he really did land on the platform the night Johnny may have died.'

Miranda started to say something but Stevie cut her off.

'Couple of things here. One, flying in bad weather ... pilots do it all the time, always have, but we need to check the weather records for that time, see if it is possible.

'The other is the logbooks. I'll see if I can get hold of them. Companies aren't always very happy to let you look at their logs and in those days it would all be on paper. Remember the company has been taken over. The new owners may not have bothered to digitalise older records, especially since the helicopters were not even in their company then. The best record would be Clement's own logbook. But, unless he's willing to show them, we'd need a warrant. So leave that for a moment.'

She shrugged and stared back at the screen, which gave her instant enlightenment.

'Why don't you go and see Sarah again, Cat. Cheaper than flying up to Shetland. She knew Clement pretty well when she lived up there. Well enough to introduce him to Ana. So, even though she was still very young she might have some input. While you are doing that, I'll get on to the company.'

'Good idea,' said Cat.

'Do you want me to come with?' asked Miranda annoyingly.

Stevie answered for Cat. 'No Miranda, I think you should talk to Peter Drayton. Not only is he the fourth husband's brother but he knows you. You might learn something from him. Also, I need you to look at the wedding photos. To see if you know anyone in them who might be of help. I've been asking you for ages!'

'OK,' said Miranda, sighing briefly, 'do you have any paracetamol?'

Cat laughed unkindly.

Chapter 49

Sarah said she would be very happy to meet Cat again and suggested she came back to her flat in Fulham. They arranged to meet at 5 p.m. on Wednesday, which suited Cat perfectly as she was meeting Caroline and Anthony, her social worker, at 3.10 p.m. the same day. Sarah said she would be at a team meeting immediately before, but if she was late Cat could wait in the park at the end of the road.

'I'll only be a few minutes late at worst,' she said. 'I'll send you a text if I get delayed.'

* * *

Anthony no longer worked as a social worker in Peckham. He had made several moves since he scared Cat that dark night in 1997. Wherever he moved, Caroline went too. Hammersmith suited her better than the others, as she now lived there with Rupert and Lagertha.

As usual he greeted Caroline with fist bumps.

'So, your mother wants to see me? Has she developed a drug problem?'

Caroline laughed. There was no aspect of her life that Anthony did not know. In all her troubles he had been her saviour and privately she called him her first love, but she knew that was not allowed and had never said a word to him.

'No, she has a detective agency, called SeeMs, and she has a question, she said a point of principle.'

'Interesting. Won't be the first crime I've been involved in.' He nodded, smiling. 'Ah, I hear her arriving. Sounds like she's early.'

'As ever! That was the effect of my father. We're all early or on time, never late.'

He smiled at her, the side of his eyes crinkling.

'It's not a bad thing, Caroline. Polite. Some of my clients are purposefully late to show how little they care for me.'

'Oh.'

'Not you though. Or, it *SeeMs*, your mother!' He grinned.

Cat walked in stiffly, her taut gait shouting out how far she was from her comfort zone.

'Hello, Anthony, long time.'

She stuck out her hand.

'Yes, and this time you know who I am!'

He took her hand and winked at her smiling. Cat relaxed and laughed. 'No one ever forgets your sins, do they?'

'MUM!'

She looked at her daughter and back to Anthony. 'I hope I've grown since that time,' she said. 'You can't imagine how much I've changed from that naïve girl.'

Anthony smiled gently. 'We can all make assumptions based on our past history. The problem is not so much making the assumption as not learning from it. Everything can be helped by talking.'

Cat pulled up a chair from the wall and sat down beside her daughter, opposite Anthony. As they both waited for her to speak, Cat felt a sense of unity between them. She wished Rupert had the same connection with his wife that Anthony had managed to achieve.

'OK, it's just a query I have – a query that keeps wandering through my head unanswered.'

'Let's hope I can answer it.' He smiled encouragingly. 'Do you mind if Caroline stays, or would you prefer she left.'

Caroline, who had been looking at the floor since her mother sat down, glanced up furiously, but Cat just shook her head.

'Oh, no problem. I'm intruding on her time.'

Her daughter smiled slightly tensely, slipping her hands under her thighs.

'It's about a diver, obviously I won't say his name, but he's not allowed to see his children, nor, as I've recently discovered, is his mother. Why would that be? Could it be child abuse? I find it hard to imagine this gentle man abusing anything.'

Anthony put his hands together as though praying, rubbed the end of his nose along the outside of his fingers.

'Don't be deceived by gentleness. All sorts of things could be involved. It might be a cover, although you might see through that, but it could also be a split personality. It is possible, he is only distantly aware of how he behaves on certain occasions when he is angry, unhappy, tired, has not taken his drugs if he is schizophrenic.'

'Drugs might be involved,' said Cat, thinking back to the discussions in Sheltand about saturation divers. 'But he has a full-time job.'

Anthony nodded. 'As to your first question, could be domestic violence against the mother, perpetrated by the father and supported or condoned in some way by the grandmother or cruelty of some description inflicted on the children; neglect of the children.'

Cat sighed. 'I wonder if being away half the time at work counts as neglect.'

Anthony rocked his head.

'Well, assuming the allegations were denied, a fact-finding, after an enquiry under Practice Direction 12J (PD12J), would almost certainly be held. If the facts were found, there would be a strong possibility that CAFCASS would not recommend direct contact.'

'Cafcass?'

'Children and Family Court Advisory Service. There is also the factor of the children's wishes to be taken into account.'

Cat looked at Caroline, who was nodding her head fiercely. Anthony continued,

'If the children don't want to see the father and his family, then that would be a strong case. The court might well rule out any direct contact, even supervised. Usually, they try and keep the door open for some indirect contact via letters or cards.'

Cat pursed her lips, thinking of the shy Marvin with his hand to his ear, keeping out the noise, spilling his tea. Could he really be a wife abuser?

'If it helps,' said Anthony, 'I can ask around, see if anyone knows about cases related to a diver. Is it important?'

'I think it might be.'

'I'll do my best.'

* * *

Even though Anthony had given her all the time she needed to ask her questions, Cat was still not late for Sarah.

She rang the bell on the outside door at exactly 5 p.m. Walking up the concrete stairway, Cat marvelled at the way council builders refused to spend their money on the public areas. Thank goodness they allowed the owners to make the interior comfortable and inviting. If she brought flowers, would Sarah be pleased?

When she reached the first floor, the door of the flat was already open and Theo, Clement's son, was waiting for her.

'Oh, Theo! How nice. I was expecting Sarah.'

'She'll be back very soon. She sent me a text, if I was around to let you in.'

'But that's great. I wanted to have a chat with you too, how brilliant.'

Theo smiled and led her to the kitchen. 'I'm having a coke, but I guess you'd rather have tea? Or coffee?'

'Tea please.'

He put the kettle on and leant against the counter.

'How are you? Have you found Ana yet? You were looking for her when we met in Lerwick.'

She laughed. 'Everything but. I've met her children.'

'Her children? I didn't know. How old are they?'

'Twenty-five and twenty-six.'

'Oh, same as me, twenty-five that is. Girls? Boys?'

'One of each.'

'Nice. You said the second husband was dead, last time. Is that their dad?'

'Yes, she's married twice since then.'

Theo made a face and turned to make the tea.

'I'm glad I know my parents. They have a brilliant marriage. So many others seem to find it impossible to live together that if I didn't know them, I'd think marriage sucked, but ...'

Cat felt stung. 'I'm a widow too. Sometimes people just die.'

Theo coloured up. 'Sorry, no ... I mean, I didn't know. It's just ... she's young ... I thought ... so many ... you know one thinks ... well, about divorce first. Lots of my friend's parents ... you know.'

He blushed so deeply his neck went red.

'Sorry.'

Cat was embarrassed that she hadn't appreciated how sensitive he was. 'No I'm sorry, I was probably a bit sharp.'

They were interrupted by the click of the door opening and Sarah came in.

'Oh, hi Cat, Theo, sorry I'm late. Everyone got tea?'

Theo made Sarah tea too. They took their drinks into the living room and sat on the sofas facing each other, Theo and Sarah on one, Cat on the other.

'What was it you wanted to know?'

'Well, it's about Clement, really,' said Cat, thinking once again she was asking a child if his parent was a murderer. How terrible it was to be a detective.

They both looked at her, even Sarah was silent.

'Everyone says what a great pilot Clement is,' she began. 'I've been talking to Billy Holecroft.' She stopped and looked at Sarah, 'Do you know him?'

'I think I know who you mean. One of the divers, friend of Clement's. If I'm right, he quite fancied Ana. He used to try and chat her up but she had quite enough with Johnny, she hardly spoke to him.'

'Sounds right. He said some things about Clement's flying, about how good he was but how even he sometimes had to divert and occasionally had to land on the wrong rig, because of the weather. Do you know anyone else who might be able to corroborate that?'

She paused. Sarah and Theo glanced at each other.

'Dad has stories,' Theo said eventually, 'pilots do, you know. They like to talk about near misses; flying in weather so low they could see the signposts. Much of it is just talk.'

Cat nodded.

'In those days there was no radar, just a radio operator on the platform, and he wasn't always there. The pilots were pretty much left to their own devices. They made their own navigation systems to help them find the rigs in murky weather ... they had Decca, but Dad said it stinks! Dad was known to be good at nav. He had a combination of memory and sense of direction. He has some hair-raising stories. You've heard them, Sarah.'

Sarah laughed. 'Of course. We all know how pilots like to talk ... *there I was, nothing on the clock but the maker's name ...*'

Theo laughed too. 'Oh yeah! Dad has one story ...'

Suddenly both of them were telling tall tales as heard from Clement.

Cat was lost in this aviation paraphernalia but clearly, she was on the right track. Bet Miranda couldn't get information like this!

'He has one about the time he took you in, in that crap weather ...' started Theo, and then seeing Cat's face stopped. 'Err ...'

'Go on,' said Cat, 'did you go onto the rig too, like Ana?'

There was a long silence. Then Sarah said, 'Look Cat this is absolutely illegal. You must never mention it, OK.'

Cat was taken aback. She felt like pointing out she was a detective, before suddenly realising they didn't know that.

'Yes, of course,' she said, crossing her fingers. Probably

whatever Sarah was going to say would be the least of Clement's worries.

'With Ana,' said Sarah. 'We shared a seat. The back of the Bolkow was down for freight, normally it has back seats, if there weren't too many oilies going in they could use it, but this one had been used to bring in machine parts ... but we were both small and skinny so we shared the front seat.'

Theo laughed. 'And when you think of how many rules you were already breaking!'

They both giggled.

'Can you remember which day it was you went on to the rig?' asked Cat. 'Or did you go often?'

'Only the once. But yeah of course I remember. I have a diary for every important issue in my life. I'll get it.'

As she went off to get her diary, Cat asked Theo how long he was staying in London.

'I'll probably be here about a week. I'm looking for more photos and pictures for the gallery. I love having Shetland stuff, but sometimes it's nice to have foreign work too. I usually do most of the research on the internet and then come down and chat to the people. They nearly always have more art than is on the web ... means I get new stuff, and they get shown in a new gallery, with a new audience. Win win!'

Sarah came back with her diary. 'We went in on 13 November 1987. The weather was dreadful. We were supposed to go straight to the Charlie platform, drop off whatever he had on board and come home, but we had to divert to Alpha. Ana was terrified. Actually, we all were. That was Johnny's platform and if he'd seen her in the helicopter with Clement, he'd have gone ballistic ... especially if he'd already drunk the whisky!'

'Did you see him?'

'No, the weather was that bad, all the oilies stayed downstairs. I doubt if any of them knew we were there. We landed, kept the engine running and then took off again as soon as there was a short break in the cloud. Clement was an islander; he knew the weather out there like he knew the wrinkles on his hands.'

'Did anyone get out of the helicopter?'

'Are you kidding? The rain was like sheets. It was pouring. Ana and I weren't scared of the weather because we trusted Clement and I guess we were young. But now ... I'd have been terrified. Then, I didn't really understand the risks ... we really thought the worst thing that could happen was that Johnny found us there! And with Clement! He'd have killed us.'

'So, no one got out?'

Sarah thrust her head forward. 'No!'

Cat said nothing.

'Two weeks later,' said Sarah, 'Johnny's body was found and we realised he may well have been already dead. It is quite creepy if you think about it. The chances are he died that night, since Ana had only put the bottle there the night before. Or, I suppose, he could have got it immediately, in which case his body would have been floating underneath us. Scary 'eh. If it had been that night, he might have gone out to get it and found us there. We were lucky in more ways than one.'

*　*　*

When Sarah let her out of the flat Cat asked. 'Does Theo often come and stay with you?'

'Yeah, whenever he's in London. It's half his dad's flat.

You didn't think I could afford a flat in Fulham on a nurse's salary did you?'

Cat hadn't actually thought about it, but obviously Sarah was right. This was an expensive area of London.

'That's nice.'

'It's brilliant. It was Clement's idea. I had trouble sharing because of the hours I keep and London's so dear. It's OK ma da saying, "Many a mickle maks a muckle," but he doesn'a live here. Then Clement said he'd like a crash pad in London, if I was willing. Was I? I told you, he is the kindest person in the world and Theo too. They are ace.'

As Cat walked back to Fulham Broadway she thought about everything she had heard. Clement could not have killed Johnny, it seemed, unless … unless Johnny came to pick up the bottle early the night before, while Ana and Clement were still there. If that happened, if he saw Clement with Ana, he might have freaked, there might have been a fight, and Johnny went over. No. Then he wouldn't have been holding the bottle. Unless he was already entangled in the tape.

Alternatively, if Clement had landed there a second time that day and Johnny was getting the bottle as he landed. And, actually, why wouldn't you pick up the bottle as soon as you could?

Sarah could be lying. She had every reason to protect Clement and none at all to tell the truth about something that happened so long ago. Or she could have jumped out and pushed him herself. Even though he was, presumably, a big man, if he was off balance even a fourteen-year-old girl might have knocked him over the edge.

Or did he just fall?

Either way Marvin was lying about the date and Billy was telling the truth. Why would Marvin lie?

Chapter 50

Miranda arrived at Stevie's house after dropping the children at school.

'Sorry I'm late, Felix's form teacher wanted a quick word about his lack of attention in class. She says he's interested in so many things he cannot concentrate on what is happening at school. The old bag seemed to think it was my fault.'

'Why?'

'Apparently, he keeps telling everyone I'm a detective and if their parents misbehave, I'll find out. He's scaring the other kids.'

Stevie laughed. 'Sorry! Am I supposed to take that serious? She must be joking.'

Miranda screwed up her face dramatically. 'No, but she ought to look out herself – smacks of a guilty conscience to me.'

'Maybe. Perhaps she is the dognapper. Have you asked her if she's got a new dog?'

'Ha, ha.'

'Come and look at the Instagram photos of the Drayton-

Rodriguez wedding. I don't recognise many people, but I expect you will.'

She led Miranda over to the computer, refusing to allow her to get diverted.

'You sit down and get looking and I'll make you some coffee.'

'Thanks.'

Miranda was soon happily ensconced in picking out friends.

'Hey look at this Stevie,' she called. 'Who knew that seedy old Doctor Morris was a friend of Tom Drayton's? I wonder if he was his GP. That would be reason enough to die. Just joking around, Stevie don't look at me like that. And blimey, Colin Hedgerow, he gets in everywhere, I bet he crashed. Old soak, no one who knew he could down the whole drinks selection in one night would invite him!'

She scrolled through some more photos.

'Hey Stevie, look! Nicholas Romero was at the Drayton wedding.'

'Why not?' Stevie shouted over the noise of the kettle boiling. 'He was her stepson, and they obviously still communicate as he will be at the Vernissage.'

'Good point,' said Miranda, and continued scrolling.

Then she stopped. She looked up puzzled.

'Hang on Stevie, can you enlarge this?'

Stevie came back from the kitchen and lent over Miranda, fiddling with the keyboard.

'A bit, I might lose resolution. Why?'

Miranda pointed to the screen.

'You see that man talking to Peter Drayton.'

'Who? Which one is Peter Drayton?' Stevie asked, moving the cursor and enlarging the picture. 'The stout one ... oh yeah, I see, you mean the guy with a beard.'

'Yes,' said Miranda, her voice slightly tense. 'That man looks like Billy Holecroft ... the diver guy we met yesterday. OK, he doesn't have a beard now, but you know I never forget a face.'

Stevie nodded. She smiled to herself. Poor Cat was feeling a bit sore about Miranda's innate talent, and yet they were the greatest friends and were a good team.

'That's a bit odd, isn't it?' said Stevie. 'I think I remember Cat saying that the guy Billy, asked her what Anastasia was doing now? And yet he'd been to the wedding. That isn't the sort of thing you forget, is it? Especially after what Mark said about the magnificence of the whole thing.'

'No,' said Miranda thoughtfully, 'which in turn makes you wonder if he was telling me the truth about Clement. Maybe he has some agenda?'

'Now you really do need to go and see Peter Drayton. He will know who was at the wedding. And why.'

'Spot on,' said Miranda, 'I'll call him now. I'd quite like to see the old devil anyway. He used to be a pal of my dad's. It's actually one reason why Phillip and I chose this area when we moved out of London. I always loved Sussex. It just has something.'

Stevie nodded. As long as she could fly away, she didn't care where she was based.

CHAPTER 51
OWLY VALE 2016

My darling children,
It is true the English say third time lucky, but I am sure it will be fourth time lucky.

The kindest man came to help me with my new house. Not all the villagers have been so kind to me: one asked if I was a flamenco dancer and another suggested I might like a job working for him: as his maid!

I told him I have a first-class degree in chemistry and he laughed. *Coño!*

Tom (the kind man) says this is just British humour, but in reality it is just rude, rude, rude.

No one could ever replace your father, who was a unique and perfect man, but life must move on. I have got engaged to that lovely kind man, Tom, he is a builder who lives near here in Sussex.

Tom is a modest man and he prefers we do not have an engagement party and even have a small wedding. *Quizas!*

Besos, your adoring mother.

CHAPTER 52
OWLY VALE 2018

Peter Drayton was very happy to meet Miranda after work. Now in his mid-seventies he refused to slow down and always worked as hard as his employees.

'Hey youngster! Yes, love to get together. Can you come to the Cock and Pheasant at 6.30 ternight? We can have a jaw.'

Miranda agreed, although she'd much rather have met in the Owly Vale pub. Going to the Cock and Pheasant meant she'd have to ask someone to pick her up afterwards. She knew herself and alcohol. Miranda would not drink and drive, but that never meant she would not drink.

'I'll bike over, Stevie. Can you pick me up afterwards?'

'I would, but I'm back on shift tonight.'

'Damn, Phillip will have to babysit and I can't get the kids out at night. Do you think Frank would do it?'

Stevie laughed. 'Come on Miranda, you know you'll have to ask Cat.'

'Bother. She thinks I shouldn't drink so much. She'll be all nannying.'

Stevie laughed again. 'There'ye go! There's an answer to everything!'

'Maybe I could bicycle home. Might rain. I wonder if I could buy an ebike by the evening.'

'Just ask Cat!'

'All right. All right.'

* * *

The Cock and Pheasant was an old-world pub with a roaring fire and small rooms. It was originally built in 1670 by the Drayton family, hence Peter's long support of the place.

'Honestly! I can't believe you know what your family were doing in 1670,' said Miranda, as he placed a glass of white wine in front of her. 'I have a hard time knowing what my father did.'

Pete grimaced. 'Yeah! Lovely man, died too young. Such a shame.'

Miranda wished she hadn't mentioned him. She could cry even without a drink thinking about her father. She usually focused on the fact her mother did such a good job bringing up Miranda and her younger sisters. She'd been such a great role model, and so supportive when Miranda fell pregnant with Jane, and Phillip wanted her to have an abortion. She took a big breath.

Pete, watching her, put his hand on her arm. He smiled at her.

'So, Miri love, what made you suddenly want to visit the Draytons' oldest pub? You know I'd love a jaw anytime but I hardly see you these days with all your youngsters, and your crazy lost-dog hobby.'

'Pah!' said Miranda pushing down her devils. 'Finding

people's stolen dogs is a very important job. You may scoff but we've helped many families.'

'So, who's lost a dog this time?'

'No one, I actually wanted to ask you about something else. Do you know someone called Billy Holecroft?'

Pete looked deeply into his beer. 'The diver?' He nodded and drank a gulp. 'I met him and that other diver at Tom's wedding.'

'Other diver?'

'Yes, Billy had a friend with a funny name ... Marley or Marney.'

'Marvin?'

'That's the fellow. We was laughing because Tom wanted a small wedding. He was worried it would be too many if he invited a few of the guys. Then, she invited half the f'ing countryside and some of his guys brought friends, like your Marvin fellow, and Tom hardly knew a soul at his own wedding. Fucking Nora!

'But you were asking about Billy. Sorry, love. OK sort of guy. Very keen on fishing, said he went up to Scotland a lot for it. That's unusual for a diver, they're away so much they usually want to spend time back home.'

'Yes, no. But he's divorced isn't he?'

'Yeah. So, no missus to stop him. But he's got kids. I know that for sure, as he told me he put his car in his kids' names, so his wife would have to walk when he had the them! No free transport for her. Funny way of avoiding alimony 'eh?'

He drank some beer.

'What else do you want to know?'

'So, is that why he was at the wedding? He was a friend of Tom's, not Anastasia?'

Pete spluttered and his calm face contorted. 'Wash your

mouth out! Don't mention that bitch here. My business ... Our business, what we worked all our lives for, what our ancestors ...'

He stopped. Took a deep breath. Drank a draught of beer and continued more mildly.

'Tom's. We were three boys, growing up, with my father wanting us all in the business. Ralph and I were a hundred percent. In there all the way. I asked to leave school early to help my dad and ditto Ralph but not Tom. He wanted to do something more with his life. He decided he wanted to be a diver. So off he went, training and the like, and then he went to work on the North Sea. It was the time, then, the 70s, when everything was happening up there, that's where all the money was, and the life! The life they led then. You wouldn't believe it. One time, he hired a helicopter to fly him home to West Sussex, from Aberdeen! And back. The money they were making. Crazy times!'

He stared down at his beer.

'That's where he met Billy. They became friends. But although Billy liked the travelling life, Tom didn't really. It cost him his first marriage and he blamed himself. So, he came back and joined us in the family firm. He was a good builder.'

'And he stayed friendly with Billy?'

'Vaguely, over the years. Then suddenly about two year ago, coincidentally the same time he met *her*, he re-met Billy, and they started doing things together. Billy only lives at Portsmouth, so they used to go out for a jar when he was home.'

'Did you know Billy had known Anastasia before?' Miranda asked. 'When she was married to her first husband.'

Pete shook his head. 'I didn't but he wouldn't have got far

there anyway. Billy was a real man, down to earth, like. Mrs Bitch was a right lah-di-dah pussy, too good for anyone or anything. But apparently not too good to take my brother's money when she killed him!'

'Killed him? You think ...'

Pete snorted. 'Nah! She wouldn't get her hands dirty. Mrs Arty Farty. But look at that ... she was forty-seven. My brother was seventy-three. A love match 'eh?'

He snorted again.

'And then, he was all worried before the wedding. Could he satisfy her?'

He looked at Miranda.

'I don't want to be crude but he was an old man ... of course he'd had girlfriends but this was different. Have you met Mrs Arty Pants?'

'No.'

'Yeah, well, some people would say she's sexy. I think she's a witch, and cold as ice.'

He picked up his beer and found it empty.

'Same again?'

'I'll do it.'

Miranda jumped up and went to the bar, returning with peanuts and snacks, as well as his beer and her wine.

'If you didn't think Anastasia killed your brother, why did you hire a detective?'

Pete made a face. 'Who told you that? Blimey. If you want to keep a secret, don't tell a builder, full of fucking leaks!' He roared with laughter. 'We hired an ex-copper, Eric Connolly. He was good. Proper man. Found that the first husband took out a huge life insurance payment on both of them when he married.'

'Both of them?'

He shrugged. 'Yeah. Who knows? Perhaps he planned to

do her in. If so, she got there first, eh.' He laughed, but not as though he was amused.

'The second husband was a right lad before he married, but settled down when he met Miss Arty Pants. Yeah right. That's what our copper said. Once a lad, always a lad, that's what I say.'

Pete took another swig of beer and looked at Miranda thoughtfully.

'He found out some rum things about the second husband. He was good, our copper.'

'What sort of things?'

'Well, that he had a heart condition for one. He took pills.'

'How? Don't doctors tell some sort of oath not to talk about their patients?'

'I have no idea. Our copper had sources in Spain. He wasn't just your average Fred Bloggs. He spoke Spanish. But that guy, the second husband, wasn't quite the straight man his children painted him in the wedding ceremony.'

He shook his head as a memory of the day returned.

'Honestly! The son talking about his oneophilia, as though that was a day-to-day word in West Sussex building circles.'

He stuck his finger under his nose.

'Can I visit your copper?' asked Miranda.

'Yes, that's the best. I'll text you his address when I get home.'

Miranda moued, silently musing.

Pete continued. 'When the second husband died, Mrs Arty Farty gave all the money back to the children, kept herself a small flat in London and an annuity. When the playboy died, she gave his son back his Sussex and Argentinean houses, flat in London to her daughter and the rest of the money to a charity for retired polo ponies. Odd, 'eh? She takes from the rich and gives to the just as rich. And you know what the bitch did to me. Wonder where my money went? To a charity for retired house builders, perhaps?'

He drank deeply from his pint.

'But killer? No, hasn't the stomach.'

'But,' said Miranda, 'She could've. She was a chemist.'

Pete shut his eyes.

'You don't know how much I'd like to think she killed Tom,' he said, opening his eyes again. 'Then I could bang her up for eternity! But, you know, I've been around, met people and I know a character or two who might kill, but bitch though she was, she was not a killer.'

He drank his beer and wiped his mouth with the back of his hand.

'Too much Viagra killed the idiot. You know what they say: there's no fool like an old fool. And the stupid twit didn't even think to make a will. You know?'

His sigh was so guttural Miranda felt his pain nestling down in her heart and joining all the other pains there. Perhaps they'd like a drink, she thought taking a gulp of her wine, trying to make herself smile.

'Did Tom have children, with his first wife?'

'No. They weren't married long. He gave her a good payoff too, and she remarried someone ... who knows, long gone ... as is the Bitch. She took half the fucking (sorry) company and left ... probably looking for some other victim now. Shall we have some supper? I'm starving!'

Over steak and chips for two and another bottle of wine, Pete told her more about his brother.

'You know, Miri, Tom was a good man. Helpful. He believed in doing things for people. That Billy you were talking about, he asked him to help on a bit of land he had, not much but he ran crops on it. Bought it to avoid alimony, I'm told!'

He grinned widely.

'Tom went over a day or so before he died to help him put down fertiliser. That's the kind of guy he was, go out of his way to help a friend.'

Miri sighed and drank deeply.

'Like my dad.'

Pete grimaced and made as if to put his hand on her shoulder. 'He was different, Miri, he wore the world's problems. He couldn't but feel ...'

'Yeah, I know,' she said and drank again. 'Tell me more about Tom ...'

'Well, this bit will make you laugh. After they'd been moving all that fertiliser the guys were thirsty, so they went into the barn for a beer. Billy had brought some in a cool bag. Great so far 'eh?'

He took a swig.

'But he forgot to put the beer in the cool bag! Great 'eh? So it was warm. Well, Tom, he don't mind, but Billy is so shocked. It's going foreign parts so much, see, they like beer really chilled. Anyway, he insists on putting ice in the beer ... what shit (sorry) 'eh ... ice in beer! Tom said it tasted shite, but he drank it anyway to be polite.'

Pete shook his head. 'He was that kinda guy, drink shite to be polite. And now he's gone. Really shit (sorry).'

As Miranda ate crème brûlée and Pete his apple crumble and custard, he asked, 'Why do they call your tall friend Miranda's Cat? Not very flattering.'

Miranda sighed.

'Guy's humour, I guess! I don't know how well you know Cat, but she married at nineteen to a chap of thirty-four.'

'Ha! Another Viagra candidate! Sorry, Miri, go on.'

'Yes, well, anyway, he got MND.'

'MND, whatsat?'

'Motor Neuron Disease, horrible wasting disease kills the body while leaving the mind healthy and able to watch your own deterioration. And it lasts a long time, he was ill for three years and every day he was a little bit weaker. She looked after him until he died, and you can imagine the effect on her, seeing the man she loved dying by increments.'

Miranda drank another gulp of wine.

'I think it wore her down, so that when he died, she thought she hadn't done enough. She felt she'd let him down, that the children did more than she did, that she let them down ... you know how it is Pete, sort of survivor's guilt.'

She stopped and thought about her own mother, before shaking herself. Took another gulp of wine.

'So, her mind must have been a bit crazy and she decided she had to die in recompense ... obviously she wasn't thinking straight. She couldn't see any way to do it without hurting her children ... you know, if they find you hanging or whatever they're warped for life. So, she decided to starve herself to death.'

'Shit! Sorry love.'

'Yes. I was really a friend of her daughter, Caroline, but after Charlie died, I used to pop over every few days, just to make sure she was OK. But then, I hadn't been around for a while, and I thought, funny I haven't seen Cat in the garden ... she loves gardening ... and there was no movement in her house for four days. You know how it is?'

She picked up her glass, realised it was empty and grabbing the bottle refilled her glass.

'You wonder, you doubt yourself and then, given my

father's history I was suddenly really worried. I went over, banged on the door ... I was yelling, threatening to break in.'

'Hum. She's got double glazing, don't break easily.'

'Ha! Finally, I remembered, they used to leave a key under a flower pot at the back.'

Pete shook his head.

'She was upstairs and in such a state. I'd never seen her like that. She just stared at me, like she had no idea who I was. Eyes wild. Bulging. The house smelt. The fridge was full of uneaten food, as though she'd bought for the family and couldn't face it. It was awful.

'Anyway. I got her dressed, made her drink a coffee. We were sitting there talking and I looked in my bag and found the Trial Helicopter Lesson Phillip's mother had given me for Christmas. Silly old bag, she knows I hate flying. She does it on purpose.

'Anyway, I gave it to Cat and it worked the trick and more. She went flying, loved it and suddenly it was all short skirts and travelling all over the shop. She was cured!'

'What!' Pete spluttered over his beer. 'Honestly, Miri, you girls do make me laugh. Miranda's Cat, 'eh! Should be Miranda's Flying Cat! Hey! I'm down, Miranda, think your mum-in-law will give me a helicopter lesson?'

He roared with laughter.

Miranda poured some more wine into her glass, realised the bottle was finished and ordered another.

'Well, I don't know how the guys know all about it. Still, you know what villages are like, we seem to know everything about each other.'

Pete shook his head. Most likely Miranda told people. Sometimes he wondered if she knew how much she talked.

When Cat arrived at 9 p.m. Miranda and Pete had

moved onto a bottle of Beaujolais-Villages, which they were finishing with some cheese.

As they parted Pete gave Miranda a shoulder hug. 'Your dad would be so proud of you, kid.'

He turned away and Miranda got into Cat's car, unable to speak.

'How did it go?' Cat asked, as she backed out the car park.

'Nice,' Miranda said after a while. 'He's a lovely man. He misses his brother. I never knew Tom but my father always spoke highly of Pete.'

Miri felt Cat mouing in the dark.

'Yeah, it's a shame we can't bring back the dead ... your father too.'

Miranda's eyes suddenly filled with tears.

'Sorry, but you know ... I miss him still.' She stared out of the window.

'Are you OK, Miri? Do you want me to stop the car?'

'No, no I'm fine. It's just sometimes .... but you know about that too. What's that phrase, on pain of death! So right. The pain of death. Poor Charlie. Poor Dad.'

Cat reached across to squeeze Miranda's knee. 'I'm sorry I was cross with you, Miri darling. You know it's only because I worry about your drinking.'

'I know.'

'It is impossible to say just what I mean ... as if a magic lantern threw the nerves in patterns on a screen.'

'Tennyson?'

'Elliot.'

'Should have realised, your favourite. Remember I left school early ...'

'So did Anastasia, but she went back later.' Cat said. 'Thinking about Anastasia, it's odd she didn't get pregnant in her first marriage. We are both examples of youthful fertility.'

Miranda gasped. 'But perhaps she did? Perhaps she lost it when Johnny attacked her. Maybe that's why she wanted to raise money for infertility, she'd had experience of the loss.'

'Oh my God! You could be right. Perhaps that was what Sarah was going to say but didn't. You are probably right. If so, she would really have hated him. And her daughter said she was a very passionate woman.

'A very angry, passionate woman.'

Chapter 53

Cat was sitting in the garden, attempting to translate one of the children's books into Dutch when Caroline rang. Her mother was relieved. Today, Dutch didn't want to appear in her head, only French.

Caroline said that Anthony had heard of a case that might shine a light on the questions her mother was asking about why Marvin, had lost custody of his children. It seems that both parents worked and the grandmother looked after the children. One night the eldest child, eight years' old, couldn't sleep, so her grandmother gave her a hot toddy.

A couple of nights later, when her mother was looking after her, she again could not sleep. So, she asked her mother for a hot toddy like grandmother's.

When the mother found out that her daughter had, as she put it: 'been guzzling alcohol with her grandmother,' she banned her mother-in-law from seeing the children. When her husband came home from work, he sided with his mother. Divorce proceedings started shortly afterwards and the father and his mother were not allowed to see the children without supervision.

Two years later, the mother remarried and moved to Australia. Neither the father nor the grandmother had seen the children since.

'Wow,' said Cat, 'a bit harsh.'

'Alcohol is a drug, Cat,' said Stevie when told the story. 'Some people feel strongly about it.'

'A hot toddy! How much alcohol is in that?'

'But why the interest in Marvin? Did you think he might have killed one of the husbands? He didn't get much opportunity.'

'We don't know that, do we?' said Cat. 'We only know where Marvin was on the day he found the body. He could have been anywhere on 12 November or 13 November. He told us the shift ended the day after he found the body, on 28 November, so we assumed that he had been underwater for weeks before.'

Stevie nodded. 'True. But, your Mr Outrage said that saturation divers do up to fifty-two days underwater, which would mean he could have gone underwater on 7 October. If so, he was underwater when Johnny fell off the rig.'

Cat prowled around the room.

'I couldn't see Clement as a murderer, so I was looking around for alternatives when it struck me Marvin might have hated Holmes for some reason. Perhaps Holmes stole his wife. We know he was a lady-killer in the 70s. Then it occurred to me that although he told us when his shift finished, he didn't tell us when it started.'

'OK,' said Stevie, turning away from the computer to listen.

'I rang Mr Outrage in Shetland ... you remember he got that huge file up for Johnny's death?'

Stevie nodded.

'Well, it seems Marvin was on an emergency shift for some problem that occurred in the pipes and this shift was very short. He was actually went onto the support boat on 13 November and went under the sea on 14 November. So, on the 13th he was available to push Johnny off the rig.'

'But only,' said Stevie, 'if the support boat was close to the rig. However, it does change things, since if Johnny fell off the rig on 12 November he was still onshore, and so unavailable for pushing. And he was the one suggesting that Johnny probably fell off the rig on the12th, not the13th. We'll add him to the list of possible suspects for Johnny Holmes' death.

'So, at the moment we have: Clement: motive and opportunity. Anastasia: motive and opportunity. Billy: opportunity but no known motive. Marvin: opportunity and possible motive if wife stolen.'

'And,' said Cat, 'Marvin was also at the Anastasia Tom Drayton wedding. Odd? Or not? He said he was just taken along, but we only have his word for it. He could have asked Mark, who was probably drunk already, to take him.'

Stevie nodded. 'Hum. Could be. Incidentally, do you want to include Sarah on the list?'

Cat stared at her daughter's email on her phone without seeing it.

'Yes, no ... no, I don't think so. She did have motive and collectively they had opportunity but she was only fourteen, and although she might be an accessory, I can't believe she was strong enough to push a fully grown man into the sea.'

'OK, we'll leave her out for now and I'll try and find out whether the support boat went to the rig on 13 November 1987.'

Stevie rolled her eyes like Miranda.

Chapter 54

Cat arrived at Anastasia's exhibition late for almost the first time in her life, and only because she had picked up Frank at Heathrow and his plane was delayed.

'Just as well Angelo left Italy yesterday,' said Frank, 'or he'd have missed his own party.'

'Oh yes,' said Cat. With all her waking thoughts focused on Anastasia, she had forgotten the Snail Man was also exhibiting at the show.

She dropped Frank at the exhibition and went to find a parking space in Berkeley Square or close by. As usual there were none. Eventually, she slipped into a space that two BMWs were waiting for and legged it before they could shout obscenities at her.

'Dog eats dog,' she thought, smiling as she ran. Or should that be Golf knocks Bimmer off its bum!

By the time she arrived at the exhibition the first crate of champagne was empty and probably the second was on its way.

The doorman checked her name against a list, and she

walked in through rows of young girls and boys holding trays full of champagne flutes. She took one, looking in vain for Frank, Angelo or anyone she knew. The room was so crowded it was hard to identify anyone but the tallest. Then she saw, close to the entrance and the champagne girls: Theo.

'Theo. We can't keep meeting like this.'

He laughed politely. Tipping his champagne glass towards her, smiling. His eyes bright.

'Yes, yes,' he said.

'How come you're here?' Cat asked.

'It's wonderful isn't it? As I told you, I've been looking for original works of artists on the web. I came into this gallery this morning because they told me there were going to be works by a Snail Man, and look what I find. He's working with the fabled Anastasia. Isn't it brilliant? My dad was so chuffed when I told him. She'd changed her artistic name from Holmes, which is why I couldn't find her.'

'Did you bring Sarah too?'

'I did. She was so excited to be seeing Ana again after all these years. We were actually the first here this evening and she and Ana hit it off right away. Isn't it amazing! It's so right.'

Theo looked so happy Cat felt scared. 'Where is Sarah?'

Theo pointed. 'Over there. She's still talking to Anastasia.'

Cat followed his finger and saw Sarah, wearing a blue mid-length cocktail dress Cat recognised from last year's Next summer sale, and talking to a very tall woman with long black curls flowing down the back of her John Galliano black satin trouser suit. Spilling with easy nonchalance down her front was a cascade of diamonds that made Cat want to ask if she was going home by tube.

'Anastasia?' she asked somewhat unnecessarily.

'Yes,' said Theo.

'Wonderful hair.'

Theo smiled.

'Also,' he said, 'if you look at her eyes, you'll see they are different colours, not completely but she has flecks of gold in her eyes.'

Cat stared at the tall shape outlined against one of the snail paintings. 'Flecks of gold,' she repeated.

'Come on,' said Theo, 'I'll introduce you. You've been waiting long enough to meet her ...'

He paused suddenly. 'It wasn't true was it? That you knew her when she was married to Perez? That's what you told us in Lerwick.'

'No,' said Cat. 'It wasn't true.'

He laughed. 'I thought not. I looked you up on the net. There's loads out there about you, about your first husband and his death of MND (sorry by the way) and about your books to teach children languages. And then I saw the bit about:

"If you want to find a stolen dog or lost child, ask for Cat, Miranda or Stevie at SeeMs Detective Agency." And I guessed that someone asked you to find Anastasia. Is that right?'

'Yes,' said Cat, 'that's right.'

'Cool. I've never met a detective before. Come on then. I won't tell Ana.'

Cat followed him almost in a daze. Finally, she was going to meet Anastasia, the woman she had heard so much about from those who loved her, and those who hated her. Those who suggested she was a murderer and those who doubted she had the guts. What could a woman who provoked such strong feelings be like?

As Cat and Theo approached, Anastasia looked up and she and Sarah turned their way. As the distance narrowed, Cat thought they were like two she-wolves sizing up the opposition. Who would win the fight?

'Oh,' said Sarah, her open smile from the heart, 'there's Cat! She's been looking for you. Finally, she's found you.' She waved. 'Hi there, Cat.'

Anastasia followed Sarah's glance and found Cat. Her eyes assessing what she saw: a woman as tall as her, taller, some ten years older, slightly greying but with eyes full of curiosity and kindness, an intelligent woman who would be better to have as a friend than an enemy.

Perhaps, said Anastasia in Spanish, if my life had been different, I would be a soft pussy like Señora Cat.

Sarah gazed up at her, puzzled.

Cat looked at Anastasia.

She saw a woman of her own height, with a haughty strength in her face, as one who has fought to live her own way. A strong woman but not, she felt, a killer. On the other hand, most definitely someone for whom people would kill. No question!

Don't be silly, Cat, she told herself, if it was so easy to tell who was a killer and who was not, we would not need detectives.

'Hello,' said Cat, putting out her hand.

Anastasia nodded keeping her hands relaxed at her side.

'*Ciao, Chica*. I hear you have been looking for me, and yet I was here all the time. Where were you?'

The she-wolf, thought Cat, had raised its lip to show her teeth. However, before she could reply Angelo and Frank came bustling up like Pinky and Perky.

'Ah, Bella, you are here, you have already met the incomparable Mrs Cat. The two most gorgeous women at the show stand together like models from the Sistine Chapel.'

Sarah giggled and he turned to her, mortified. 'But, you too, young Sarah, who I met tonight with such joy, a bundle of information and happiness, you too are in the Sistine Chapel. An angel, I think, a full and beautiful cherub ...'

Sarah burst out laughing. 'Oh, Angelo thank you, but I'm not sure I like the idea of being a cherub on the Sistine Chapel. I'm on a diet you know, usually am ...'

As the two loquacious members fought for verbal domination, Cat drew Anastasia aside. 'I wonder. Could we meet tomorrow? I'd like to ask you a few questions, if you don't mind, but I don't think this is the place.'

'*Coño*,' said Anastasia in fast Spanish undertone, 'British always stick their noses in where they are not wanted.'

'Oh,' replied Cat in Spanish, 'but I'm half French.'

Anastasia gave a burst of laughter, waving her hands incomprehensibly.

'I forgot! My son told me.'

She gave Cat a card, Anastasia Rodriguez on one side, an address on the other.

'My studio. Come tomorrow II a.m.'

Then she turned and walked towards some new arrivals, her stride elastic and her head held high. Cat watched her feeling ambivalent.

Chapter 55

The next morning, Cat found herself walking down Montague Street, opposite the British Museum. Passing through black double doors, which stood open invitingly in the old block, she walked up five floors. If there was a lift, the builders had hidden it well and as Cat puffed up the steep stairs she wondered if Anastasia had carried her furniture up here. Hope someone helped her.

At the top of the stairs there was only one door. It was open and it led straight onto a large open-plan room. Anastasia was sitting on an elderly leather sofa sorting photographs in front of her on a table. The other side of the table was a bed, neatly made up and pushed back against the wall. Cat walked in and sat down beside her, without speaking. She looked at the collection.

'These are good.'

Anastasia glanced up. She smiled. For a moment she looked happy and then the veil of hauteur returned.

'Thank you.'

After a silence, she said: 'Coffee?'

'Please.'

Anastasia got up and pushed a panel behind the sofa. Hidden from view was a small kitchenette.

'How neat!' said Cat, springing up to look.

'There is one the other side, too.'

Anastasia indicated a second panel, which, slightly opened, showed it was a clothes cupboard.

'Wow. I had no idea. What a brilliant idea to make use of a small space.'

'Like so much in life.'

'What?'

'Hidden from view until we stumbled across it. Isn't that what you and your friends do? In the SeeMs Agency: "Where we go behind the seemingly true and smash the assumption." Find the hidden?'

'Sometimes the best hiding place is out in the open.'

'You may be right, Mrs Cat, but for me the open is too wild a place. I prefer my studio with its protective walls and upper floor silence.'

Cat followed Anastasia into the kitchenette, curious about its size. On the rail was a twin to the tea towel she bought in Shetland, with pictures by Peter Coutes. Cat picked it up.

'A memento from Shetland?' she asked, her heart beating. These had only been made for two years. How come Anastasia had one? Had she slipped over to Shetland to visit Clement? Were they in this together? Had Clement been involved in all the murders?

Anastasia looked at her curiously.

'Yes, Sarah gave it to me yesterday.'

She said nothing further but Cat absorbed the satire in her smile. She took her coffee and went back to the sofa.

'Thank you. Do you live here? Nicholas Romero said you had a flat in Chelsea.'

Anastasia snorted. 'Did he? Or did he say I had stolen his flat in Chelsea?'

This time Cat said nothing.

'I've given it to my daughter. There seemed a nice irony in that, since she introduced me to Nicholas's father. You English would call it squaring the circle.'

'It's a very neat flat,' said Cat, looking around the small flat reminiscent of a monastic cell.

'Neat,' Anastasia smiled to herself, 'English euphemism. In Spain we are more direct. My friends say: "Why do you live like a nun?"'

She pulled out a photograph. It was an elderly woman with an appealing face. Cat looked and immediately felt she would like this woman.

'Her name is Emmy,' said Anastasia, 'she was from one of those Dutch families who colonised Indonesia before the Second World War. They had enormous luxury, for the period. Then, during the war, Indonesia was overrun by the Japanese. So, Emmy and her ilk were put into concentration camps.'

She sighed. 'They were not pleasant places. We've seen them in films now, we've heard the stories, but do we really feel what they felt?'

She looked at Emmy's photograph as though asking her to respond.

'When I photographed her, she was living in Holland, in The Hague. She was in a small flat, but she had oversized furniture, presents from friends who didn't want the pieces any more. We talked a lot, while I took the photographs. Her father was an amateur photographer too and she showed me some amazing pictures of Batavia, which was what the Dutch called Jakarta. Taken in the 1920s, there were pictures of horse-drawn transport, of earthen streets, of colonial houses, of the jungle, of an era so different. That was the time of the Dutch East Indies. The Dutch were the masters then. Then the Japanese came and they became the slaves.

'She was a lovely woman. She said: "Once you have had everything and lost it all, you no longer care about things."'

Anastasia looked at Cat. 'I feel the same.'

Cat nodded.

'Can I ask you about Johnny Holmes?'

Anastasia half smiled. 'Always the terrier. What do you want Madam Catherine? And why?'

Cat was momentarily taken aback. Then she thought openness might be the best response.

'Angelo is a close friend of my boyfriend. His sister is worried. She employed us ...'

Cat stopped speaking. She'd been too impetuous, that was so unlike her. She was turning into Miri. What *had* she been going to say? That Gia employed us to see if you were a killer?

But Anastasia pre-empted her. She looked at Cat, dropping into Spanish she said quietly, 'You think I killed Johnny, Carlos, Romero and Tom. You worry for your friend the Snail Man. You think I will kill him too? I am, as you British say: the Black Widow spider pulling innocent men into her web.'

Cat said nothing. As with Anastasia's son, she again felt that a more serious helmsman had taken over the boat.

Anastasia's eyes flashed.

'*Coño!* I have not killed anyone. Indeed, I was as distraught about Carlos and Tom's deaths as anyone. The others, I admit, left me cold.'

Cat struggled. She was losing ground here.

'You were responsible though.'

Anastasia looked at her, a sneer damaging her beautiful face.

'Responsible? What is that? Are you a child? A child who, on hearing his parents are divorcing, thinks he is responsible? A dog that feels his owner's pain as his own? Señora Cat, you have a lot to learn in life.'

Cat recovered. 'No. Wait. If you are totally innocent tell me about everything and let me be the judge.'

Anastasia half smiled. 'The Cat has claws. What do you want to know?'

'Start with Johnny Holmes. Why did you marry him?'

Anastasia rested her chin on her hand.

'When I met him, he was charming, so, so charming. And I believed everything he told me. You are my generation, Mrs Cat; you remember the 70s, the 80s. You could not investigate a man's claims so easily then. And, we were naïve. We were children of Franco. Franco only died in November 1975. Suddenly we had this new freedom. Obscene postcards! A boom in the sex industry. You may not believe me, but I lived in Marbella at that time and I saw the changes and they were not all a benefit. I saw tourists come for the cheap booze, the sand and the whores who sold themselves to the tourists with money.'

She sighed and pulled a photograph from the pile. A handsome man, he vaguely resembled Thomas Anders of Modern Talking. He stared arrogantly at the camera, his half smile already showing possession. He leant against a large maroon coloured Mercedes.

'Then our Johnny arrived on the scene with his Mercedes and his money. Money everywhere. Nothing was too much or too much trouble.

'So, we trusted this Scottish laird. My parents were delighted. I would be off their hands but also with a kindly, handsome charming husband who had wealth and property. I was seventeen years old. Why would I not fall in love?'

She looked out the window at the roof of the British Museum. Two pigeons circled before landing on a gutter.

'It lasted three weeks, my love. We were married, we had a magnificent honeymoon in Marbella and then we started driving back towards Scotland. I offered to drive. He agreed, but I had only been driving for a few minutes when he told me to stop. He shouted. I was dangerous. I got too close to other cars. I was shocked. In my family we sometimes screamed at each other, but not like this, with love. He was angry. *Incandescente*. And why? It is not such a fault to drive badly at seventeen.'

She brought her gaze back from the museum and on to the photographs. She picked out a small black and white picture of a large ferry with Townsend Thoresen embossed on its side. Although it was quite an amateur work, it showed the potential of the later photographs.

'So he drove, stopping only for petrol, until we reached this boat. Two days on the ferry, we slept on the chairs in the film room. I was puzzled. Why was my rich husband sleeping so rough? Why didn't we have a cabin? But when I tried to ask, he ignored me, and I started to become slightly ... slightly afraid.'

She shuffled through the photographs and found one of the docks at Portsmouth. Heavy raindrops sat like warning tears on the camera lens.

'So, we arrived in Great Britain, and we drove again. We drove through the rain. When he was tired, we pulled off the road and he slept in the car. Slept on the backseat, while I curled up in the front. Eventually we arrived at Aberdeen.'

'But,' said Cat, 'but if he was a rich oil man ...'

'Yes, it's true, but perhaps he had spent so much on

wooing me. Or perhaps, he wanted to put me into the right frame of mind. Who can think like Johnny Holmes?'

She laughed sardonically and pulled out a picture of the Aberdeen harbour. It was still fairly basic, not as busy or full as Portsmouth. And it wasn't raining.

'On the ferry to Lerwick we had a cabin. He slept like a child and awoke charming again. Here we had sex for the first time. He was rougher than I expected, but I had no experience to offer. I felt we were moving together and I thought, I hoped, it was just the journey, the tiredness that made him so angry. I looked forward again to a happy life in our laird's castle.'

She pulled out a photograph of Lerwick in 1987. A much smaller town than the one Cat visited a couple of months ago.

'My introduction to The Shetlands.'

The boat had a large logo P & O on the side and a smaller name *St Clair* on the stern.

'He took me first to the Co-Op. 'Go shop' he said. 'You will need to provide me meals for ten days until I go offshore.'

'He stayed in the car.

'We had two more ferries before we reached Fetlar, where I was to live. I remember we drove up from the ferry port, and a large house appeared on the right of the horizon. 'Brough Lodge,' he said.

But instead of pulling into it, as I expected, he drove past, laughing. And kept on driving. Laughing more. He used that laugh many times in our marriage ... I hear it still echoing like music stuck in my head. Only it is not musical but maniacal. Eventually, we arrived at a dilapidated two-storey house sitting alone on the side of a track.

'Everything was OK until we got inside. Then, he saw my shopping. 'Where is my food?' he said in a quiet voice.

'I laughed. I thought this was a joke. I had bought a combination of luxury things. Of course, there was no Spanish food available then, but I bought tasty snacks, fruit and berries, I may even have found some olives. Some Italian wine.

'That time he did not hit me, he grabbed me here.'

Anastasia grabbed Cat by the scruff of the neck. Cat stiffened reflexively and Anastasia let go, smiling ironically.

'He pushed me back outside and into the car. I hit my head on the lintel and started to complain. He said, "Shut up, cunt! Or I'll give you something to whine about". He drove me to Sarah's father's house. She told you the rest. How she taught me to cook. However, it still wasn't good enough, and he beat me again. She was a good teacher. She could do everything. Although she was fourteen and I was seventeen, I was the baby, she was the grown-up.'

Anastasia pushed some photographs aside and found one of Sarah. She was standing by a hide on the beach. Fish was cooking on a fire pit dug into the sand next to her feet. The photographer had caught the way smoke drifted in gentle circles.

'Sarah built that. She was a real ... American's call them backwoods men.'

Cat examined the photograph. There was something about the way Sarah stood, both kindly and in charge that Cat recognised.

Anastasia looked back at the British Museum. The pigeons had taken off and flown away.

'I thought I was dead then. This would be my life for the next seventy years, if I lived that long in the cold damp weather, with its harsh, biting wind and constant driving rain.'

She shook her head and looked back at Cat, who said.

'Did you get pregnant?'

Anastasia blew a bubble of air. 'You know, of course. You had a child at nineteen. Don't look at me like that ...'

Cat was raising her eyebrows.

'I had dinner with Theo and Sarah last night. Theo wants to be a detective himself now.'

She gave a wry laugh.

'He said you left a deep trail on the internet. A detective but not a spy!'

'Did you?'

'Ah, *coño*! What do the English say: like a terrier on a scent? Yes, the day before we took the boat up to Muckle Flugga I realised all the sickness and fainting must be a baby, and I was scared.'

She found a group of photographs: a lighthouse taken from the sea. In some the lighthouse was high above them, in others it ducked down: it was not a calm day.

'I was so sick on that boat. Even Sarah was scared. She was so young, but she knew about animals. *Pues*, the herring boat saw we were in trouble and brought us back to Fetlar.'

Another photograph. Steely woman, thought Cat, still taking photographs while feeling like death.

'Sarah told you, how he beat me and raped me, and then the bleeding started. He left for his drinking friends and when he came back and raped me again, ignoring the blood that coloured our bed. I suppose he was too drunk to know or care. The next morning, he went off early, either for drinking or whoring, I did not care either by then.'

She found another photograph. It was a small boy with red hair.

'I saw this boy, his name is Magnus, and told him to go and get Sarah. She had to sneak out of the house as her father had gated her, but she came. And when she saw all the blood she understood immediately.'

Anastasia shook her head. 'I at seventeen didn't really understand, but Sarah at fourteen knew about life and death.'

'You lost the baby?'

Anastasia nodded her head. 'I'm so glad I had Isabella and Mateo or I would have had a lifetime wondering about that child. As it is, I sometimes worry if his soul was developed enough for Heaven.'

Cat looked up surprised, but Anastasia was looking back at the museum. There were no pigeons.

Cat thought of the desolate empty place in Shetland where Anastasia had been living.

'Odd that there was a boy there?'

Anastasia looked at her. 'Yes,' she said slowly, 'he liked helping Clement and I sometimes wondered if Clement sent him to guard me. But perhaps he was sent by my guardian angel.'

Cat realised she was serious.

'And then what happened?'

She looked outside again, and then back at Cat.

'Holmes only came back once more before he died, a week after he left. I had no idea where he was, or if he even realised what he had done. He picked up his clothes. He hardly looked at me. He said, 'I'll be back on 13 November.' And he left.

I never saw him again. On 14 November I reported him missing.'

'Why?'

'Why what?'

'Why did you report him missing? He often didn't come home. He left without telling you where he was going.'

'Sarah thought I should.'

'Really. Why?'

'I told her that in spite of my religion I wanted a divorce. In Scotland people got divorced. In England. Even in Spain. My family wouldn't like it, but I could not cope with any more ... she thought I had grounds for divorce and it was good to get him on neglect as well as abuse.'

'Funny,' Cat thought, that Sarah had not said anything about divorce. But then she hadn't mentioned the baby either. Perhaps she felt those things were too private to be discussed with a stranger.

'So,' Cat said, 'Clement took you out to the Alpha platform in the days before Johnny should have come home? The day you left the whisky bottle. And again, on the actual day Johnny should have come home. Two days in a row? Is that right?'

'Ah, but the second day was the weather. On 13 November, Clement was taking Sarah and me to Charlie platform, not Alpha where Johnny worked, but the weather was dreadful and we were diverted.'

Stevie had examined the weather reports and said it was true. The weather was awful. Here, at least, Cat knew Anastasia was telling the truth.

'It was a huge adventure.' Anastasia was saying. 'I loved it. Although we were scared that we might see Johnny, it was still fun. We were young girls. Can you remember that sensation? When life is at the same time dreadful and yet things make you laugh?'

'Did Clement get out of the helicopter on the rig?' Cat asked. 'The day you were diverted?'

'*Pues*, you are serious? It was terrible weather. Sarah and

I had no idea it was so dangerous. Or I hadn't anyway. What did I know about flying? About weather? But when we were sitting on the wrong platform, with the rain teeming down I did wonder if I would live to see my parents.'

'Did Clement get out of the helicopter?'

'Oh, the terrier again. I've told you. Sarah has told you, and no doubt if you asked Clement, he would tell you too. Nobody got out of the helicopter.'

'How did you know Sarah had told me?'

'She told me last night. What do you think we talked about? Honestly! Cat the Terrier Dog! We talked about Shetland. We talked about you. Are you surprised?'

Cat grimaced. So much for getting individual stories.

'Tell me about putting the whisky bottle under the platform jacket. How come Holmes could ask you to do that?'

'He didn't ask me. Women weren't allowed on the platform, or indeed anywhere on the rigs. And he would have killed Clement if he knew I went in the helicopter. No, he asked Clement, and Clement told him he had done it.'

'How?'

'How what?'

'How did he ask Clement; you didn't exactly have text in those days.'

'No, Mrs Cat-Terrier, but they had other ways of talking to one another. Johnny asked Clement when they were on the helicopter together, and Clement left a message for Johnny via the radio operator saying: "The pipe has been delivered." All delightfully *Boy's Own*, as you English say.'

'Secret Squirrel, more like,' said Cat. 'How did you leave the whisky there?'

'It was on a rope. Before we left Scatsta, I wound the rope around the bottle, it was both a disguise and a vehicle. I got out on the platform. Threw the bottle out and it curled down like a diving bird. I thought it might hit a leg and break, but it didn't. I tied my end to a post, and then I got my camera.'

'Didn't anyone see you?'

'Almost certainly, but no one said anything. Clement was unloading the machine, there were lots of men around but they didn't speak to me.'

'No one?'

Cat thought Billy Holecroft had mentioned he had shown her around, she had better check that in her notes.

'No one.'

Anastasia turned to the photographs again. She rifled through them. 'Ah ha!'

She put a photograph in front of Cat. It was hard to see what the photograph was of, but as Cat focused she saw it was taken from inside the helicopter, its screen steamed up with droplets descending down the curve of the Plexiglas. In the distance, it was just possible to see a bit of the platform building, with huge ropes of rain streaming between.

'Now you see the rain on the last day we went out to the rig. I gave all the other photos to Clement, as a thank you. But this one I kept. A memorandum. Something to remind me to be careful where I put my love!'

She snorted. 'How well I learnt, Mrs Cat. And how little.'

Cat compressed her lips. 'Before I knew that you and Sarah were on board, I thought Clement must have killed Johnny,' she said. 'Saw him bending over and kicked him off the platform.'

Anastasia laughed, simultaneously shaking her head.

'If it was true, neither Sarah or I would have told you. Clement would not kill like that. Perhaps in war, Clement would shoot a man at short range, perhaps if his family were threatened. But Clement would not take a coward's action.

You do understand what I mean. Johnny was a bad man. God gave us justice and you shall not take it away.'

Cat moved in her seat. She too glanced out at the British Museum and saw the pigeons had returned and were necking.

Chapter 56

'How did you meet Carlos?' Cat asked.

Anastasia's face softened for a brief moment, before the veil again descended on her eyes.

'Carlos was sent to me from Heaven.'

She shook her head.

'I thought I had done my penance for whatever had made God angry, and now we would live forever in the sun. But I did not understand people; men.'

She searched through the photos and found a picture of a man in his forties; fit and supple he dominated the camera: a man who made things happen.

'We were happy for twenty years. Then, even though he had his wine, his company, his brilliance and his children, he grew jealous of my photography. My little piece of freedom.'

She shrugged.

'You know the rest. My son. My daughter. They told you everything. I am lucky in my children.'

Her face took on a strangely blank look and Cat, feeling as much as seeing the pain, decided to return to Carlos later.

'Do you know if Romero was using tramadol?'

Anastasia found a photograph of Romero senior; Cat noted how like his son he looked.

'He was a sportsman who did not wish to grow old. He thought he was soothing away his pains. I told him no, his doctor told him no. Tramadol does nothing, nothing except ease your short-term pain. But he believed no one.'

She shrugged.

'What about his drinking of Carlos's old champagne stock? Why did he do that?'

Anastasia bit her lip.

'He was a foolish man, and a jealous man. I told him and his son, if they went on playing that game, I would leave but they apparently liked to tease me ...'

She pulled out the photograph of Nicholas.

'He liked to rile me, and he easily worked up his father. Did he show you the video he made, the day his father died?'

'Yes.'

'He would. He sent me a copy, with a threat. He said he knew that I had killed his father, and he would see me in jail.'

Cat gasped. 'What? Blackmail?'

Anastasia snorted. 'Blackmail is for the weak,' she said, but her right eyelashes flickered uncontrollably. 'I would happily have killed Romero after his performance that day, but I didn't have a chance. The fool killed himself first. I told Nicholas that.'

'And yet,' said Cat. 'You invited him to your wedding with Tom Drayton.'

Anastasia shrugged. 'That was Tom. He was a kind man. He felt sorry for Nicholas. No father, no mother. He didn't want him to feel left out.'

'What did Isabella think? Didn't she mind?'

'Maybe. What she said was he could come as long as his current girlfriend was left behind. I forget her name. She was some kind of hospital technician.'

Anastasia shrugged.

'How did you meet Tom Drayton?' asked Cat.

Anastasia found yet another photograph. A kind looking man with dog-like eyes, he stared hopefully at the camera. He was large, probably six-foot four, and muscular with far too much flesh and a pregnant stomach.

'You can see he was a sweet man. He came over to give me some advice on the house I bought in Sussex.'

'Ah, yes. What have you done with the house in Sussex?'

'I rent it out. One day I will live there. Until then I have my studio. This is enough for me.'

Cat looked at the clock and saw it was already 3 p.`m. They had missed lunch.

'What do you think happened to your husbands?'

Anastasia took the photos of all four men and laid them in chronological order on the table. She pushed the photo of Johnny higher than the others.

'I do sometimes wonder about Johnny. Had he already been drinking? If he could get whisky, others could too. Did he then stagger out onto the platform, looking for his bottle? Grab my line, pull it and fall?'

She pushed Johnny back into line and pushed up Carlos. She didn't speak immediately and Cat waited watching her eyes. Eventually, she spoke very quietly.

'A heart attack. Too young. Too cruel. We would have loved again. With Teresa and Romero gone, our passion would return.'

Carlos returned to the line and the photograph of Romero was elevated.

Anastasia snorted. 'What is there to say here? His own foolishness killed him. His own arrogance. *Coño!*'

Romero too returned to his place and Tom was pushed up.

'Poor Tom, a good man. I don't know why that evening he suddenly wanted to eat so much, why he took Viagra at all. We had sex that evening. He went to sleep. He never woke up. *Eco*, the best way to die? *Quizás*? Perhaps?'

She piled up the photographs, putting Tom on top.

'I thought this time it would be OK. But, I was wrong. There is the Dog of Death that follows me like a loyal hound.'

Cat looked at her. 'That's not a good feeling?'

'No. *Lo siento mucho*. Sometimes, I fear it will be my loyal companion forever, and then I am frightened to see my children. You understand?'

Cat felt a wave of sympathy. She too had known death, but nothing compared to Anastasia.

Chapter 57

The former policeman, Eric Connolly, lived in Berkshire and when Miranda looked up the address, she was relieved to see it was close to the railway station. It might be the copper was a teetotaler, although that wasn't her experience of policemen, but just in case he wasn't, better to take the train.

She arrived at 12 noon as he instructed and was greeted at the door with:

'Sherry? I always have one at this time.'

'Yes, please. Don't tell me it is from Jerez?'

He laughed.

'Spot on, Mrs Zielinski. May I call you Miranda?'

'Yes, of course.' Miranda blushed at such old-fashioned courtesy, while simultaneously noting he pronounced her name correctly.

He led the way to the sitting room and Miranda observed him with interest. He was extremely small and delicate, thin and wiry. The sort of man you would overlook. Given his age, his police career seemed impossible: in the past policemen had to be taller than five-foot eight, didn't they?

'Military police,' he said reading her mind. 'By the time I joined the regular police force I had skills they needed.'

'Ah.'

Was, she wondered military police a euphemism.

'So, you are interested in my friends in Jerez. And their erstwhile maid.'

'Maid?'

'Yes.' He smiled at her again. 'You will stay to lunch?'

'Love to.'

'Excellent. I'll tell my girl. I never married and I like my food.' His eyes twinkled. 'Life has been good to me, and I can afford a cook.'

While he went to the kitchen, Miranda wandered around the room looking at the books and pictures. Eric seemed to like discreet drawings, landscapes and paintings of horses. His books included biographies and textbooks, all in alphabetical order. There was a large section on tactics including a lot of books by Liddell Hart. She pulled one out and it fell open at the Battle of Sedan.

Eric came back from the kitchen. As he refilled her glass he said: 'Brilliant man. We had to read him at Sandhurst.'

She put the book back and returned to her seat comparing how quickly he noticed what she was reading with her husband: for Phillip to notice something she would have to leave his supper sitting on it, and even then ...

'Tell me,' Eric said, breaking in to her thoughts. 'The SeeMs Agency, how did you come by the name?'

How indeed! For the girls the name had been so important, so integral to how they saw themselves and to who they actually were, but to outsiders it was just a handle to distinguish them from others. Miranda didn't try and explain the philosophy but moved straight onto the epithet.

'It's a compilation. See.' Miranda held up her fingers in the letter C, 'for Cat and M for Miranda and S for Stevie. Also, we are not exactly what we *seem* to be. We want to move beyond the assumption. And, Ms itself is important because, unlike Charlie's Angels, we are not run by a man but are our own bosses.'

He raised an eyebrow. 'Very clever. Now, what would you like to know about our friends in the south?'

Miranda moved into a more comfortable position in the armchair, put her sherry on the table in front of her and looked curiously at the man sitting upright yet relaxed in the chair opposite.

'Well, let's start with why I might want to know about the maid.'

'Not the maid,' he said, 'Anastasia's maid. She employed her (Teresa Garcia was her name) in 2011, when she was twenty-two.'

He sipped his sherry.

'By all accounts Teresa was devoted to her mistress.'

'And this was the maid with whom Carlos had the affair, once Anastasia spent too much time with her photography?' Miranda asked.

'Correct.'

'Why?'

'Why did he have the affair, or why did she?'

He sipped his sherry, watching her.

Miranda crossed her arms across her front. She noticed her legs were already crossed, perhaps she, like Liddell Hart, had automatically taken a defensive position.

'I sense I'm not going to like any of the information you are about to tell me.'

'The world can be a duplicitous place,' said the former policeman, 'and worse.'

'Even though I think I know the answer, tell me,' said Miranda.

He nodded.

'Peter Drayton told you Carlos was a man about town before he met Anastasia.'

'You've talked to him?'

'We have become friends. He's a clever man, Peter. In my opinion the best builder in the country.'

Miranda picked up her sherry and took a gulp. She had never much liked sherry, but it was alcohol: soothing.

'Teresa is a beautiful woman,' said Eric, 'and, I am told, the very imprint of her mother.'

'Her mother?'

'Yes, her mother was from Andalusia, where all the most beautiful women originate. She was working for the Perez estate as a fruit picker from 1987 to 1989.'

He sipped his sherry, watching Miranda's reactions over his glasses.

'Carlos had an affair with her, but by 1989 he had tired of her, so he got her a job in a shoe factory in Seville. She moved. The affair ended, and, presumably, Carlos thought that was the end of the matter.'

'But she was pregnant?'

'You are very quick,' he said, still watching her.

Miranda dipped her head modestly. 'Go on.'

'Shortly after she started work in the shoe factory she married. Her husband was what was in those days was called *chingar*. As an interesting aside I might tell you the word originates from the Basque verb *txingartu*, which means to burn with coal.'

Miranda wrinkled her brow. 'You are saying he was gay?'

'I am.'

'And they had a child,' said Miranda, 'which presumably pleased them both.'

'I'm not sure how pleased he was,' said Eric, sipping his sherry. 'He only stayed around for a few years. However, I was able to track him down and he was quite convincing on the possibility of him being Teresa's actual father.'

He raised an eyebrow.

'I see. So, no chance Carlos was not her father! So, Teresa was brought up by her mother alone, on her income from the shoe factory?'

'Yes, and as soon as Teresa was old enough to work, she too started work in the shoe factory.'

'So, she isn't particularly well educated? Like me, in fact.'

Eric moved his head in assent.

'Sadly, when her daughter was twenty, her mother died of cancer. But Teresa had previously given up her job to look after her mother, so she was living on welfare.

After her mother died it was difficult for Teresa to find employment.'

Miranda nodded, imagining how much Teresa must have suffered.

'Then, Anastasia offered her a job as a ladies' maid, with training and a good salary. A personal maid is a very special person.'

'Whoa, hang on a bit! How did Anastasia find her?'

'In my opinion, we may be verging on coincidence. Or as Anastasia would say, a gift from God.'

'Yes.'

For a moment, Miranda thought about Cat's deeply devout mother. Would she consider finding her husband's illegitimate daughter a gift from God? It would certainly enliven family conversation.

'Isabella, Anastasia's daughter, likes music.'

'Oh, right.'

'Teresa, who still did not have a job, joined a group of travelling musicians playing the shoes.'

'You are not serious?'

'There is an interesting irony, certainly. But perhaps it was the only instrument she could find. *'Music with Shoes'* started in Japan and became popular in certain circles in Spain.'

'Wow.'

His eyes twinkled. 'Indeed.'

'So, go on,' said Miranda. 'We still have a big step between playing the shoes and meeting Isabella.'

'Isabella heard her play. In my opinion, she already had some knowledge that Teresa was her sister. Perhaps girls have an instinct for it or perhaps she was already looking for her. The Perez family employs servants, many of whom have done long servitude with the family. Servants talk. Anyway, she showed a lot of interest, and they became friends. Then Teresa showed Isabella the only photograph she had of her father.'

'So Teresa knew?'

'In my opinion, she did. I met both women and, in my opinion, they have a familial resemblance.'

'So, who was manipulating whom?'

The policeman shrugged. 'Sometimes things work that way. A situation benefits both of them.'

'So, just to back up a little.'

His eyes twinkled. 'Yes.'

'You said that Anastasia offered her a job. Did Isabella introduce Teresa to her mother?'

'Yes.'

'But I don't understand. She loved her parents. Why

would she do that?'

Eric lowered his vision to his glass, considered it, picked it up, took a sip and then continued. 'Have you met Isabella?'

'No, Cat met her.'

'Ah, then I must explain. In my opinion, while she is extremely clever, she seems, shall we use the label autistic – with people? I talked to her for a long time. She had no idea that I was an English detective: my Spanish is fluent, my mother was a Basque and I speak Spanish with a Basque accent, so, many Castilian speakers think I am stupid. Similar to the way the English assume those with Irish accents are stupid.'

'I see. Go on.'

'In my opinion, she knew she was causing a problem. Remember she had also introduced her mother to Romero.'

'Yes.'

'However, in my opinion, it is doubtful that she realised her mother would react in the way she did.'

'Really. Go on.'

'Teresa started working for Anastasia. While Anastasia was busy photographing polo matches in Argentina, Teresa started cooking for Carlos.'

Miranda frowned. 'You said she was Anastasia's maid, why would she cook for Carlos? Didn't he already have a cook?'

'Anastasia liked travelling light. She did not want to take her maid. She asked Teresa to cook for Carlos, perhaps because she wanted her employed, or perhaps because she wanted him watched. In my opinion, she thought Teresa would protect Carlos from other women. I very much doubt she expected the girl to sleep with her own father.'

'I doubt it too,' said Miranda, feeling extremely uncomfortable.

'Carlos was attracted to his new cook. They started an affair. Then, one night she told him not only that he was her father, but that she was pregnant.'

'Oh blimey,' said Miranda, 'I knew I wasn't going to like this.'

'Yes, sometime that night he had a heart attack and she was so badly injured she lost the baby.'

'Oh, my God. What did the police say?'

'There were no police. Carlos had a known condition: angina. He was taking medication for the condition. He had seen a doctor a few days before. In such circumstances no police are necessary.'

'But what about Teresa?'

'The family paid her off. They are very rich. She signed a NDA.'

'NDA?'

'Non-disclosure Agreement. I met her. She is now living with a group of flamenco dancers and playing the shoes. She refused to talk to me, but she seemed to be living very comfortably.'

Miranda sighed. Then something occurred to her.

'Wait! Didn't Teresa in effect kill Carlos?'

Eric looked at her for a long time. He said, 'I can only suppose that Mateo did not think so. They are not a family who like scandal.'

Miranda felt queasy.

'Why would Teresa sleep with her father?'

Eric put his fingertips together while he considered the question. Miranda watched his hands moving up and down like children playing spiders.

'In my opinion,' he said, 'although I was not able to talk

to Teresa, and hence could not form a personal view, she was very angry. I suspect that her mother, who was, after all, Carlos's girlfriend before Anastasia arrived on the scene, thought she was in line for the top job. In my opinion, she thought she would one day be mistress, not just of Carlos, but of the Perez vineyard. When she was displaced, her anger knew no bounds. We do not know if she told Carlos about the baby but, in my opinion, she did, and he decided to ignore it, to suggest it was not his. She would probably not have known about DNA, nor would she have had access to it, so it was only her word against his, and his was clearly the stronger voice.'

He lifted up the sherry bottle invitingly, gave Miranda a top-up and put some more in his own glass.

'So she was dumped on her *chingar*, who subsequently left, and she had to make her own way. In my opinion, her anger grew and grew and was transmitted to her daughter, even with her milk.'

'And this was the only way Teresa could find to get her revenge?'

'Possibly she had been plotting for years, then this seemed like a gift from God. Again!'

'But the baby? She wouldn't have wanted to kill her own child.'

'No, but in my opinion, and as I say, my opinion is formed without personal knowledge, she was so blinded by her desire for revenge, not only on Carlos but on Anastasia, who replaced her mother, that she did not think about the possibility of pregnancy. Nor did she think that his reaction to her news would be so fraught that he would accidentally, or otherwise, kill her unborn child. In my opinion, she hoped only to make him extremely unhappy. Perhaps she hoped the child would have some place within the family. Without talking to her on the subject, we cannot know.'

Miranda looked at the light dancing on the sherry in her glass. She was finding it hard to breathe and wondered if she was descending into a state of shock.

'And Anastasia?' she asked.

'She came straight back from a photography job in Argentina. In my opinion, she was genuinely heartbroken.'

Miranda put her hands over her mouth. 'And Isabella?'

'Yes, also, in my opinion. There are many people, even, or perhaps especially, very clever ones, who have no idea what effect their actions will have on others.'

Chapter 58

When Cat arrived at the Hall, Stevie called over the old dog.

'Come for a walk,' she said.

Cat raised her eyebrows. 'I didn't think Ozzy did walks at her age; she doesn't look very keen.'

'We're not going far. I just wanted to show you something I saw a couple of days ago.'

'OK.'

They walked through the village to the large country cemetery that served the unified eight parishes. Unusually for a country village, as well as the scattering of small tombstones with sad epitaphs, it also had two large elegiac tombs owned by important local families and full of descending generations of dead.

Stevie stopped outside one with a flamboyant angel holding a brick in one hand and a bag of money in the other. Between the angel and the money was an iron gate that prevented entry.

'Odd decoration,' said Cat, running her hand over the angel.

'Victorian, I think.'

Stevie told the exhausted dog to sit and wait, and it collapsed down panting. She produced a large key from her pocket and inserted it into the lock, which turned smoothly.

'We have lift off!' she said, incorrectly.

They walked down some slimy stone steps with moss-covered walls, into the chill of the inner sanctum. There, there were rows and rows of sarcophagi, presumably all of which held one or two bodies.

'Prolific family, the Draytons,' said Stevie.

'So I see.'

She walked over to an internment niche; on the plinth was a beautiful ornate jar with a lid.

'Inside,' said Stevie, 'are the remains of Tom Drayton, builder and part owner of Drayton's building firm.'

'He was cremated?'

'Yup. A family first.'

'Why?'

'We need to send Miri on another job.'

'Yes, although ... why would Anastasia want to have Tom cremated?'

'It's a good question. I've been racking my brains for hours.'

'Is that the same as surfing the internet?'

'Ha, ha, but yes, actually.'

'Cremation is much cheaper, but that wasn't an issue here, was it?' said Cat. 'Especially if they are all expecting to go into a great and groovy tomb.'

'Groovy! Ooh, la la!'

Cat ignored her. 'My father was cremated but Charlie was buried. The difference mostly seemed to be that you could do burial straight away, because if necessary, they could dig up the body and do any investigation they might have missed, but you had to wait for cremation. Waiting until everyone was entirely sure there had been no funny business going on.'

'What even with your father?'

'Yes, because he hadn't seen a doctor for two weeks. As soon as he died, a policeman came and sat with us until the funeral director removed the body.'

Stevie put her hand on Cat's arm sympathetically.

'Well, that would surely be the same with Tom. It didn't sound as though he'd been to the doctor recently, except perhaps to renew his prescription of Viagra.'

'Yes. Maybe you are on to something there. Perhaps he OD'd on Viagra. Is it possible?'

Stevie nodded. 'Not exactly, but if you mix sildenafil, which is Viagra to you and me, with nitrates, it can cause massive drop in blood pressure, which with someone with heart problems would be lethal.'

Cat nodded. 'Where do you find nitrates in daily life? Fertiliser?'

'Could be, they are found in bacon.'

'Of course, preservatives. Did Anastasia give him a huge amount of bacon for dinner? Gammon?' Cat started to laugh. 'Sorry, murder by bacon butte. It just doesn't hit the mustard.'

'Ha ha,' said Stevie, 'but you have a point hidden in there! I had a chat with your daughter-in-law Gloria, she suggested I talked to a friend of hers who works in geriatric medicine and he suggested nitroglycerin.'

'What? The explosive?'

'Same. Ironically, it is used in hospitals to treat angina. To prevent heart attacks. And yet, if mixed with Viagra, because they both reduce blood pressure, it has the opposite effect.'

'You may be right, but where would she get it from?' said Cat. 'You can't just walk into a chemist and ask for a kilo of nitroglycerin, can you? You'd go straight down on the terrorist list.'

'Yes, I asked him for an alternative. He didn't know, but put me onto his girlfriend, who is a pharmacist. She said you can buy ammonium nitrate quite easily. Apparently, frozen ammonium nitrate can be used to freeze things and is used in cold bags.'

Cat squished her nose, thinking.

'Ah, maybe. So, what do you think? She cuts into a cold pack, pours it over some ice and gives him the ice laced with nitrates in his whisky that night? Plus the Viagra and plus some alcohol. An explosive combination for their love life. She's a chemist. She'd know the effect and how to do it and presumably that it would not show up in the autopsy. But something doesn't feel quite right.'

They turned and walked out of the tomb. Cat paused and stroked the dog.

'What else have we got?'

Stevie locked the iron gate to the tomb and turned for home. The dog heaved itself up and followed her. Cat fell into step.

'The two most controversial husbands were cremated,' said Stevie. 'Not Johnny, obviously, or Carlos.'

'Hum,' said Cat, 'since learning about Teresa I'm starting to consider Carlos pretty controversial too.'

'OK, fair enough. But Johnny we know lies ten thousand fathoms deep, or did. I expect Anastasia's family buried what bits they had left in Fetlar. There didn't seem to be any other family.'

'No, and Anastasia's family were probably glad to put that all behind them and be away.'

'Yes,' said Stevie. 'Carlos had a great flamboyant funeral with black plumed horses driven through the vineyard. Must have been quite a spectacle and certainly plenty of witnesses.'

Cat laughed. 'I expect Anastasia took photographs. I'm surprised she didn't show them to me.'

Stevie raised her eyebrows. 'I doubt the grieving widow is allowed to jump around taking photos? Or wanted to? Do you?'

They walked further down the village, greeting locals on the way.

'Romero had no autopsy and was cremated. And Tom was cremated against his family's wishes.'

'So, no chance of retrospective autopsies.'

'Just so.'

'But. I'm baffled,' said Cat. 'I was so sure that she was innocent. That Nicholas had killed his father for money ... but now?'

They arrived home and Ozzy collapsed on her bed and fell asleep. Cat and Stevie went into the kitchen.

'Oh yes, that's something else I meant to tell you,' said Stevie as she flicked on the kettle. 'Nicholas has his own money. When his mother died, she left a trust fund in his name. She, apparently, was one of the few who did have a will.'

'Oh,' said Cat, 'so he didn't need to kill his father for money. Unless he's spent it all. Has he ever worked? Any idea?'

'Dunno. Hard to see him as a banker or accountant, isn't it? Acting perhaps?'

'Hum,' said Cat, her mind still running over the money. 'Remember that Wallis Simpson quote, "You can never be too rich or too thin!"?'

Stevie laughed.

Cat stirred her over-hot coffee, watching the liquid circle in her mug, trying to cool it with motion.

'Hang on! Didn't Miri say that Billy had given Tom beer with ice after his help on the smallholding? Even though he said he didn't mind warm beer?'

'You're right. She did.'

'And,' said Cat, 'it tasted shite.'

Stevie nodded. 'Yes, but why would Billy want to kill Tom? They were friends and had no rivalry we know about. Besides, Billy wouldn't have been relevant to whether Tom was cremated or not. Anastasia made that decision.'

'You're right,' said Cat, 'my mind had gone away from why Tom was cremated and on to how he was killed, if he was killed.'

Stevie tapped the computer, which sprung into life.

'We'd better look a bit deeper into their friendship. They were divers together long ago ... perhaps something happened then.'

'Maybe,' said Cat. 'How about ... Billy owed Tom money and Tom wanted it back now he was married. Money is always a great incentive.'

'Could be. I'll see what I can find out. I may have to go into seedy part of the net to look into bank accounts.'

Cat swallowed. 'I don't think I want to know, especially not how.'

Stevie swivelled on her chair and said, 'I'm talking to Mr Charleston later on Skype. I wanted to find out what he discovered about Romero from the autopsy doctor.'

'Oh, good,' said Cat, fiddling at her mobile. 'Miri could ask Peter about the family's reaction to Tom's cremation.'

'And you could ask Anastasia why she had two of her husbands cremated, even though that was a family first.'

Chapter 59

Miranda hated shopping with the children. Her son kept filling the basket with things he'd seen on TV.

'We must have this Mum, it makes you clever. This one makes you handsome. You could lose weight with this one ...'

'Put it back, Felix. Put it back where it came from!'

And her daughter liked to sit on the floor and contemplate life.

'Get up Peta, we are in a hurry.'

'Yes, Mum,' Peta shuffled her feet and rolled over on the floor, dissecting the tiles with her fingers.

'Come on!'

A boy about ten years old stopped in front of her. 'I know you,' he said loudly.

'Do you darling?' Miranda asked, lifting a box of cereal into the basket. 'Am I a film star?'

She quite liked being confused with a celebrity, which one she wondered: Kiera Knightly, Helena Bonham Carter, yes, that was probably more likely. She asked the boy.

'Nah, you're too fat! More like Nigella.'

Brat! Who was it said the only good children are asleep upstairs?

'Nah! You were with Dad. Mum, Mum, this is the lady with Dad.'

A thin woman, wearing a large floppy hat that covered her face, turned and dragged her trolley, full of pre-packed meals, towards Miranda.

'You silly cow,' she said, 'whatever he told you is lies. He's all promise and lies.'

Miranda felt in need of a drink. Unable to see the woman's face she could not place her. Could this be something to do with Nicholas Romero?

'Who? Who is full of promises and lies? Who is this man?'

The thin woman snorted.

'You know very well. I know your type. Other women's husbands, that's what you like. All the perks, none of the pain! You were in our Billy's house last month. We saw you lolling on the settee, drinking beer, chatting up the boys in your short skirt, you tart!'

'Oh, good Heavens,' said Miranda sharply, so that's who it was, context can be everything. 'You mean Billy Holecroft, the diver.'

'Yeah,' said the woman, but she looked a bit puzzled. 'Did he tell you he made £1,500 a day? That's what he said to me, when we met. What he didn't say was he spent £2,000 a day.'

'No, I was there asking him questions about a murder in 1987. He was a witness.'

The boy looked sceptical. 'Oh yeah? You a policewoman? You don't look like a rozzer. Where's your uniform?'

'I'm not.' Miranda wished she'd used the village shop.

She hated these huge busy supermarkets anyway. 'I've never met your Billy before, OK.'

'Ditched you, has he? He always does. Yeah, you aren't his type anyway,' said the woman raising her shoulder, 'he likes 'em slim.'

'Thanks.' This really was not Miranda's day. 'I'm not that fat, my husband says I'm just a bit cuddly.'

'He must be a nice man. But Billy ain't, and he's funny with women. Dead jealous! So you avoid him, right.'

And she and the boy swept off, leaving Miranda's children gawping.

'Are you going to leave Dad for a diver?' asked Peta.

'No!' said Miranda, 'now get off the floor or I'm going to leave you to work here.'

Peta burst into tears, drumming her heels on the tiles.

Once they made their way through the supermarket, got Peta off the floor several times and put back all the extras Felix wanted, Miranda was exhausted and in need of a glass of white wine. She considered stopping at the café and having a quick glass, but she suspected Felix would tell Phillip, who would be annoyed.

Deep in thought they stepped out of the supermarket at last, and were nearly knocked over by a car WAR 923. Inside, she saw Billy's ex-wife and son. Why, she asked did she ever use the supermarket?

Chapter 60

Cat sent Anastasia a text asking if they could meet again. The speed of her reply surprised Cat.

'I'm going to the gallery tomorrow night. Pick me up at 6 p.m. and we can go together.'

'Great,' thought Cat, 'that will give me an excuse to invite myself to stay with the Little Family in Bloomsbury.'

The Little Family was her nickname for the throuple of her son Victor, daughter Vanessa and daughter-in-law, Gloria, and their son Charlie. Cat could still not bear to use the term throuple itself.

She rang Gloria.

'Stay as long as you want, Cat darling,' said Gloria immediately. 'Charlie keeps asking if you are coming to see him soon. He's made you something special to have with your breakfast.'

As usual, Cat was early for the rendezvous with Anastasia. She sat in the car, not quite outside the flat but a few spaces back, as the road was full of vehicles and there was no room outside the entrance.

She started checking her emails, half an eye on the black

double doors in case Ana came out early. Glancing up a second or third time, she realised a man had been standing on the opposite side of the road, staring up at the flat for about fifteen minutes. He was wearing a hoodie and it was impossible to see more than his outline in the deceptive dusk. He lit up a cigarette, which shone on his face but he was too far away and Cat didn't recognise him. She wished Miranda was there. She'd recognise him even at this distance. She laughed to herself.

'Honestly, me and my petty jealousies!'

At 6 p.m. Cat sent Anastasia a text saying she was outside. The reply was: 'Five minutes.'

Cat cursed herself for always being so early. Normal people were late!

About fifteen minutes later, Anastasia came out of the flat and looked around. Highlighted by the lamplight, her elegant three-quarter length jersey dress and boots made her seem like a fashion model. Cat was glad she had changed out of jeans, but still felt scruffy.

As Anastasia's eyes searched for the car, Cat saw the man watching the flat cross the road and approached the woman. Cat felt a cold chill. She started the car and drove out of her parking place without looking first.

PAAAAHHHH!

A yell as loud as an elephant's call hit the street, accompanied by excessive honking.

'Fucking woman!' yelled a voice, 'don't *any* of you have driving lessons?'

However, he had stopped in time, hadn't hit her and when she reversed back into the space, he sped past a finger raised in praise.

Anastasia rushed up to the car. 'Are you OK, Cat? *Que coño*!'

Cat laughed. 'It's what I'm always telling Miranda not to do, and I did it.'

Anastasia laughed with relief. 'I'm glad you are all right. *Culpa mea*! I should have texted you to say I was on my way down.'

She got into the car.

'Who was that man?' asked Cat.

'What man?'

'The man who crossed the road towards you?'

'Oh, yes, your excitement put it out of my mind. He asked for a light.'

'Oh, how odd, he was smoking already.'

Anastasia looked at Cat in the gloom of the car.

'Was he? I thought he did look familiar ... did you recognise him?'

'No.'

'Oh well,' said Anastasia, 'probably just a bum.'

But Cat felt cold again.

They parked outside the exhibition. There were very few people there now the private view was over.

As Cat got out of the car, she saw the number plate of the car in front: WAR 923. Anastasia saw it too. 'My initials,' she remarked. 'Unfortunate ones as you see.'

'What's the W for?'

'Waleska, it means Glorious Ruler. Poor parents ever hopeful! I quickly changed to Anastasia. Both the initials and the actual name with its royal connection do me no good.'

They passed into the gallery.

'Have you sold many photos?' Cat asked as they walked in.

'No, they come to see, to chat, to drink, to party but not to buy. It is OK.'

They went into the back and sat down in a room with computers. It was empty of people but had strip lighting above, which made the space seem harsh and unattractive.

'What did you want to ask me, little Gatto?'

Cat plunged in with the question. 'Why didn't Romero have an autopsy?'

'He did.'

'What do you mean?'

'There was an autopsy. In Argentina they always have one in sudden deaths, it is the law.'

'But ...'

'I assume there was a report but I returned home after the cremation. I didn't see a report but the body would not have been cremated without one. On this one, you need to ask Nicholas. He stayed in Argentina and organised everything.'

Cat nodded. Something was not right here. Vanessa needed to do more searching.

'Isn't it unusual to be cremated in Argentina?'

'I don't know. We didn't discuss it. Nicholas took charge of everything.'

'One more question?'

Anastasia inclined her head.

'Why was Tom cremated? Peter Drayton said he was the first in a long line of Draytons ever to be cremated.'

Anastasia laughed. 'And now it is evidence of my guilt?'

Cat saw she was genuinely amused.

'Tom was unusual. He was a good, good man. But he was, as you like to say in England, a normal man. Not, as he would have put it, a *posh twit*. He thought Peter and the others, with their mausoleums and their fine houses, were becoming the new aristocracy. And he didn't like that. It was bad enough having a wedding where he didn't know half the guests. He wanted his body cremated, so it didn't have to go and lie in state like the Queen.'

She laughed again. 'He did have an autopsy. Again, sudden deaths in England must have them. I remember it said he died of a heart attack. I'm sure you can find it online somewhere ... you seem to find most else.'

Chapter 61

Cat had her answer and was about to leave when Anastasia said:

'So, Mme Cat, any more questions? Or shall we have a social drink? Dinner?'

They left the gallery and walked to a restaurant in Dover Street. Anastasia seemed oblivious to the cold, although she pulled the dress hood over her head, but Cat shivered and wished she had brought a coat. Going into the warmth of the restaurant she felt relaxed for the first time since she'd seen the man watching Anastasia's flat.

Anastasia ate very little, ordered only a roasted squash salad and kept her one glass of wine for the whole meal. In another era, she would have smoked constantly; instead, she talked, her hands transcribing each thought into dance.

'Why did you choose to study chemistry?' Cat asked, 'Clearly you are a linguist too.'

Anastasia shrugged. 'I wanted something I could use. I knew I would always take photographs, it was my passion, but I thought then I would have a career. Then I met Carlos and life changed. However, when Carlos discovered my knowledge of chemistry he was overjoyed. "We will dance ahead of the competition," he said. We used nitrous oxide for changing the taste of the grapes, and dry ice. There were other things. Sometimes they worked, not always. He was a great enthusiast. Then I fell pregnant with Mateo and he said: "Hurrah, we celebrate with a new champenoise that we make ourselves, now we are a real family."

'I had been worried and Carlos was worried too, though, of course, he never showed fear, only talked about our future successes.'

'He knew about the miscarriage?'

'Of course, I told Carlos everything. We had no secrets,' she paused, 'then.'

She took a sip of her wine. 'When Mateo was born it was pure joy, and he grew up such a star, so interested in everything about the vineyard ... at seven and eight he was going round checking the men's work. Carlos called him his Perfection Manager. Isabella was less interested in the wines, but she loved reading ... she would find out things we hadn't known and tell us ... from the beginning you could see they were clever. By the time she was six, she spoke three languages and this improved. She has a linguistic talent. Now she speaks perhaps eight languages but, oddly, she is more interested in their construction and inter-relationships than the abilities language gives you to understand other cultures.'

Cat ate her mussels in white wine, while Anastasia talked about her life. But when they were finished the main course, she asked. 'Why did you marry Romero?'

Anastasia snorted. 'Why does one marry? With Carlos we had a perfect union, but he grew jealous of my photography. When I was photographing for him, I was the best photographer in the world, but I wanted to test my skills, to photograph sport, action, landscapes and even people. When I needed to grow with my work, he hated that. So he took my maid as his plaything, *puta*. I hated him then. The children were worried. They thought if I took a lover, Carlos would be so jealous he would drop the maid. But Carlos despised Romero ...'

She sighed.

'In the beginning there was passion with Romero. But then ... we do things with the best intentions, but they have the worst results. It was a bad time. I must have married him for pride ... you have some English saying "a man who marries his mistress creates a vacancy". So I am not alone. But I grew to hate the whole Romero family ... and then the fool died and I was happy.'

'Ah,' said Cat, glad her main course had arrived.

'So, tell me about your little fat friend with the beautiful face who drinks too much,' said Anastasia.

'Miranda?'

'That's her ... you call her Miri. Miri means bitter and I wonder if somewhere inside that is it?'

'No,' Cat said, 'definitely not. Miri is the kindest person in the world. Kinder, perhaps, even than your Clement.'

Cat waited to see if using Clement's name got a reaction, but was disappointed.

She continued. 'Miri's father was a builder. He worked across Sussex, all the way up and into London in the 70s and 80s. He was immensely successful but then the recession started in the 90s. There were fewer projects and he started gambling to keep up payments. He even tried to get Miri's mother to release the home he gave her. She refused. There were huge arguments and one day he walked out and threw himself under a train.'

Anastasia gave a gasp.

'Miranda's mother started a shop in the bottom of their house. Miranda gave up school to help her. Together they put the other two children through school. Then Miranda met Phillip and fell pregnant. He wanted her to have an abortion. She refused. He left, but later he returned and they married. Whatever she seems like on the surface, underneath she is a strong woman with determined morals.'

'Oh,' said Anastasia, 'then she is Miranda, worthy of admiration, not Miri the bitter.'

Anastasia's phone bleeped with a text and she looked at it. Her face lit up.

'Mateo. He's in town.'

'That's nice.'

'Yes, very nice.'

'Does he stay with you?'

'No, I have no room. He will stay with his sister in Romero's old flat. There is plenty of room.' Anastasia laughed. 'Perhaps I will stay there too, tomorrow.'

She picked up the mobile, dialled a number and got up.

'Excuse me.'

She walked outside.

Cat was toying with the menu, when she noticed someone standing across the road. He was smoking, the light of the cigarette giving his nose an eerie prominence under his hood. She looked back at the menu, and then up again. It looked like a man, and he was now stubbing out his cigarette with his foot.

Something tickled her memory and she sent Miranda a text.

Anastasia returned to the table and sat down.

'Ana, is that the man who asked you for a light, standing over the other side of the road?' Cat asked.

Anastasia followed her gaze onto the street.

'There's no one there.'

The space was empty. Perhaps it was just a smoker forced into the street by the law. She felt a chill from the window.

'I'll give you a lift home,' Cat said decisively, 'it's on my way.'

'Thank you.'

She would wait until the woman was safely ensconced in her flat.

'Mateo is going to join us at the flat for coffee,' said Anastasia.

'Oh, excellent. But would you rather I left ...'

'No, no,' said Anastasia, 'Mateo is looking forward to seeing you again.'

Cat smiled. How would Mateo feel finding her carousing with his mother, the detective, the woman who suggested his mother was a murderer, with the accused? Would he be freaked out or take it in his stride?

'Why?' asked Anastasia, signalling for the bill, 'did you start a detective agency? You seem to have enough work, both you and Stevie, and Miranda has her children.'

Cat smiled. 'It started with Miranda, she was in the pub and a woman came in panting and crying. She said her dog had been stolen.'

'Had it?'

'Actually no, it was a dispute with her ex-husband. He had taken the dog, she wanted to get him into trouble.'

'Why didn't she go to the police?'

'I don't think the police take stolen dogs very seriously, especially not when it is part of a domestic.'

'And you resolved the problem?'

'Yes, Miranda talked to both the husband and wife. The husband agreed to allow the wife to keep the dog, provided she gave him the money to buy another one. It seemed to work.'

'So, Miranda got a taste for solving disputes, and you went in to support her?'

'Yes, and she needed Stevie for the internet, Miri is not very technical. I was getting bored of translating. I wanted a challenge. But my languages are useful.'

'So I am your useful dog, and your start into a new dynamic world of death!'

The bill arrived and Anastasia lit a cigarette, ignoring the no smoking sign. Cat looked up, surprised.

'I know them here, the owners are Italian, they understand.' Anastasia lifted her chin, her eyes challenging Cat to disagree.

Cat shrugged.

Anastasia paid the bill and they collected their things together. Cat picked up her handbag. She looked outside to see if the man was still there. If so she could defend herself with her bag.

As they walked outside Cat's phone bleeped with a text from Miranda. Cat looked at it. Nodded. Put the phone back in her bag.

Chapter 62

As they walked back towards Cat's car Anastasia asked. 'Tell me about your husband, Cat, he was older, like Carlos, no?'

'Yes, Charlie.'

'Nice: Carlos, Charlie. We have a strange mirroring you and I, no?'

Cat thought for a moment. How to describe Charlie in a few words?

'He was kind,' she said, 'humorous. But he did like his girls to follow his lead. It was different with Victor, the boy. Victor was to be a leader too.'

She looked at Anastasia, wondering if she was boring her but she was listening intently.

'You are my generation. You understand things have changed.' Cat sighed, unlocking the car.

'My children, even my friends don't really understand. They ask why I didn't stand up to Charlie when he wanted things his way, but what can I say ... I married at nineteen. Charlie took over from my parents. I probably was immature.'

Cat put the car into gear.

'I see the car with my initials has moved,' Anastasia said.

Cat looked up and saw she was right.

'Perhaps he was a buyer. Let's hope they went home laden with photographs.'

Anastasia laughed. 'So, you were telling me about your children.'

Cat went on, wondering why Anastasia cared.

'Vanessa, the youngest of the twins, didn't need me, she was so strong herself. She made her own way. Head girl at school. Got a first at Oxford, came top in her year at Law School.

'And Caroline, the older twin, despises me for not having stood up for her sufficiently when Charlie told her to sink or swim. Although, that is a little unfair as I did my best. But perhaps for your children your best is never good enough.'

Anastasia nodded.

'And Victor, has he been a leader? A success?'

'A success? I'm not sure. He has his own business. It keeps him well. But they, my children, are still young, like yours. Both my daughter and my son love the same woman. All three live together with their son Charlie.'

Anastasia raised her eyebrows but anything she might have said was lost as they arrived back at the flat.

Cat panted her way up the five flights, but Anastasia leapt up several steps at a time. Mateo was already in the flat, sitting on the black sofa, leafing through the photographs. Anastasia saw him and her laughter filled the flat with joy.

'Cat, my son!'

Mateo got up, gave Cat his hand.

'Delighted to meet you again, Madam Cat.'

As he smiled, the mother and son's strong resemblance

washed over her, as did how happy and relaxed Anastasia looked in his presence. She was like another person. A happy person. Someone without a horrible past.

'Coffee?' Mateo asked.

'Please.'

He walked behind the sliding panel and Cat could hear the click of the kettle.

'I wonder,' said Cat, 'do you have any of your wedding photographs? The Drayton wedding. We saw some on Instagram but I would love to see the real deal.'

'Of course.'

Anastasia went to the cupboard and brought out a photo album. She laughed.

'I keep wedding photographs, although, of course, I did not take those, perhaps you think I am crazy!'

Together they went through the photographs, which were quite different in style. Cat stopped at one, of Tom talking to Billy; Billy Holecroft with a beard, in morning dress.

'Do you recognise this man?' Cat asked.

Anastasia looked thoughtful. Mateo brought in the coffee.

'I remember him,' he said, 'he and his friend were divers. Tom asked me to talk to them, as they would not know many of the other guests.'

'His friend?' Cat queried. 'Have you a picture of him.'

Mateo took over the album and searched through the photographs. Finally, he found a picture of a small man, almost outside the edge of a photograph of someone else. He stood alone and he was holding a glass of wine.

'He looks lonely,' said Anastasia, 'no friends. But he knew Tom?'

Cat looked at the photograph and saw it was Marvin.

'Did you meet either of these men? At the wedding I mean? I know weddings are busy times for the spouse.'

Anastasia swished her hair.

'I'm not sure about that one,' she said, pointing to the small picture of Marvin. 'I don't remember him. I am not good at remembering people. In photographs, yes. But in real life ... *Vaya* ... they look similar. But yes, I do remember this one with the beard.' She pointed to Billy. 'Tom introduced me to him, and the man said:

"Oh, I know Anastasia, we were friends in Shetland." And I laughed, I said: "I had no friends except Sarah."'

Cat gasped. 'What did he say?'

'I don't remember. No doubt someone else came up and talked, could be I walked away. You remember ... your wedding is a very busy time!'

'Yes.'

Cat looked down at the photo again. 'So you don't remember him from Shetland? He remembered you. Said he showed you around the rig.'

Ana laughed. 'No one did that. The men just stared at me. They must have known Clement brought in a woman, but they did not say anything. It was thirty years ago but I still remember their stares!'

Anastasia looked at the photograph again.

'*Pues*, why are we looking at his photo?'

Cat sucked her lower lip.

'You remembered that car registration WAR 923 outside the gallery?'

Anastasia nodded.

'Well,' said Cat. 'I remembered where I had seen it before. It was outside Billy Holecroft's house. Miranda says she saw it too, with Billy's wife and children in it. She just sent me a text. We knew that the car belongs to the children, for alimony reasons, but here is the odd thing: Marvin is also on the insurance. He too can drive the car.'

Anastasia frowned. 'What? The lonely little man in the picture? Why?'

'Billy drinks. Presumably he put Marvin on the insurance so he can get home when he's drunk. The way I drive Miranda home when she has too much onboard.'

'And you think this Marvin is a client? That he bought some of my photographs? I didn't have any of Shetland, but there were some nice ones of children.'

Cat sighed. 'It is possible ... or he might be the person watching the flat. Or it might be Billy. Or even Billy's wife if she has the children.'

Mateo had been looking at the photograph of Marvin but now he looked up sharply.

'Is someone watching the flat?'

'I'm not sure,' said Cat honestly, 'but I did see someone outside when I arrived and again outside the restaurant. It looked like the same hoodie.'

Mateo nodded. 'There was a man outside when I arrived. Not a woman. He was smoking, so I thought he was just a smoker. I didn't look at him closely. He didn't have a beard though. The man in the photograph has a beard.'

Cat nodded. 'But last time I saw Billy Holecroft he was clean-shaven.'

'But,' said Anastasia, 'these Billies, these Marvins why would they be watching me?'

'Either of them might a stalker?' Cat said.

Anastasia shrugged.

'Pah, what could a stalker do?' She shrugged but again her right eyelid fluttered convulsively.

'A lot, Mother,' said Mateo, his voice echoing with

concern. 'Don't take stalking lightly, it usually points to men with mad delusions. It can lead to killing.'

Cat nodded, thinking. Or could they be looking at the wrong angle? Could money be involved?

'We know,' she said, 'that Tom saw Billy and Marvin on the night he died? Did he say anything about either of them when he came home? Is there any chance one of them owed him money? Tom wanted to claim back a loan?'

Anastasia looked surprised. 'Tom was very relaxed about money. I don't think he would have insisted on a loan being returned.'

'Did he say anything at all about Billy or Marvin?'

Unexpectedly, Anastasia blushed. 'Yes, he did. I wanted to use his phone for something and I picked it up. He took it back quickly, avoiding my eyes. I was devastated. We'd only been married such a short time. I thought he must be having an affair. I spoke out. Then Tom was embarrassed. He showed me ...'

She shrugged. 'He and his diver friends had been watching porn on his phone. He thought I'd be shocked.'

'Oh,' said Cat, 'I guess he often ...'

Anastasia spread her hands. 'Men. Old men. They like to watch!'

'Nitrates, porn, Viagra, eating heavily. Could it lead to death?' Cat spoke almost to herself.

Mateo however, was more interested in his mother than Marvin or Billy.

'If this man, this Marvin is a murderer. If he killed Tom then he could kill you.'

'*Coño*. Why?'

'Don't dismiss this lightly, Mother. He may believe you are his girlfriend.'

'Yes,' said Cat. 'He might actually have killed Johnny and Tom because they were in the way.'

Anastasia spread her hands. 'Tom died two years ago, why start now?'

'Because,' said Cat, 'you've just become engaged to Angelo.'

Anastasia looked at her son. 'And you think this madness is true, too?'

He nodded. 'You must come and stay with us in the flat. You cannot stay here, alone.'

Anastasia shook herself.

'Come, Mateo, this is nonsense. Tomorrow I will come and stay with you. You and your sister may protect me. Until then, we will think about these divers. Now, I will have some sleep, and you should too.'

She kissed her son gently but firmly and ushered both guests out the door.

'Goodbye Cat, nice to see you again.'

Chapter 63

After they had gone Anastasia continued to drink her coffee. Why did Cat and Mateo, both reasonable people, have such paranoia when it came to Tom's old friends? It made no sense. She looked again at the wedding photograph. The Billy looked like an affable sort of man. Tom liked him. The Marvin was less cheerful but perhaps he was a little shy.

Finishing her coffee, she took the cup to the kitchenette. Looked out of the window at the dark street. No one was standing by the lamppost now. They must have been wrong.

She sighed. Cat would be back with her family now. Mateo at his sister's flat. Only she was alone.

There was a noise behind her. Mateo must have come back for something.

She turned smiling. 'What have you forg ...?'"

The question died on her lips. It was not Mateo standing there but a completely unknown man and he was taking off his shirt.

Who?

'Hello, darling, did you miss me? I'm back now. And we are going to have some fun.'

He dropped his shirt on the floor and advanced towards her.

Anastasia drew herself into her full six-foot Pilates position.

'Get out of my house!'

'Oooh, she *is* a nasty one. Orders! Orders! I know you've missed me but no nasty tempers now.'

She stood still, mesmerised by his tattoos, partly hidden under the hair of his body.

'You've been a naughty girl, haven't you?'

He took another step forward. Anastasia started to say: 'Leave immediately or I will call the police ...' when a phone rang on the other side of the room.

They both started. Then the stranger said: 'Only if you can get to your phone ... come on, darling, try to get past me.'

His laugh brought back a memory ... this *was* the man from Tom's wedding. The man who said they were friends in Shetland.

Anastasia's phone was in her pocket. But how to get it to dial Mateo's number without alerting the man. If she spoke to Siri, even in Spanish he would hear her.

'Leave now,' she said, 'and we will forget this whole business. I will let you go.'

The man laughed again but this time his eyes glittered too. 'Will you indeed? You and who else?'

His voice deepened and he took another step towards her.

'OK bitch,' he said, 'I've had enough. Strip! Take your clothes off. Let's see what all those men died for! Come on Black Widow show me your web.'

He lifted his right hand. Something flashed in the lamplight.

The man had a knife.

Anastasia froze. Thirty years ago, a seventeen-year-old girl was staring at a man who looked like an angel but with a devil in his eyes. He hit her so hard she flew across the room, something warm spurting from her mouth. She tasted blood. He was on her hitting and punching. He hit her belly with a passion and he was yelling: 'Who were you meeting?'

And even as she wondered if he knew that a lighthouse stood on a barren rock, she felt something warm seeping down her legs.

'Come on baby!' The man's coaxing voice surprised her.

He was still standing opposite her with the knife raised.

He stepped towards her.

There was a muffled noise by the door.

And Anastasia saw a flash of red stiletto heels.

Chapter 64

Cat parted with Mateo at the black oak door, which he shut firmly. They both looked over at the lamppost but the space was empty. Cat felt relieved. It must have been her imagination.

'Good night, Mateo.'

She walked to her car and started the short drive to Bloomsbury, where she was staying with the Little Family.

Arriving she parked the car. Locked it and, approaching the house, went to get her keys out of her handbag.

Only. No handbag.

Without her handbag she had no keys and no phone.

Was it in the restaurant? No, because she'd thought of defending them against the unknown stalker.

Could it be in her car?

She retraced her steps. Looking in through the car window. Nope.

Must be in Anastasia's flat. She only left there five minutes ago. Anastasia would still be up. Cat could not wait until morning for her bag. Gloria had given strict instructions not to ring the bell in case she woke Charlie. In the past there were phone boxes but now they had all gone, changed into emergency units for defibrillation equipment. No phone, no call. Not all progress was helpful.

Sighing, she got back into the car and drove back to Montague Street. Parked right outside the door. At this time of night the door would be firmly shut. Indeed, she had seen Mateo do it.

There must be a bell knob on the left of the door.

There was indeed a knob, but before she could lift her hand to ring it, she saw the panel next to the door was broken. Shattered glass covered the floor inside.

Had that been like that when she left Ana? Only yesterday she had admired the art deco decoration on the glass. It was not broken then.

Had the panel been broken tonight? Since the moment Mateo slammed the door?

She felt sick. Looked back at the lamppost where the stalker had stood.

Empty. Still empty.

It could be nothing. There were other flats, as well as offices in the building.

Someone might have forgotten the key. Decided to break in rather than call an emergency locksmith.

She pushed the black door. It swung open. Her stomach joined her heart.

Mateo had shut the door firmly.

She couldn't ring anyone. Her phone was in her handbag. After tonight she was buying one of those dresses with pockets for your phone.

The most tragic word in the English language: phoneless.

Never again would she be phoneless.

The open door might be an accident. She walked into

the hall. Her red stilettos went clack clack on the tile floor. *A noise to awaken the dead*? She really hoped not. She kicked off her shoes and hugged them to her body.

If this was a mistake, if it was just some idiot who forgot his key, then she and he would laugh over a glass of champagne.

But, in case champagne was not the solution, she ran up the stairs, hardly noticing how many floors there were. As she neared the top, she heard Anastasia's voice.

'Get out of my house. At once! Before I call the police.'

She could hear a low reply but could not decipher the words.

However, the intonation was clearly English not Spanish. It was not Mateo. *Who else could be here at this time of night?*

Cat crept up the last flight of stairs feeling sick.

The door was wide open. Blocking her view of the window, and Anastasia, was the large body of a man. Shirtless. Covered in tattoos.

Cat stopped. Why no shirt? Where was his shirt? Then she saw it, dropped on the carpet the arms inside out. Mesmerised she stared at it. It came from M&S. Then the man moved. She saw the streetlight reflected on a knife in his hand. A knife! Her organs did another little dance.

She dropped one shoe silently down onto the carpet. Held the other high in front of her like a sharp-edged hammer. Thank Heavens she'd worn stilettos this evening, even though it made her six-foot four. Flat shoes would be hopeless.

Creeping forward, Cat saw muscle movement in Anastasia's face. The woman knew she was there. But ... that big black sofa was in between her and the man. Should she climb over it or go round it? A moment of indecision. She put her foot on the sofa, and it creaked. It was only a slight noise but enough. The man turned and Cat saw the knife flash towards her.

She gasped. It was Billy!

Instinctively, she thrust the stiletto forward and down, just as he lunged towards her with the knife. Although she was much taller than him, his movement meant she missed his head. The shoe hit his hand. The knife fell on the floor.

'Oh! It's the beautiful Catty bitch,' said Billy, rubbing his wrist. 'Sorry, Ana darling, she must be jealous. But I'll get rid of her ... although two lovely little girls would be fun ... perhaps ... next time darling we could ... gnngh.'

Shiny pieces of light exploded in the streetlight, something spurted upwards in little fountains and then dropped downwards covering the upholstery and the floor. The man pitched forward. With an odd noise like a dog being sick he fell on to the arm of the sofa. From there he slid on to the floor.

'Oh,' breathed Cat.

Red wine dripped over the sofa and on to the floor.

She looked up. Above the man hovered Anastasia, holding the neck of a broken bottle in her hand. Both women stared at it as though it might suddenly go off in another spasm of street-lit showers.

'I should have chosen a bottle of white,' said Anastasia. 'Now I'll have to get carpet cleaner.'

'Is he dead?' asked Cat.

Anastasia lifted one of his arms. It fell back loosely.

'I don't know. I'll get a silk scarf. We can tie his arms, just in case.'

'Silk?'

'Much stronger than cotton.'

'Oh.'

Cat saw her handbag next to the sofa and picked it up. Grabbed her phone from her bag.

'I'm calling the police.'

Anastasia nodded. She sat down abruptly and Cat saw she was shaking so much the chair wobbled on the floor-boards. The noise like a cuckoo's warning cry. Too late.

* * *

By the time the police arrived the women had tied Billy's arms and legs. Anastasia had phoned Mateo and Cat sent a text to Gloria explaining the situation and saying she might be back quite late.

Billy groaned and the women looked at him.

'He's alive,' said Anastasia.

'Good,' said Cat, wondering if Ana's voice was regretful. 'I didn't fancy a manslaughter charge.'

'It would be me, not you, on charge,' said Anastasia. 'You see how easily this can happen! Only this time it would be a lost burglar not a husband.'

And then she laughed and laughed and laughed.

Chapter 65

It had been a long night by the time Cat got back to Bloomsbury. Gloria and Vanessa were still up and ready to hear the story. Cat extremely happy to tell it.

* * *

Two constables arrived at Anastasia's flat exhausted and sweating, having run up the five flights of stairs. The younger one walked in but the older one was so puffed he had to stop and put his hands on his knees to get his breath.

As soon as the younger policeman approached Billy, he started shouting.

'My darling Anastasia and I were having a quiet drink, when this Cat broke in. She hit me with her shoes. The bitch! She knocked me out.'

He struggled around and sat up. Anastasia jumped back. She had stopped her laughing and instead her eyes watched him intently.

'She's jealous!' he yelled. 'That Cat's been stalking me. Came to my house uninvited. Twice!'

He moved his wrists against the silk, but the bindings held.

'She broke a glass panel by the door to get in,' he screamed at the policeman. 'Tell her it's true, darling,' he said blowing Anastasia a kiss.

Anastasia stared at him.

The young policeman wrote it down.

'Please don't touch anything,' the older, now recovered, policeman said. 'If you ladies would come with me.'

Both girls went in the back of the Panda Car, as Anastasia called it. Speaking in quiet Spanish, Cat asked Anastasia if she was OK.

'I'll have to tell them everything,' she said, 'in some ways this is for the best.'

Anastasia was silent, looking out of the window at the dark streets passing them. Cat remembered how little that family liked publicity.

When they arrived at the station, with one of those quirks of life Cat was recognised.

'Hello,' said a young voice. 'It's the language Cat.'

Cat turned round smiling.

'Andrew, what are you doing here?'

'I'm on secondment from Sussex. It's so good. Different or what? Are you translating for this lady?'

'No ...' Cat started, but the older policeman broke in.

'Andrew, if you don't mind, a word.'

Andrew made a face at Cat and went to talk to his colleague. Meanwhile the girls were led to separate interview rooms.

Cat was told a CID man would be with her shortly and was given a preamble which she remembered from her job with the police, translating the Perjury Act 1911 and the Criminal Law Act of 1967.

When the CID man came in, Cat told him the full story. Why she was at Billy's house, her connection with Anastasia and all the other deaths. After a while the constable stopped the recording and asked her to wait. He returned with a detective and they both asked her lots of questions.

'What sort of questions?' asked Vanessa. 'You should have asked for a lawyer at that moment. You might have implicated yourself in something. The police aren't infallible.'

Cat made a face. 'I thought you weren't interested.'

'Huh! Is that the thanks I get for introducing Stevie to Mr Charleston?'

'Sssh, Vanessa,' said Gloria, 'let Cat tell her story.'

'Well that was it, really,' said Cat. 'I guess there will be further questions later. I took a taxi back to Anastasia's flat to pick up my car and found Anastasia and Mateo just leaving. They had been fetching her clothes before taking her to Isabella's flat. After he put his mother in the car, Mateo came to talk to me. He said his mother had hardly spoken a word. He said she seemed very shocked. He would have his doctor look at her tomorrow. He said he'd take her back to Spain with me for a while to rest.

'Good place to rest, a vineyard,' said Vanessa.

Gloria frowned at her girlfriend.

'Probably Anastasia is indeed suffering from PTSD. I'll check you in the morning too. You seem OK at the moment, but these things suddenly hit you. Do you want to stay with us awhile?'

Cat shook her head.

'Thanks Gloria, but no. Billy may be out of the way for a while, but the girls and I still have a case to investigate. We still need to know who killed Father Romero.'

'Ironic,' said Vanessa, 'that you started planning to prosecute Anastasia and ended up protecting her. You really are everyone's mother, aren't you, darling?'

Chapter 66

While Cat and Anastasia were in and out of police stations, Stevie was sleeping in happy ignorance. She was flying the Tiger through the Amazon chased by bandits, when the robber's phone went off. It rang and rang and rang. It was giving his presence away and now the tables were turned: Stevie would be able to find him.

Opening her eyes, Stevie realised it was her phone. Why did the bandits have her phone? She stared at it. The face said: Vanessa.

Stevie pushed the button across groggily.

'Hello?'

'Stevie?'

'Oh, Ness, what time ...?'

'Sorry Stevie did I wake you? It is 9 a.m. I'm at work.'

'Yeah, now I'll never find the only Tiger left in the rainforest.'

'What?'

'Nothing! I was dreaming. Don't worry, I never really know which time zone I'm in, even when I'm home!'

'Oh, good. Now, wake up and start thinking. Billy Hole-croft's been arrested. Mum and Anastasia had to give witness statements. The police are looking into Tom Dray-ton's death once again. Mum's back home now, but it was quite a night.'

'What? What happened? And how come you let me sleep through it?'

'Yeah? Well I wish I'd slept through it myself, frankly. My mother loves attention. You should have heard her. She was quite the hero, saving everyone here and there. I reckon she was flirting with the policemen.'

'Come on Ness! Leave it out.'

'Sounded like it to me,' said Vanessa darkly. 'You know my mother thinks old is just a better form of young!'

Even though they were a phone call away, Stevie knew Vanessa was smirking. 'Well, at least she's got over her Catherine Cougar stage. Such a relief she met Frank, even if he tells the worst jokes I've ever heard.'

The young women giggled. Stevie was fully awake now. She needed to get up and dressed. Although she was sorry to have missed the excitement about Billy, she had a lot to tell the others. Her Skype call with Mr Charleston had proved very informative.

Chapter 67

When Stevie, Cat and Miranda finally got together that afternoon they had so much to say they fought to speak first, falling over each other's voices, stopping to apologise, before hurtling on again.

Cat got in first. Hers must be the most important. Telling them all about Billy and her interview in the police station.

'What did the police do with Billy?' Miranda asked.

'He was there in the station. I saw him arrive not long after us, but they wouldn't tell me what would happen now. It's so frustrating. We're clearly no longer relevant to his case, the police are in charge.'

'Wait and see,' said Stevie sitting back calmly. 'They, like as not, will want to ask some us questions, as well as Anastasia.'

'Let's hope,' said Miranda. 'Disappointing to lose control of the case now, just as it was hotting up.'

'Now,' said Stevie, 'I got some information from Mr Charleston, the lawyer Vanessa and I met in BA.'

'Brilliant. Tell us.'

'Well, first thing is there *was* an autopsy. Mr Charleston spoke to the doctor who did it. He remembered the work. Apparently, there were large deposits in Romero's muscles, typical of someone taking painkillers over a long period. He knew Romero was a top-level polo player and he said it added to his belief that sport at a high level should be for the young. Like tennis, he said, before they get too old.'

Miranda laughed. 'Obviously no one told Federer that! Or Serena Williams. Or Tiger Woods or ...'

'So, what else did the autopsy say?' asked Cat.

'Evidence of lots of old injuries, apparently. There were other things. They talked about it for quite a while, but Charleston said there was nothing much of relevance. The doctor did remember that Romero had tramadol and champenoise mixed in his stomach. Bad mix, he said, makes you very sleepy. He was not at all surprised Romero fell off his horse. Of course, it was bad luck that the other horse rode over him.'

'Yes.'

'What happened to the autopsy report?'

'It was lost.'

'Lost? How?'

'That itself is an interesting connection.'

'Really?'

'Yes. The guy whose horse ran over Romero, is the brother of the hospital technician who helped Dr Silvester with the autopsy.'

Cat had to grapple with that one: 'Is that relevant?'

'Yes, because the hospital technician is being blamed for losing the autopsy report.'

'Why?' asked Miranda. 'I mean the technician wouldn't lose the report on purpose would he?'

'She, her name is Maria Arinez.' Said Stevie.

'Oh!' said Miranda. 'The girl Nicholas dumped Isabella for? I'd forgotten she worked in the hospital. Small world! But why is it relevant? I'm still lost.'

'I don't know whether it is or not, but she has just become engaged to Nicholas Romero.'

'Has she?' said Cat. 'Given what a creep he is I can see you might think she's trying to hide something. But realistically, perhaps she just loves him?'

'Maybe. Or maybe there is a reason the autopsy got lost?'

'We need to find it. Do you think you can do that, Stevie?'

She shrugged. 'I'll try.'

'So, finally,' said Miranda, 'my pennyworth, although it's not really relevant now, I guess. But re Peter Drayton and Tom's cremation.'

Now she finally had the floor she could take her time. She took a long slow sip of coffee.

'Pete said he wasn't really surprised when Anastasia insisted on the cremation. The family didn't want it that way, they were all planning to be buried in the vault but Tom was always the different one. None of them are devout believers.'

'How about Teresa?' said Cat. 'I think I should go and talk to her. Can you find out where she is and if she'll agree to meet me?'

'I'll find out,' said Stevie, 'and I'll keep fiddling around on the internet, it's amazing how it stimulates thought.'

She grinned.

Chapter 68

Cat made a Skype call to Anastasia and Mateo telling them about Nicholas and his father's autopsy.

'You are not suggesting Billy Holecroft killed Romero too?' asked Mateo, who had become Anastasia's voice since she wasn't talking much at the moment. She sat looking at Cat her eyes slightly glazed. Cat wondered if she was even listening to their conversation. Had the Dog of Death finally bitten her?

'Unlikely. Although, since he travels a lot, not impossible.'

'Then you agree? Romero's death was an accident.'

After the back and forth this morning Cat was starting to feel unsure. But still it seemed too fortunate.

'No, I don't. Did you know that the hospital technician who worked on Romero's autopsy was the sister of the man whose horse ran over his body?'

'*Coño*,' said Anastasia. Obviously she was listening.

'Who are they? This family?' Mateo asked.

'They are called Arinez,' said Cat.

Mateo took a breath. '*Madre de Dieu!*'

Cat looked at him. 'You know them?'

Mateo snorted. 'Of course. They were one of the most notorious families in Argentina in the 1980s, responsible for many crimes. But why should they care about Romero? Was he involved with gangs? He was stupid enough.'

'No,' said Cat, 'but Nicholas Romero has just got engaged to the girl.'

Mateo moved closer to his mother and put his hand on her shoulder.

She spoke quietly. 'These are just names from the past. We have to live. The days of Argentina's dirty wars are over. Are we finished?'

'Before you go.'

'Yes?'

'Nicolas's mother. Mateo, you said she fell off their yacht?'

'Yes.'

'How old was Nicholas when she died?'

Mateo answered. 'Seven or eight, why?'

'I just wondered. Was he close to his mother? Maybe, money was not the only reason Nicholas had for killing his father.'

Mother and son looked at each other. Eventually, Anastasia said. '*Quizás.* Perhaps. Nicholas was much troubled. His father the playboy! *Coño!* No good for a child that his father plays. That his father ... *vaya...*'

She shrugged, moving her hands expressively.

'Nicholas turned to the church. He would come with me to mass. He loved confession! He said he would be a priest. But, *vaya,* he followed nothing through. He was a boy of ideas but no reality, no action. He needed someone to direct his life. The church is not your mother.'

'And now,' said Mateo, 'he has moved to the religion of the gangs, *quizás*, perhaps?'

Anastasia gave a spurt of laughter. 'Perhaps this Arinez has become his mother. His church!'

'Maybe,' said Cat. 'Maybe.'

'Thank you, Catherine,' said Anastasia. 'You have been very kind. I am going away for a while, but when I return, we will become friends.'

'Thank you,' said Cat. She smiled.

As she was about end the call she stopped.

'Anastasia.'

'Yes?'

'Do you still have the video Nicholas sent you?'

'I deleted it.'

'Oh.'

'Why,' asked Mateo, 'do you think it is important?'

'I'd like to look at it again. To see some details.'

Mateo nodded. 'I'll look on my mother's computer, I can probably find it. If I do, I'll email it to you.'

When they had left her screen Cat pushed her glasses on her head and sat looking at the shiny rectangle in front of her. What would happen to Anastasia now? Would Angelo be able to understand such a complicated wife? Cat rubbed her forehead. Had any of her husbands understood her?

Chapter 69

'Was Teresa happy to talk to me?' asked Cat.

'No, not interested. She didn't even answer the email I sent her. A friend wrote back that that part of her life had finished and she had moved on.'

'In English?'

'Ha Ha, Google Translate. I'll forward it to you. Maybe it has hidden meanings in the Spanish.'

'So, back to Nicholas Romero,' said Miranda.

'I still cannot work out why Nicholas had his father cremated, or indeed why the autopsy was lost,' said Cat. 'It's not illegal to take tramadol or to drink champenoise. Even though he died from the accident, not the drugs, cremation would not change anything. Makes no sense.'

'Well, this may see a bit far-fetched,' said Stevie, 'but Gloria did suggest that since Romero died without absolution, he should not really be buried in a Catholic graveyard.'

'I can't see Father Romero being very religious, or minding about that,' said Miranda, 'can you? Although play-boys may not consider it irreligious to have numerous girl-friends.'

'I wonder,' said Cat slowly, 'do you remember Nicholas saying: Miri, save my father's soul? We now know he is, or was, the religious one. It is possible that he didn't want his father's body to achieve the resurrection? But to be sure of that we need to know if the ashes were put in sacred ground or not.'

'Wait,' said Stevie, 'the ashes! What did you just say about putting them in sacred ground?'

'Oh,' said Cat, 'it's all around the final resurrection. The Catholic Church used to insist that believers had to be buried, so that on the day of the final resurrection they could be reconstructed in their final form. Recently, however, the Vatican has decided to alleviate this require-ment, since God is potent enough to reconstruct them, even from ashes. So, Catholics may be cremated but the ashes must be kept in holy ground and not dispersed like Protes-tant ashes, nor kept at home.'

'And yet Nicholas had his father's ashes in his house in Buriton.'

'Did he?'

'Well, put it this way, there was a funerary urn there. Don't you remember? You saw it under the polo sculpture, the one with a crucifix round its neck. Who else could it be?'

'Of course. I forgot!'

'I'm getting lost,' said Miranda, 'are you two seriously suggesting that Nicholas had his father killed, and kept his ashes on unholy ground as revenge for the death of his mother?'

'Actually, yes,' said Cat. 'Remember I was born a Catholic. The power of the future life is strong. I know it sounds crazy, but it could be a motivation if you think of him as a lost boy desperately clinging to the church for security.'

'I see. But even if I give you that one, it still doesn't explain why they lost the autopsy.'

'Nope. We need to find it. I'll get on to it,' said Stevie.

'At least Anastasia has escaped their machinations,' said Miranda. 'Instead she will have Angelo to protect her. Once Mateo stops protecting her in Spain, that is. I wonder if my son will do that for me in the future.' She laughed. 'I can't imagine what Felix would consider protection. Building me a Lego fortress?'

'Oh bother,' said Cat. 'I'd quite forgotten about Angelo. He's coming to stay again.'

When Cat arrived home, she could see Angelo was already there. Although she could not remember what sort of car he drove, the way he parked was unique. Most visitors put their cars carefully at the sides of the small space, allowing room for other cars, but Angelo's Lamborghini sat in the middle of the yard, as though he dumped it and ran. She sighed and squeezed her Golf past it, into a space by the wall.

'*Hombre!*' she muttered. '*Hombre de sombrero!*'

Inside the house, she found Angelo in an even higher phase of excitement than usual, while Frank appeared to be finding it difficult not to laugh.

Angelo threw his arms around Cat and hugged her deeply.

'Oh, *mio gattina*! Mio *cucciola*. The best and the worst have happened and I do not know whether to laugh or cry. My heart is distraught and yet my heart is given a prize so I long to celebrate. I am a man in turmoil.'

Frank, managing to release Cat from Angelo's embrace,

kissed her. She could feel the vibration on his lips as he tried not to laugh.

'I have to tell you what happened,' said Angelo. 'You who have soul will understand, while my friend, my erstwhile friend, Frank finds it funny, you will see the pain and the power of the gift.'

She nodded, hoping she looked sympathetic.

Angelo sighed. 'So, this morning I receive a delivery. First the man calls me, "are you at home? I have a very important delivery and you must be there to receive it." I am as you say, all agog. I say bring it on.'

Frank could hold it in no more and hastily rushed to the kitchen to get Cat a glass of wine and burst into fits of laughter.

'OK,' said Cat cautiously. 'Go on.'

'Bah! So, the man, he arrives and on his enormous van, which I might say he can hardly fit into my small drive, is written: Live Delivery. I cannot guess. I stare in imagination. I long for the moment the doors are open and a huge elephant emerges.'

Frank brought in Cat's wine.

'Well, he goes to the back of this enormous van and he brings me a box. Like this'

Angelo drew a box about six inches wide in the air.

'So small. Where is my elephant? Why such a large van?'

He threw his arms open.

'So, I have to sign for it. And on the paper is written: Gift from Anastasia Rodriguez. Card enclosed.'

'I buzz with excitement. My darling! My love! What could she have given me? I go inside. I open the box. Inside is another box with holes and inside that, cosily nestling in straw is Cerion Nanus.'

He looked up at Frank and Cat. Frank once again dissolved into laughter while Cat stared amazed.

'What is Cerion Nanus?'

'Oh, *Gattina*, you have never heard of Cerion Nanus? You have not lived. Cerion Nanus is the smallest snail in the world, it lives only on islands in the Caribbean, and is so seldom seen ... well a gift like this is just the way to lift my heart to Heaven. As it will yours when I show you. Which I will when you come to my house.'

'Yes,' said Cat, sighing, 'for your imminent marriage.'

'Ah,' said Angelo, and tears sprung into his eyes. 'Alas, no. For with one hand she gives, while with the other she takes away.'

'What?'

'I say there is a gift card in the box too. It is from the love of my life, second only to Cerion Nanus. My darling Anastasia says: "Darling Angelo, I shall love you forever, and as a token of that I give you this, Cerion Nanus, which I know you have longed for all of your life. Sadly, I cannot marry you as I have decided to join a charity of scientific nuns investigating male infertility. For a while I shall be living between the Caribbean and Spain." Oh and she put a PS. It is a bit odd though. She says to tell the Cat, you I suppose, that she has taken My Dog for a walk. Do you understand? Why should you care that she has taken her dog for a walk?'

'Yes,' said Cat. 'I understand. I think you are right Angelo. She is a good woman, but ... why do good people do bad things?'

'Ah, *Gattina*, if I could tell you then I could have all the rarest snails in the world and live with them in harmony.'

After Angelo had gone to bed, and Frank had taken the dogs out for a last walk, Cat sat down to write a report to Gia.

As she hesitated over her laptop, an email popped into her inbox. It was from Gia.

* * *

'Congratulations,' it began. 'Angelo rang me this evening to explain he was no longer getting married, so I see you have done your work and protected my brother from mariticide. Thank you.

'As to the budget: there being only a few pounds left, I must congratulate you on your honesty and efficiency. If only my team were as good at planning as you, we would have reached our goal by now.

'If you have any questions, please contact me. Otherwise, I shall consider our commercial work concluded and hope to meet you socially next year.

Best wishes, Gia.'

* * *

So, thought Cat, Angelo is safe. Free to turn his fancy else-where. But Anastasia, forever dogged by her past, will never be free. And yet, Cat did not want to think of Anastasia as a victim, but rather someone who kept fighting back in spite of her past – a heroine.

* * *

The sound of the cuckoo alerted Cat to a WhatsApp message. It was Miranda.

'Just to let you know I met Billy's wife in the super-market again. We seem to have become besties! She told me Billy has been formally arrested for the murder of Tom Drayton. She is moving into his house in Portsmouth with the kids, she says it is much nicer than the place they were at. It's an ill wind ...'eh! I expect the police will be in contact with you soon. Wonder if you can pin Father Romero's murder on him too. Haha Cat, just joking! LOL.'

Another email pinged into Cat's inbox. It was from Mateo and included a short apology for having taken so long; the video was attached. She clicked on it and found herself looking at Nicholas's face and then on to his father and Anastasia.

'Odd video,' said Frank, who had walked in quietly behind her, 'didn't you say it was a promotional video?'

'That's what Nicholas called it.'

'Then where are all the wide shots of the clubs, close ups of the individual players etc, etc?'

'Published a book on promotion?'

'Ha Ha. What do you think publishers do? Just sit back and drink the profits?'

'Ah, so you've seen a few ... too few to mention?'

Frank said nothing, watching the video. 'And it's been edited, not that that's unusual, particularly given the content.'

'How can you tell?'

'Look, see where Romero jumps on his horse, rides off, then falls, the shadow is from the left ... now it starts again with the horse thundering by ... the shadow is overhead. If you look closely, you can see that the body has gone. That bit was a rerun of the horse's gallop and put in at least an hour later!'

'You are right. How did we miss it?'

'It is well done. It's only because I spent years looking at promotional videos that I didn't think it looked right.'

'So, Nicholas, or more likely Maria Arinez, doctored the video.'

'Wonder why?' said Frank, 'can't be just editorial conceit!'

'For the same reason they lost the autopsy,' said Cat. 'Presumably, both the autopsy and the original bit of video show that Arinez's mallet hit Romero on the head. Even if it *was* an accidental hit, that would make it manslaughter, instead of a horse-induced accident. Arinez probably didn't want to risk being implicated, and Nicholas wanted the stress to be put on his father's fall and what induced that: hoping we would conclude it was due to Anastasia's poisoning.'

'And yet she wasn't even investigated.'

Cat stopped the video. 'I can only suppose the Arinez family no longer have the pull they did in the 1980s or that they were so chaotic that the incriminating evidence they provided was ignored.'

'Or that Mateo was a good son to have in these circumstances.'

'You think? He was in Spain, not Argentina. Could he have such pull?'

Frank shrugged. 'Either way, Anastasia is in the clear.'

He put his hands on Cat's shoulder and rubbed his cheek against hers.

'So, did she kill any of her husbands?'

'I don't think so. In some ways she was as much the victim as the dead men. Trouble is,' said Cat, 'we make assumptions. Because all her husbands died mysteriously, and she profited from their deaths, we assumed she killed them before we made any investigation and that blinded us to the truth for quite a long time.'

'Nicholas Romero was also at the wedding.' Frank said. 'Do you think he and Billy met, planned something together?'

'You know, Frank, for a while I did wonder if there was a connection. Then I realised, whatever that dotty boy might have wanted to do, Maria would never let him get off the point. They wanted Romero's money. Killing Tom would not have helped them at all. The little extra suspicion thrown on Anastasia wouldn't help their case enough to be worth it.'

'OK. So it was the contaminated ice from Billy, followed by the Viagra when Tom got home?'

'Yes, when Anastasia said Tom admitted he and Billy watched porn on his phone, I wondered if Tom might have dashed for Viagra and then on to bed with Anastasia! Anastasia said he ate a lot at dinner, the pharmacist told Stevie that eating a lot with Viagra means more absorption and hence greater effect.'

Frank sighed. 'Poor Tom, the effect of a younger wife.'

Cat, who was eight years older than Frank, swatted him. '*Coño!*'

'Oooh, I love it when you talk dirty in Spanish.'

Frank kissed her.

'Why did you ask "why do good people do bad things" if Anastasia didn't kill anyone?'

'She took advantage of people.'

Cat felt Frank moving his head against her cheek.

'Don't we all? Didn't Teresa take advantage of her?'

'Perhaps. Anastasia did take Romero's money and the Drayton's money, half their business. A business they had spent generations building up. Isn't that a bit unkind?'

'But most of it she gave away.'

'So? So, she should be called Anastasia Hood?'

'In which case you girls are her Merry Wo-men.'

'Funny boy.'

'Oh!' added Frank, 'and what happened to the red-haired boy? The one who helped Clement and later fetched Sarah, when Anastasia had her miscarriage?'

'What? Honestly, Frank, you are weird. How can you remember that boy? Amazingly, though, I have the answer. Sarah told me that Magnus was going to be a pilot, but he changed his mind after seeing Anastasia in such pain, and became a doctor. He still works in the islands.'

'Anastasia seems to have had a phenomenal effect on everyone she met.'

'Yes,' said Cat sleepily, 'perhaps if you'd met her, you'd become a successful comedian.'

'I did meet her. My purr-fect Pussycat!'

Cat opened her eyes. 'So your jokes *are* better.'

Chapter 72

The three girls met again the next morning to discuss Romero's death.

'Mr Charleston sent me a copy of the autopsy,' said Stevie. 'Seems that what was lost was found.'

'And?'

'Clear damage to the skull. With that information the police went into Buriton Manor with a warrant. They found the original video, the one that Nicholas doctored. Typical of Nicholas to keep it! It seems pretty clear that Father Romero was killed by a blow to the head. At the very least this looks like a potential manslaughter charge.'

Cat shut her eyes and lent back in her chair.

'Do you think she is Cat napping?' asked Miranda.

'Ha Ha. No, thinking. Pity she doesn't like surfing.'

Stevie swung her chair back to her friendly screen, while Miranda got up, looking for something to read.

'Where was Nicholas?' asked Cat suddenly.

'Come again?' said Miranda.

Stevie frowned. 'When.'

'On the yacht. Nicholas's parents were on their yacht when his mother fell off. Where was their only child?'

'They probably had a nanny,' said Miranda trying to keep the envy out of her voice.

'Probably did,' said Cat, 'but wouldn't nanny and child be on the yacht?'

Stevie spun her chair around in loops.

'Why?'

'Nicholas was how old when his mother died? Anastasia thought six or seven.'

'Well,' said Stevie, stopping her spinning chair at the screen and getting up a timeline.

'Mother Romero's will was read in 1989. Nicholas was born in 1983, in November, so yes, he was just short of six years old.'

'Certainly old enough to travel on yachts and go places with his parents.'

'Yes. And?'

'Bearing in mind that Mother Romero, what was her name, I can't keep calling her Mother Romero?'

'Maria.'

'OK, Maria Romero was very religious, so, however much her husband's behaviour pained her, it is unlikely that she would commit suicide. Just suppose that Romero did push her, and suppose that the child was watching.'

The girls looked at her.

'You think he had been wanting revenge since he was six?' asked Stevie, her tone suggesting that she thought this a bit far-fetched.

'Given,' Miranda added, 'Nicholas's extravagant temperament, are you suggesting that he waited some thirty years to enact his revenge? Really?'

'No,' said Cat, 'I'm not. I actually don't think that the

troubled boy was capable of organising anything, let alone a successful murder. But I think his girlfriend, Maria Arinez, might well.'

'Why?'

'Money. Maria knows the Romeros are rich. Nicholas no doubt talks endlessly about all the money he will inherit from his father. And at some point he will have told her he saw his father kill his mother.'

Cat sat up and put her hands on her knees.

'Well, the Arinez family are far too used to justice and the law to think there is any point trying to link Romero to a death thirty years ago. Instead, Maria and her brother look for ways to get rid of Romero without any blame attaching to Nicholas. Then along comes Anastasia with her troubled history and difficult present.'

'Perfect,' said Stevie. 'God's scapegoat!'

'Nicholas has no trouble getting Isabella to introduce him to her mother, and then he introduces Anastasia to her father. Bingo.'

'So they do the deed. Planned by both siblings, enacted by the one and covered up by the other. The only problem, however, is that their cover up of the murder is too good. It is put down to an accident and no one is blamed. Anastasia gets off scot-free and, worse still, she takes the lolly instead of Nicholas.'

'Indeed,' said Stevie, 'obviously neither Nicholas, nor the Arinez siblings realised that Romero's marriage nullified the original will, so now they need Anastasia to take the rap for his death.'

'Then guess what?' added Miranda, 'he's at an art show, thinking of nothing much and along comes a patsy detective who fancies him. Hell's teeth! I'm never flirting again!'

Cat laughed, but Stevie added. 'But don't say that

Miranda. It was exactly because you flirted with him, that he thought he could deceive us into thinking that Anastasia was guilty. And he was wrong. We nailed him.'

'He didn't realise,' said Cat, 'that people, like things, are not always what they Seem!'

Chapter 73

There were only five non-locals on the ferry from Puerto Rico to Vieques: three nuns and two laywomen. Nobody talked very much. The nuns were singing. If they wondered who was doing the fundraising for their charity, when both chief benefactors were on the boat with them, that was not the focus of the song: instead they were singing a satirical Spanish version of Geronimo's Cadillac' written specially by one of the nuns, who was hoping for a record label.

As the ferry approached the dock, the singing stopped and both laywomen looked up. On the shore, a young man was holding two horses.

One of the women waved.

The man smiled and the horses nodded their heads, perhaps in acknowledgement but perhaps against the flies.

The singing nun asked. 'Will you join us in 'Geronimo's Cadillac', for the journey up to the nunnery, señoras?'

She indicated the elderly Ford awaiting them near the jetty.

Gia smiled. 'We will ride the horses; it is the best way to

see the island.' She turned to the other woman. 'I am so glad you decided to invest in our project but I am sorry it didn't work out with my brother.'

Anastasia threw her head up and down like the horses.

'*Vaya!*' she said. 'You know when something is right. When something is almost right but not there, then you let it go. I'll enjoy the ride. It is nearly forty years since I was last on a horse, but now I am starting a new life.

'So, I shall ride again."

ACKNOWLEDGMENTS

When you publish independently there is a perception that you have just written a book and put it up on the Internet, but this is far from the reality. I wanted this book and the whole series to come to be as professional as possible and so I consulted and worked with a large number of people in the industry. It is definitely a learning experience. Thank you to so many people, in particular to:

Kat Gordon for her superb editorial, author Shaun Baines for his irreplaceable advice, Elizabeth von Aderka, and Colleen O'Brien from the CWA, and Catlin Macleod from Fiverr, for Beta reading. Sam Jordison and all at Jericho Writers, a company which hugely improved my writing and my understanding of the process.

Jill French for copy editing and John Martin for proof reading.

For medical expertise, thanks to Caroline Veitch and Janie Grant. For information about the oil rigs, Geoffrey Knowles. For police procedures, Graham Nunn, and Graham Bartlett. For family law, Richard Budworth. For knowledge of the Polish language, Robin Dabrowa

For cover and all aspects of design, Kari Brownlie

The Alliance of Independent Authors for invaluable advice.

Malvina Nicca for all her help and encouragement. To my long-suffering friends for their useful advice and most of all to my husband Gerald Cheyne and the dogs for their invaluable support.

ABOUT THE AUTHOR

Gina Cheyne has previously written children's books about dogs but this is her first crime thriller.

She has worked as a physiotherapist, pilot, aviation journalist and dog breeder. She lives in West Sussex with her husband and dogs.

She also writes aviation and children's books under a different name.

ALSO BY GINA CHEYNE

Biscuit and Oscar Learn to Fly

Max and Biscuit Fly to India

Pugwash Runs Away to Sea